P9-DGQ-359

Battle Lanterns

Battle Lanterns

by

MERRITT PARMELEE ALLEN

Decorations by
Ralph Ray, Jr.

DAVID McKAY COMPANY, INC.

NEW YORK

ALLEN
BATTLE LANTERNS

PUBLISHED SIMULTANEOUSLY IN THE DOMINION OF CANADA

First Edition March 1949
Reprinted August 1949
September 1950
May 1953
July 1955
May 1958
May 1960
November 1962
May 1964
May 1966
October 1967

Printed in the United States of America
Vail-Ballou Press, Inc., Binghamton, N. Y.

Battle Lanterns

CHAPTER I

THE ship's boat trembled and lay rolling lazily among the small waves. "Aground she is!" a sailor growled, and fell to cursing the blackness of the night. Oarlocks creaked, sea boots scraped on planking, men grunted and strained, but the boat only rocked.

"She's fast," said the same voice. "I'll sound with an oar." And, after a moment of probing in the dark water, "It's a bar."

"Damn the British!" another muttered, as though the enemy might have laid the ridge of sand under the sea.

"I'm goin' over the side," the first man said. "I've a whim I can walk ashore. Give me the line."

"Aye, sir."

"Pay it out as I need it." The men heard him slip into the water and the boat raised slightly on the side where his weight had been.

Toward the stern a weak voice asked, "Where are we, Bill?"

A boy answered, "Entering Charles Town harbor, Mr. Wilde. We'll soon be with friends."

"Cold, so cold!"

"That's because you are wet with spray, sir."

"Is it winter, Bill?"

"No, sir. Don't try to think for a while."

"I say, is it winter, Bill?" The delirious voice said angrily.

"No, Mr. Wilde, no," the boy answered gently. "It is June. You remember now."

"To be sure I do — June, 1752."

"Yes, yes. Can't you sleep for a while, sir?"

"It is 1752, ain't it, Bill?"

"No. But never mind."

"What year *is* it, then?"

"1776."

"So cold! So cold!" The voice trailed away.

"Sounds like the old boy's castin' off," a sailor said under his breath.

Another whispered, "Stow yer gab fer sake of the lad."

After that, as the minutes passed, they sat in silence for the most part. Mr. Wilde was sleeping or in a stupor, it was too dark for Bill to tell which. A night bird called, a fish splashed, little waves smacked the sides of the boat, making sounds like lips too tired to speak distinctly. The breath of the marsh was warm and smelled of salt mud as it rode the languid northeast breeze.

Suddenly a voice came down the wind, sharp and threatening: "Who's out yonder on the water?"

"Friends," the man in the sea answered quickly.

"That's as may be. British or Americans?"

"Americans."

"Tories or honest folk?"

"Honest folk from New York. Our ship was sunk by the

British outside the harbor. We've a sore-wounded mate in a small boat and want to land."

"Stay whar you be till I fetch th' major."

"Backwoods Johnny," a sailor remarked in an uncomplimentary tone.

"Shut yer hatch," another snapped. "They're jumpy as cats, what with the fleet knockin' on their door."

"There is ice in the Hudson," Mr. Wilde mumbled. "Cold!"

"How is he, lad?" a sailor whispered.

"I wish I knew," Bill answered.

How could he know, there in the dark? He was not a surgeon, but a boy and a badly scared one at that. Even the old salts were so fidgety they started and rattled the oars when another night bird squawked close overhead. And when a light appeared approaching on shore there was intense silence in the boat.

The light stopped, and a deep voice hailed, "Who are you out there?"

"Survivors from the ship *Dancer* out of New York," the man in the water answered. "She was sunk by the British outside the harbor. We have a man bad wounded."

"Fetch him in," the voice ordered.

Leaving two men to handle the boat, the others waded to the beach, carrying Mr. Wilde as gently as possible. They were met by an officer and three soldiers, evidently militiamen.

"Follow me," the officer said. "We have a doctor in camp."

"Beggin' yer pardon, sir, he's past that need," said the

sailor who was supporting Mr. Wilde's head.

"Ah!" The officer raised his lantern and looked at the dead man's face. "Yes, so he is." The voice was deep and gentle. "We will take him to my tent." He struck out across the sand.

They followed silently. The boy came last, stumbling now and then because of the mist in his eyes. Out of the darkness they entered a stretch of dim, bulky shapes, which the lantern showed to be tents and huts. Men slept between them and in doorways or sat up and blinked when the company dogs barked.

The officer led the way into a small tent and motioned them to lay the body on a bunk made of poles and blankets.

"I will post a guard here for the night," he said, as though these were friends rather than strangers. "You gentlemen will kindly accompany me to the Commandant."

The boy stepped forward, hesitated, and said, "I ask your permission, sir, to stay here with — with him."

"Granted." The officer offered no embarrassing sympathy, merely nodded to the sailors, who filed out after him. He knew how to spare a fellow's feelings.

Bill sat on an upturned water bucket and held his head in his hands. Had he been at home he would have cried, but in a man's world tears are contemptible. And it had been a man's world since he left New York months before. He wished now they had traveled on horseback, even if people did say the roads were awful and the taverns worse. Post riders made it in five weeks from New York to Charles Town, mighty good time, with the good earth under them all the way. But Mr. Wilde had been all for sailing. The romantic streak in him made him scorn the thought of going after buried treasure in anything but a ship.

The devil take that treasure! It was the boy's by law, so naturally he wanted to recover it, but long ago it had cost more suffering than it was worth, and now to that price was added the life of one of the best of men. Of course, the gold could not be directly to blame because those who sought it had set out at a time when there was trouble with the British. They should have waited a while. Still, in the beginning, it had not seemed reasonable to expect outright violence from Englishmen. From pirates, yes, but not from men of one's own race. Even if they had known Charles Town was blockaded they would not have looked for this brutal treatment. For the first time the boy was glimpsing the fact that armed forces were not always one with the people. But he was too sad and too weary to think much about it then. In spite of his trouble, he leaned against a tent pole and dozed.

He awakened at the sound of a step and heard the officer saying in his soft, deep voice, "You had best stretch out for a while, lad."

Bill stood up, for he was not sure if he should sit in the presence of a commissioned soldier.

"If you don't object, sir," he said, "I would rather watch out the night here."

"As you wish, by all means." It was somehow comforting to be the focal point of this man's large black eyes. "Was the gentleman your father?"

"No, sir; he was a very good friend. His name was Wilde. Mine is Bill Barlow."

"I am Major Francis Marion of the South Carolina Militia." He bowed slightly, for he was a graceful man though far from handsome, being small and swarthy. And he was the kind who did not find it beneath his dignity to introduce himself to a boy.

"I thank you for your kindness, sir," Bill said.

"No thanks are necessary. Who wouldn't give all possible aid to shipwrecked men?" Marion sat on a block of wood and motioned Bill back to the bucket. "You were trying to run the blockade?"

"No, sir. We didn't know there was a blockade. They sank us without explanation."

"British arrogance." Marion snapped his fingers, a way he had when angry.

"We got off in three boats, but were separated in the dark. Are we far from Charles Town, sir?"

"You are on Sullivan's Island, across the bay from the city. We are building a fort here, racing against time to finish it before the enemy fleet moves in."

"Then it is real war, sir?"

"Nothing else."

"We thought at home, when I left, things might be patched up."

"It's past the patching point." Marion's large black eyes glowed. "We don't want war, the best Britishers don't want war, but mulish old King George will have it rather than admit he made a mistake by pushing us too far." He stood up and kicked the block of wood.

"My father was against kings as far back as I can remember," Bill said in an attempt to sound mature.

"How old are you, lad?"

"Fifteen, sir."

"Nigh thirty years behind me. You have been in Charles Town?"

"No, sir, but I am going there to see a friend of my father's, John Stewart, Esquire."

"The importer and merchant?"

"Yes, sir. Do you know him?"

"It pleasures me to say I do. A grand gentleman. I'll send you to him in the morning."

"You are putting me deeper in your debt, sir."

"Nonsense!" The major smiled, and he had a smile that won the hearts of everyone from children to old soldiers. "There are no debts of that sort between friends." He turned quickly and left the tent.

Bill sat out the night and by morning felt twenty years older. In his mind he had evolved from a dependent boy to a man on his own in the midst of war. It was his war, too, for his people back north were patriots, but until this day he had never taken hostilities seriously. It had been mere political talk, with enough fireworks to give it spice. Now it was the real thing. If these South Carolinians, poorly equipped amateur soldiers, had the courage to stand up against mighty England the other colonies were, or soon would be, doing the same thing. There would be no backing down, either, once they got started. It would be a fight to the finish, and he was already in it. It was no place for a boy; he must be a man.

His sudden mental transition may have changed his appearance unfavorably, for when Major Marion came back at dawn he took him by the shoulders and pushed him outside the tent.

"You need breakfast and a fresh breeze through your brain," he said in explanation.

"I should stay with Mr. Wilde," Bill protested.

"It will do him no good and yourself harm. I'll send a messenger to John Stewart and have him arrange the burial in Charles Town."

"Why can't I go and talk with him, sir?"

"Later. Tories are under a cloud now. It would take time to get you a pass."

"Is Mr. Stewart a Tory!"

"Yes." Marion smiled at the boy's consternation. "But that is not unpardonable. Many of our good people are Tories. It is no reflection on character, merely a difference of opinion." He turned and hailed a passing officer: "Is mess ready, Pete?"

"The cook has just passed the happy word."

"Good! Bill Barlow, this is Captain Horry." He pronounced it "O-ree."

"I am honored, sir." Bill bowed stiffly.

"Pleasured, I'm sure." Horry showed his white teeth in a quick smile. "You're from the north, I hear."

"Yes, sir."

"We don't see many from up there."

"England is north." Marion grinned. "They" — he jerked a thumb toward the sea — "are calling on us in considerable numbers."

"They'll find the tea hot," Horry promised. He was a

handsome man of about Marion's age, an easy-going planter in peace but a fire-eating soldier.

They put away a whopping breakfast served by Negro boys at a log table under the palmettos. Several junior officers were present and Bill gathered from their talk that Major General Charles Lee, who was in command, was as popular as the itch.

"I'll bet a hat when the shooting starts he has business in Charles Town or some more distant place," Horry said bluntly.

"I hope so," a young lieutenant said vigorously. "Give us Colonel Moultrie and they may keep their Continental generals."

"Aye, give us Moultrie," another seconded. "He doesn't need to be trimmed with gold braid to make him a soldier."

"That's the difference between a patriot and a politician," Horry said bitterly. "Statesmen may be soldiers, but politicians are too petty to stand the test of battle. Am I right, Francis?"

"Right as rain, Pete, as a rule." Marion stood up. "But, gentlemen, it is our cause, not our commanders, that we serve. And there is plenty for us all to do." He tapped Bill on the shoulder and they left the table.

It was part of the major's duty to make the rounds of the works at frequent intervals to see that the Negroes who brought the rafts of palmetto logs across the cove wasted no time. The race against the British was so desperate that soldiers, civilians and slaves worked together on equal terms. If anyone moralized on this democratic spectacle he did it silently, saving his breath to swing an ax or shovel.

In days to come Bill would remember the fort as he first saw it that morning, more like a lumber yard than a fortification. It was a square, with a bastion at each angle, designed to accommodate a garrison of a thousand men. But it was far from completed. Only on the southeast and southwest were the walls their full ten feet above the platforms. They were built of palmetto logs, one on another in two parallel rows sixteen feet apart, with the space between filled with sand.

Marion slapped one of the logs with his hand, almost affectionately. "Providence made palmettos for defense work," he said, with a suggestion of pride, as though he might have shared the original idea. "They are tall and straight, without a branch, and a foot to fifteen inches through."

"But they are soft wood," Bill objected, making an unfavorable mental comparison between them and the oaks along the Hudson.

"Aye, that's their virtue." Marion picked at the bark with his thumbnail. "They're spongy, almost like cork. They stop solid shot without cracking or splintering."

"Yes, just the logs for this business," Bill said wisely, as though he had spent years instead of a few hours among them.

"If we can finish before the ships move in, they can't blast us out. And we must finish! We must hold this fort, lad, regardless of the cost or liberty will suffer. Liberty is the only thing in the world that is worth fighting for to the death. Liberty!" Marion spoke the word with a fierce tenderness the boy had never heard before. The major's eyes burned and his pale cheeks flushed for a moment, giving him, briefly, an heroic, almost glorified, appearance. As he would do many times in later years, Bill marveled at the way the man's spirit could show in his face. The glow faded as suddenly as it came and the major became commonplace again, hurrying away to work on the walls.

Bill followed him along the platforms where the great guns were set — nine-pounders, twelve-pounders, eighteen-pounders and twenty-six pounders, with higher platforms between them where riflemen could stand at loopholes. The flag flew from the southeast bastion, a blue field with the word *Liberty* emblazoned in white. Five heavy guns were close under the staff. Back to the east, through an opening in the wall, showed the tents and huts of the camp. To the boy the place, unfinished though it was, looked impregnable. A few minutes later he said something of the kind to Captain Horry, who came by with a basketful of spikes for pegging the logs, for Horry was the essence of democracy, speaking and being spoken to by everyone.

"You and General Lee don't agree." The captain grinned in that quick way of his. "He says it won't stand gunfire for half an hour."

"But all those mighty big guns, sir!"

"Yes. Perhaps twenty-five of them can bear on a target at one time."

"Have the British as many on their ships?"

"Well" — Horry looked good-naturedly at the youngster — "it is believed that Sir Peter Parker's squadron of ten or a dozen ships carries upwards of two hundred and fifty guns."

"Holy smoke!" Bill gasped. Then he rallied and said, with a great show of confidence, "But we have an army here, too."

"To be sure, to be sure, we mustn't forget the army," Horry agreed solemnly. "A few less than four hundred untrained men with a handful of gunpowder and a few bullets made from window weights taken from houses in Charles Town."

"You're codding me, Captain."

"No, Bill."

"Anyhow, the British haven't *any* army here."

"Not on the spot, no, but not so many miles from here, on Long Island, Sir Henry Clinton has three thousand regulars. We expect a call from them presently."

Bill's eyes widened. "What can we do, sir?"

Horry laid a hand on Bill's shoulder. "Don't worry, lad," he said. "In guns and men they outnumber us ten to one, but we are from South Carolina, which makes the odds in our favor."

At that moment the stirring long roll rattled from all the drums in camp. Men sprang into action everywhere and Major Marion ran down the platform, his face shining.

"They're coming, Pete!" he shouted. "Battle stations!"

"A right pleasant sound to hear!" Horry laughed aloud and raced toward his post.

Marion pulled up beside Bill. "Make your way to the dock beyond the camp and get a ride to the city on a barge."

"I want to stay here, Major." Bill threw back his head.

"You are too young for battle."

"It's my war as well as yours. Age doesn't count."

"There's no denying that spirit." Marion wheeled. "Come along with me."

CHAPTER II

STRANGELY enough, in spite of the commotion, Bill was aware of the clicking of Marion's heels on the oak planking of the gun platform. He followed easily, for he was almost as tall as the little major and ten times as excited. At the southeast bastion they met a quiet gray-eyed officer who, in spite of a limp, was almost strolling along, carrying a telescope in one hand.

"This looks like *the* day, Major," he remarked as casually as he might have mentioned the weather.

"Yes, Colonel Moultrie, they're moving in at last." Marion glanced through an embrasure.

"Try the glass, Major."

"Thank you, sir." Marion took it and studied the fleet, which, to Bill's naked eye, looked like a flock of white birds swimming on the ocean. "About a mile and a half offshore. Coming fast with the wind and tide."

"Nicely timed. Splendid sailors," Moultrie commented.

"Gad! One is anchoring."

"The glass, please." Moultrie reached for it. "I have watched them so closely the past few days that I recognize — yes, that is the *Thunder,* a bombship. We'll soon hear from her."

"The one leading the line is presumably Sir Peter's flagship," Marion guessed.

"The *Bristol*. Our Tory friends say she carries fifty guns. So does the *Experiment*. And there's the *Active* — and the *Solebay* — twenty-eight each. The same for the *Actaeon* and the *Syren*. Over there — "

A shrieking whistle cut the air and ended in a clap of thunder. Moultrie looked at his watch.

"The *Thunder* has landed the first blow," Marion remarked.

"With what effect?" Moultrie asked, and both officers hurried away.

Bill stood trembling on the platform between two cannon. He knew he was trembling, and it seemed very natural because he was as scared as a rabbit. It was the way he had felt when the British fired on his ship the day before, only worse. Then there was a chance of getting away in a boat, but here he was cooped up in a pen and a whole squadron was getting set to blow the place to smithereens. He wished he were back in that boat with the friendly darkness reaching out to cover him.

A second shell landed at a distance behind the walls. He saw the sand scatter from the impact, then leap straight up in a cloud when the explosion came. The noise of it was terrific and it all seemed to take place inside his head. The earth shook and the vibration ran up his shaking legs to his quaking stomach, making him feel sick and cold. Could anyone stand such a strain, he wondered. Obviously they could, for on three sides he saw men working rapidly and quietly bringing up powder from the magazine, which was covered with sandbags, loading the guns and making other preparations. They were stripped to the waist, with kerchiefs tied around their heads, and sweat was running down their backs, for the weather was sultry. Strange that a fellow could shiver under such conditions.

Another shell whistled out of the sky, but before Bill could locate it someone caught him around the waist from behind and swung him flat on the planking.

"What do you think you're doing!" he grunted, but his voice was wiped out by a roar.

The man who was holding him down released him and whooped like an Indian. Bill jumped up and squared off at a big awkward man who defended himself with a broad grin.

"Who're you?" Bill shouted.

"Jasper — gunner's sergeant."

"That doesn't give you the right to throw me around."

"Easy, banty." The big fellow's words were slow and soft. "That shell hit kerplunk onto th' mag'zine."

"It did!"

"Shore. Had it tetched off th' powder an' us been standin' up hit mighten blowed our lights out. I didn't have time to interduce myself an' explain th' sitcherashun."

"Oh — I see. Thank you." Bill felt cheap. "Then the shell didn't pierce the magazine?"

"Shore not, elsen we'd a went up in a chariot of fire like Lisher — or was hit Liger?"

"I don't remember. Then the magazine must be bomb proof."

"Yep." Jasper jigged a few steps. "We hain't got that to fret over when th' fightin' starts."

"Starts!" Bill stared at him. "What do you call this?"

"Jest a fleabite to what we'll see when th' Britishers git to unloadin'."

Bill liked the gunner, he was so human. Besides he was someone to talk to, which was important right then.

"I'm scared," he confided. "I don't care who knows it."

"Shore you be." Jasper nodded. "We're all scairt."

"But soldiers are used to battle."

"Sojers — huh! None of us, not even the colonel, has did more'n a little Injun fightin' — most of us not that."

"Then how can you keep so cool?"

"We hain't cool, don't fox yerself."

"Why don't you run for home? Honest, I believe I would if I lived near here."

"Wal," Jasper glanced at the flag, flying almost over his head, "I cain't read, but I know them white letters spells Liberty. We've stuck that flag up thar, an' we plan on keepin' hit thar."

"I want to help."

"I need a extry hand with my bat'ry."

"What can I do?"

"Peel off yore shirt an' tie up yore ha'r. When th' music starts you holp pass powder from th' mag'zine."

"Yes, sir." Bill set his jaw to keep his teeth from chattering.

He had always imagined soldiers as fighting in trim uniforms, not stripped down like longshoremen, but if that was the thing to do he would do it. He folded his jacket and shirt and laid them under a cannon, for in the back of his head was the thrifty thought that he must take care of them as he had no others this side of New York. Hoping to do his part in destroying a fleet, yet careful of his own shirt! Human nature in a nutshell. And he took his time at it, forcing himself to move slowly while waiting for more of those bombs. The fear was wearing off a little but he was by no means sure it would not return tenfold when the ships were within range. If he could only keep from breaking when the real test came! Men like Sergeant Jasper could stand up to anything in defense of the Liberty flag, but the boy had not yet learned the source of their strength.

The Negro workmen had disappeared. Along the walls the gunners stood behind the loaded cannon, with lighted matches in their hands. The crews waited in knots, keeping their courage up, laughing and laying bets on this and that. It was something like the moment before a horse race. Bill looked through an embrasure and saw the great ships *Active, Bristol, Experiment* and *Solebay* coming in fast. They appeared immense and irresistible.

The tide tugged and the wind pushed the ships to make their bid to destiny. Finally they were within range. The gunners stood tensely watching Marion, who had his eyes on Moultrie farther along the wall. His arm went up. Marion wheeled, and shouted, "Commence firing!" The matches glowed and almost in one voice the guns of the battery spoke.

The noise was tremendous, but to the men it was a joyful sound. They were striking back, throwing their metal, lashing out at the arrogant enemy who thought they ruled the world.

"You drew blood, boys!" Marion yelled, and the crews cheered as they reloaded.

They fired independently, each when ready, after taking deliberate aim. At first only the bombship replied.

"Why don't they talk back, Major?" Jasper shouted.

Marion turned on the firing step, where he had been looking through a loophole. For the second time Bill saw his face glowing with that strange light.

"They are forming their line," he answered. "We shall hear from them presently."

He jumped down from the step, took some loose papers from his pocket and, with a cannon for a desk, wrote on one of them with a clumsy pencil such as planters used for tagging cotton bales.

"Bill," he called, "deliver this to Colonel Moultrie in the southwest bastion and wait for an answer."

"Yes, sir."

Bill was not sure what a bastion was, but guessed it was one of those towerlike things, so he ran along the platform to the one that stood where the south and west walls met. Moultrie was talking to another officer, a sea captain by the look of his rig.

Bill saluted self-consciously, for it was his first attempt, and held out the note. "From Major Marion, sir."

Moultrie read it and stood thinking. Bill looked over the wall and gasped. In spite of the heavy fire from the fort, the squadron was coming in under full sail. The *Active* had outdistanced the others and was at that moment letting go her anchor and clewing up her sails. She was not more than four hundred yards away when she delivered a broadside. The crashing thunder of it, with the smoke and flame, and then the shiver that ran through the wall when the solid shot crashed into it were too much for Bill. His knees gave way and he sat on the plank floor with a thump. The officers glanced his way but did not stop talking and he got up red-faced and aching with shame.

While he waited he heard the strange officer ask, "What do you think now, Colonel?"

Moultrie answered calmly, "We should beat them, Captain Lemprière."

"Sir," the captain said, "I know naval guns, inasmuch as I've handled them myself, and I tell you those ships will knock this fort down in half an hour."

"If that happens," Moultrie answered, "we will lie behind the ruins and fight off their landing parties." He turned away and wrote a reply to Marion's note.

After that Bill was on the jump acting as handyman for that part of the fort. Did someone want a message delivered, a pail of water, a handful of spikes to peg down a loose plank, it was, "Hey, boy, shake your boots!" In that way he saw more of the battle than did the men in the batteries. He had a feeling that the enemy's guns followed him wherever he went and that he was never more than twenty feet from every shot that landed in the place. As they fell faster and faster his fear gave way to defiant exultation. Let 'em come, the more the merrier! If the whole British fleet, the whole British Empire, commanded by old George in person, was out there throwing everything it had at the little log fort he would not be afraid. The men behind the fort's guns were green fighters, a handful of farmers and merchants and mechanics, but they had something, an indefinable something, out of which Moultrie and Marion had made a defense that weight of metal and numbers could not batter down.

Perhaps not, but it was taking an awful pounding. An *awful* pounding. Buckets of sand had been brought up to give better footing on the bloody platforms, wounded men were crawling to the rear, and those who died were dragged aside like fallen trees. In quiet times such scenes would have been horrible, but under the stress of battle they seemed as natural as falling leaves in a windstorm.

The powder smoke was so thick between the fort and the ships that sometimes the gunners had to wait for it to blow away before they aimed. During one of those pauses Jasper called out, as Marion walked past, "How's the enemy line, Major?"

"In close order." Marion rested a hand on a cannon. "The heavy ships are anchored in front, the lighter ones back, opposite the gaps."

"What's them two 'crost from us?"

"The *Bristol* and the *Experiment*."

"Gawd pity 'em effen our guns don't bust!"

As he spoke the fort trembled as though a mighty fist had smashed into it. Splinters whistled through the air, smoke and dust swirled and twisted. Part way down the line a twenty-four pounder sat back on its haunches and two men behind it clawed the air as they fell. Then in from the sea came a rush of sound like all the noise of a thunderstorm packed into one blast. Marion glanced at the magazine and smiled. Moultrie came striding down from the bastion, feeling the logs with one hand as he passed.

"They're holding, Major!" he shouted.

"Like rocks, Colonel. What hit us?"

"Seven broadsides together. I happened to be looking when the whole line blazed together."

"The flag's down!" Jasper bellowed.

He leaped on his cannon and from it to the wall. The bastion flagstaff had been cut by a ball and the flag was hanging by a thread over the edge. Just before Jasper reached it it fell outside and he followed without hesitation. The officers looked at each other. A man couldn't live out there. It was the vital part of the wall, the target for the heaviest guns. Within two minutes it would again be blasted by hundreds of guns.

It was blasted, but Jasper came back, climbing hand over hand with the flag over his right shoulder.

"A sponge staff, Bill," he shouted from the top log.

"Gad! Don't keep him waiting!" Marion ran along the platform.

Bill caught up a sponge stick and heaved it to Jasper. Standing there, he tied the flag to it. Solid shot were falling in the sand between the logs and covering him with dust, but he planted the staff and tamped the earth around it with his heels. Then he shook his fist at the fleet, gave three cheers, and jumped down to the gun platform. Bill hugged him.

The battle continued savagely, for the British must knock the fort to pieces before they could take Charles

Town, which was the key to the southern campaign. True to tradition, the sailors fought their ships heroically. They were close in and taking a wicked raking fore and aft. On the *Bristol* alone, over a hundred men were dead. Her masts were down and she was so badly hulled that in order to keep her afloat carpenters were brought from other ships and set to work among the gunners.

"Gad, Francis, my hat is off to those lads!" Horry shouted.

"Noble fellows." Marion nodded.

"I've been watching 'em with the glass. Twice the quarter-deck has been cleared of every living man except Sir Peter Parker himself, and by the looks of him he's hit. They've lugged their captain below — dead, I judge — but still they fight."

"The other ships are as good," Marion answered. "Look at the *Experiment*, she's a slaughter pen."

"But slugging back."

"The sad part is, Pete, they're our kinsfolk."

"I'm proud of 'em, Francis! Call that treason, if you will."

"Why couldn't this thing have been settled sensibly? Why must men with brains fight like wild animals?"

"God knows." Horry turned partly around and stopped short. "May I be a tadpole's granny! We have a caller. Major General Charles Lee has curled his wig and powdered his nose and come all the way from Charles Town to our party." He looked contemptuously at the far bastion where a stout man in glittering uniform and snowy wig was standing with Colonel Moultrie.

"Easy, Pete, he's our commander," Marion cautioned.

"He is *not*!" Horry retorted. "We're not in the Continental line, but in the South Carolina Militia. President Rutledge and Colonel Moultrie give orders here, and don't you forget it."

"It doesn't matter at the moment," Marion said soothingly. "Shall we go up and pay our respects to General Lee?"

"And get a sour look down that long nose? No thank you. I'm on duty with my guns."

"There is enough for all of us to do here," Marion answered. He took the match from a wounded gunner and resumed work.

General Lee stayed a few minutes and then returned to Charles Town. Since coming to the city he had ridiculed the fort and its defenders. Once he had ordered it abandoned, but President Rutledge had flatly refused, reminding him it was garrisoned by local troops who took orders only from their own officers. At that, Lee was petty enough to remove from the fort such part of the powder as he had control of, hoping that when the battle came the stubborn Southerners would lose and he could humiliate them before Congress. Such was the man, babied by Congress and detested by General Washington, who all but lost the war in the South, and who was later charged with cowardice and openly suspected of treason.

That day Lee's narrow-mindedness or treacherous intentions nearly offset the heroic work of Moultrie and his men. About three o'clock in the afternoon the officer in command of the magazine sent word to the colonel that, at the rate it was being used, the powder would not last an hour.

Moultrie despatched messengers hot-foot to Rutledge and Lee on the mainland, explaining the situation and begging for powder. With all speed, and doubtless with secret satisfaction, Lee replied to spike the guns and abandon the fort as soon as the powder was gone. Moultrie showed the order to Marion.

"Abandon the fort!" To Bill, who was near by, the little major seemed to grow a foot. "God in Heaven! Tell the living and the dead they have fought in vain today!"

Moultrie was a quiet man, but his eyes, red-rimmed from smoke and sweat, burned with anger.

"Marion," he said, "General Lee's ignorance of South Carolina character is pitiful."

"His arrogance is insufferable!" the major exploded. "Congress or no Congress, he has no authority here. You will disobey that order, of course, sir."

"No" — Moultrie smiled slowly — "I shall obey it to the letter."

"What! Do you mean — "

"Not so fast, Marion, not so fast." Moultrie's eyes twinkled. "I shall withdraw when the powder is exhausted, but I shall see to it that it is never exhausted. I will bury an ounce or two of it myself." He started toward the magazine, then turned. "Order the gunners to fire only once in ten minutes. Collect all axes, knives and other weapons and distribute them among the men to be used in hand-to-hand fighting."

"Yes, sir!" Marion threw back his head and laughed aloud.

After another round the slugging stopped, as the Americans seemed to have met a death blow. The fort was almost silent, only occasionally did one of its guns speak. Encouraged by what they supposed to be approaching surrender, the British bore on harder. The timbers in the walls trembled, but still the soft palmettos absorbed their punishment and held. However, such endurance could not last forever; sooner or later those hundreds of great guns would pound the place to dust and scatter the dust in the wind. Already one end of the line was beginning to crack, and there three twelve-pounders were abandoned after the wall fell and the crews were killed, for they continued to fight without protection until the last man went down. And only at long intervals did the other cannon sound. Their defiance was magnificent, but the weight of their metal was only a fraction of what was needed.

Tempted by the weakening opposition, three ships from the second line tried to round the point and attack from the rear. It would be fatal to the men behind the walls, who, if caught in a cross fire, would be wiped out completely. But there was nothing they could do about it, for their whole supply of powder was not enough to stop one ship. Hollow-eyed under their masks of powder stain, the men watched, cursing Charles Lee, and praying for a miracle that would give them a fighting chance.

It came with the sureness of divine action. Though manned by veteran seamen, two of the ships collided and in the confusion all three went aground on a sand bar.

"An omen!" Moultrie cried, and his voice rang like a bugle. "Gad, gentlemen, our promise of victory has been renewed!"

Five minutes later a mule team galloped up from the wharf, running belly-to-the-ground, and pulling a wagon carrying five hundred pounds of powder from President Rutledge. It was every ounce he could scrape up in the city and with it was a note stoutly reaffirming his faith in victory. As a postscript, he added: *Do not make too free with your cannon — cool and do mischief.*

Eagerly the weary, battered garrison took up the fight that had seemed so near its end. Their fire was still dangerously restricted, but they planted each shot with deliberation and did fearful damage. Had there been a sea running the gallant *Bristol* and *Experiment,* and perhaps other ships, would have filled and sunk. As it was, their crews fought on through one of the cruellest days in naval history. Masts were down and bulwarks shot away, and amid the debris officers and men lay in heaps and red streams ran from the decks into the ocean. Still the flags flew and the cannon answered.

"It's race suicide," Marion said in anguish. "Anglo-Saxons slaughtering each other when they should be standing together against the rest of the world."

"It may be the way to understanding," Moultrie answered. "You don't appreciate a man till you fight him. The same holds with nations."

Bill was so tired that when no one was looking he leaned his head against a log and sobbed. All day he had thought himself a man and now he was crying! A fellow must be tougher than that if he were to hunt buried treasure and perhaps fight pirates. All that seemed so far away now, a fanciful dream that had given place to the reality of war.

Money was a mean, cheap thing in this new light. It was not what these men were fighting for. They were giving their lives for something that could not be wrapped up in a purse. It had neither weight nor shape, it was invisible, yet it burned forever before their eyes like a torch. It was the finest thing in all the world, that one word the women of Charles Town had worked into the homemade flag—*Liberty.*

"Gone to sleep, Bill?" Jasper's big voice was hoarse but still hearty.

"No; just thinking."

"Rest yore brains by footin' down to Cap'n Huger's bat'ry an' fetchin' me a new swab."

Captain Huger had one arm in a sling and blood was dripping from a splinter cut on his chin. He fired a cannon and retched as the smoke blew back in his face.

"Get a swab for the boy, McDonald," he said faintly to a man at the next gun.

"Shore, Cap'n." McDonald paused to wipe his blackened face, and mutter to Bill, "He's been that sick with pain fer two hours, but he won't quit."

He reached for the swab, twisted like a leaf in the wind and fell headlong from the platform to the ground. A solid shot had nearly cut him in two. Bill, Captain Huger and two gunners tried to raise him, then laid him back hopelessly.

"I'm goin'," he whispered. The men looked at one another miserably. Suddenly he came up on one elbow and smiled at them. "I'm goin'," he repeated in a stronger voice, "but don't let liberty go with me." He dropped back dead, and they returned to their work.

Bill did not know when the sun went down. The sultry air was so full of smoke that day and night changed places behind it unobserved. By seven o'clock the firing had slackened and just before dark the fleet began to withdraw.

"Give them the last kick, Major," Moultrie shouted, and Marion fired the final shot, a forty-pounder, at the *Bristol*.

Bill crawled under a cannon and fell into a dead sleep. He awoke shortly before sunrise and ran to the wall for a look around. The fleet was at anchor beyond range, all except the *Actaeon,* which was aground about a mile offshore. Her crew had set her afire and left her, her guns facing the enemy and her colors flying.

Major Marion came along the wall, freshly washed and shaved. He looked almost dapper and Bill marveled then, as he would so often in years to come, at the little giant's endurance.

"A fine morning, Bill!" he hailed.

"Yes, sir." Bill looked back at the fleet. "They're licked, aren't they?"

"They lost the engagement, but they are not licked."

"We did pretty well yesterday, didn't we, sir?"

"Nicely. It's possible history will remember the day."

"They may not forget the battle of Sullivan's Island. I know we won't."

"The battle of Fort Moultrie," Marion corrected. "President Rutledge has sent word that the fort has been christened for the colonel."

"I'm glad I was at the christening."

"By the way, Bill, what are your wishes for the burial of Mr. Wilde? Has he kinsfolk in the city?"

"No, sir, none nearer than New York."

"If I may be useful, please command me."

"Thank you, sir." Bill glanced up at the blue and white flag. "I thought about it during the battle. I wish he might be buried with the men who fell here. Could such an honor be arranged for him?"

"Yes, and it shall be."

"Thank you, sir. I guess that's the most we can do for him. He couldn't lie in better company."

CHAPTER III

IMMEDIATELY after the battle of Fort Moultrie neither Bill, nor anyone else, had more than a vague idea of its importance. Only time could show it to have been one of the three decisive victories of the American Revolution, the others being Saratoga and King's Mountain. At the time, the Carolinians merely knew they had driven off some of the best ships in the British navy and saved Charles Town and the hinterland from an invasion by Clinton's troops. And they had done it despite the loan of General Lee by Congress. Had Rutledge listened to Lee the battle would not have been fought, nor would it have been won without the leadership of Moultrie and Marion. That much was clear at the start.

When the debris of battle was somewhat cleared away General Lee appeared and reviewed the garrison. Bill stood in line with the others, stiff and hot and uncomfortable. Lee, who was always at his best when the shooting was over, spoke eloquently of the defense of the fort, then spoiled it all by calling it "our" victory. The men took it in silence and rolled their bloodshot eyes at their officers. Moultrie, who had one hand bandaged, moved slightly as though in pain, Horry opened and closed his mouth, and

Marion stared at the sea. And the sea sparkled in the sunlight as though winking its understanding of the situation.

When Lee had strutted his little part President Rutledge came over from the city and was met at the water's edge by the cheering troops. In spite of the jubilation he looked pale and worn, for as President of the General Assembly of South Carolina, he had taken the brunt of raising the militia, building the fort and providing for its defense. The lion's share of glory was his, but in his own opinion he was no lion. He did not review the troops, but met them as neighbors, for he knew many of them by name. Spotting Sergeant Jasper, he took off his own sword and handed it to him.

"It is the symbol of trust placed in me by the people of South Carolina," he said. "From them, through my hands, it is a token of gratitude to the one who saved our colors at the risk of his life."

Jasper stammered and blushed and twisted his leather cap for a full minute before he could speak, and then no one heard what he said because everyone was whooping it up for him.

"Sergeant," Rutledge continued, "in personal appreciation of your heroism, I shall issue you a lieutenant's commission."

Jasper shook his head. "I'm greatly obliged to you, sir," he said, "but I'd rather not have it. As I am, I pass well enough with the boys, but effen I had a c'mission I'd have to keep higher company. I can't read or write, sir, and I'd look plumb foolish hangin' out more'n I washed."

"A hero and a sensible man!" Rutledge put out his hand

impulsively, and the men cheered with more gusto than if Jasper had been made a brigadier.

When the ceremony was over, Bill felt so let down that he wanted to cry. Men were everywhere, but he was painfully alone. The experiences of recent days and nights had shaken him so that he had the unreal feeling of being outside himself and trying to get back in. New York seemed as far away as the moon, war had replaced peace, the world he had known and supposed to be stable had ended with a bang, and in its stead was a place of tumult and death that lacked reason or reality. Such things could not happen — yet they had.

He went down to the shore and washed his hands in the ocean that floated the British navy, the traditionally invincible navy that had bumped its nose against the palmetto logs and backed off, bleeding and groggy. That did not seem right either. He was elated by the victory his side had won, but he wished the enemy were not British. They were his people by blood and heritage and he could not understand their desire to kill. Major Marion had blamed it on King George. Was the whole English nation afraid of one man? That might be the great difference between the old world and the new. Was that why men like Marion took this so seriously? Would they rather die than subscribe to ideas in which they did not believe? Now that the heat of battle was over, would they go on?

Turning these new and troublesome thoughts in his mind as he would have turned a strange fruit in his hands, Bill fell asleep under a sandbank. He was so dog-tired that the stars were out when he awoke. He rolled over and looked up at them, wishing he might reach them and pull himself up where the air was cool and free from the stench of gunpowder and blood. Camp sounds came to him faintly; singing and yelling and ax blows. The men must have a big bonfire and its light picked out the top of the sand hill above him. There, a man seemed to rise out of the ground against the lighted sky as he walked up the other side of the dune and stopped on its crest. Bill recognized Marion. The major stood with his head thrown back and his hands clenched low in front of him and there was something so intensely dramatic in the unrehearsed pose that the boy tingled all over.

"Lord of hosts," Marion spoke, as he supposed, to an audience of One, "if war must come, I thank Thee that I have been given a part in it. I hate war, but I hate tyranny more. I can not turn back. I must go forward. There is no choice. Give me the strength and the courage and the faith to meet what is before me. And, though I be denied all else, may I not fail my country!" He spread his arms wide and stood for a moment against the sky, then walked away.

Bill felt the tears smarting in his eyes. In the space of a moment Francis Marion had become his hero, the epitome of all that was fine in a man, the symbol of the nation's righteous fight for liberty. In that one minute the boy's doubts vanished; Marion and all who shared his spirit would go on. No matter what happened, *they would go on.* He looked at the stars again and prayed to what he believed was beyond them: "Let me go with them. And don't, please don't let me do anything that will make Major Marion ashamed of me."

It was the next afternoon when Marion, who would not leave his wounded men until he had done all possible for their comfort, found Bill eating with Jasper, both sharing an iron kettle by a fire.

"I am leaving for Charles Town presently," he said. "If you are ready, I will acquaint you with John Stewart."

It was characteristic of him to keep every promise he made, even to a boy who was a stranger. Bill looked at his own battle-torn breeches and his shoes stiffened and discolored by sea water and gunpowder.

"Am I fit to be presented to a gentleman?" he asked.

"He will recognize the livery of war."

"You say he is a Tory. Now that I am his enemy, will he receive me, sir?"

"Of course, of course. A man of Stewart's ilk will receive the son of an old friend regardless of politics."

"Then I'll go with you, sir."

"An' keep yore eyes peeled," Jasper cautioned. "Whar's one good Tory six're waitin' to knife you."

Marion might have had himself rowed ashore in a staff boat manned by soldiers or slaves, but he prefered to paddle his own dugout. As planter and sportsman, he had traversed innumerable streams and marshes on business and pleasure during a considerable part of his forty-three years, and he could handle a small craft beautifully. It was easy even for Bill to see that his skill was remarkable.

"Ever use a paddle, Bill?" Marion asked over his shoulder.

"No, sir, but I'll try."

"Not now, please."

"Is it hard to learn?"

"I don't know. I can't remember when I learned." Marion's arms were working as smoothly as the legs of a swimming duck. "I was a puny child so my parents gave me great doses of exercise for medicine."

"It worked," Bill remarked, wondering if it were good manners to speak familiarly to an officer.

"Mighty well, too. By the time I was sixteen I was tough enough to ship before the mast to the West Indies. We collided with a whale and spent six days in an open boat, living on the flesh of a dog. Two men died. I had my fill of seafaring."

"As I will have when I get home," Bill said.

"That may be." Marion did not press for particulars as to why Bill left home in the first place, and the boy was not free to bring the subject up.

They landed on the tip of the peninsula on which Charles Town stood, between the Ashley and Cooper rivers. Bill was amazed to see acres of stores and warehouses level with the ground.

"Did the British guns carry this far?" he asked.

"No." Marion tied the canoe to a ring in a wharf timber. "The buildings were razed so they wouldn't provide cover if the ships passed the fort."

"That cost a heap of money!" Bill's Yankee thrift was staggered.

"War is always expensive."

Bill looked back and forth. "The trade here must be immense to use all those wharves."

"Yes, I have seen three hundred and fifty ships in the

harbor at one time." Marion dusted his breeches with his palms.

"Flags from all over the world probably."

"Including the Jolly Roger."

"Pirates?"

"Plenty of 'em in the old days. In 1718, forty-nine were hanged here in one month. Twenty-two in one day, including the notorious Steve Bonnet. Spicy characters they were." Marion glanced about. "And still are, for that matter."

They had been stepping along as they talked, out of the ruined warehouse district up into the residential section. The streets were full of people, all in carnival mood. Sedan chairs and carriages bore ribbons and flags in the state colors and people waved to each other in passing, horsemen cantered along to the jingle of spurs and bridle chains, pedestrians kicked up a happy dust with their cowhide shoes or their bare feet, and everywhere the mellow voices of Negroes stood out like blossoms of sound. The Whigs were gay because they had taken a fall out of mighty Britain and the Tories concealed their true emotions inasmuch as they knew what was good for them.

Marion was as familar with the city as with his plantation in nearby St. John's Parish.

"This is the street." He put in an extra stride to keep step as they turned a corner.

"I hope Mr. Stewart is at home," Bill said.

"Tories are required to be at home these days."

"Under guard?"

"No, on parole."

Most of the houses stood flush with the street and had side entrances, but the Stewart place was larger and stood back, facing out over a high brick wall. Marion swung open a wrought-iron gate and Bill noticed the S and C motif gracefully woven in the ironwork. Beyond was a garden, set with trees and plants whose names the boy did not know, then a tall white door between fluted white pillars.

A Negro servant opened the door and bowed low in a friendly rather than a servile manner.

"How are you, Noah?" Marion handed him his hat and motioned Bill to do the same.

"Ah'm fine, Massah Marion." The man grinned and with a flourish dropped the hats on a table.

"Is your master engaged?"

"Hisse'f an' Massah Graves are writin' lettahs."

"Show us up."

"Yes, suh."

They went up a stairway that spiraled easily for all its great width. Bill, the thrifty Northerner who did not appreciate a Southerner's love of expansive living, wondered why they built it wide enough for a platoon, and when he reached the top and looked down the well he wondered again why the floors were so far apart.

At the far end of the upper hall Noah knocked on a polished door, opened it a hand's breadth, and announced, "Gen'mens to see yo', suh."

"Bring 'em in," a deep voice answered.

"Yes, suh, hyeh dey is." Noah swung the door wide open and bowed them through.

Across the room Bill saw a huge, florid man in powdered wig, blue suit, white ruffled shirt, green stockings, and shoes with flat silver buckles. Behind him, beside a writing table, stood a young, sallow clerk, with black eyes too close together.

"Drop me down!" the big man rumbled, coming forward. "Major Marion is welcome."

"Thank you, Mr. Stewart." Marion bowed. "May I present my friend, William Barlow."

"Pleasured to know you, young man, mighty pleasured!" Stewart spoke rapidly, a characteristic of Charles Townians. "Graves," he said over his shoulder, "the letters can wait."

"Yes, sir." The secretary's voice was soft, with a sort of forced smoothness. He gathered up his papers, quills, ink horn and sand shaker, and backed noiselessly through an inner door, which he closed a moment later.

"Sit yourselves down, gentlemen." Stewart set the example.

"No, thank you," Marion said.

"I recollect you are one of those natural oddities, a dry Whig." Stewart chuckled. "But wet or dry, not to be criticized by a mere Tory. Congratulations on your victory, Major."

"The Almighty was good to us."

"You and Moultrie and Rutledge don't take the credit due you. Drop me down, sir! When we thrash you, as we're sure to do, we shall claim the glory."

"You, too, may need a bit of Heaven's aid before that day comes," Marion retorted affably.

Bill marveled at the way they chaffed about such a serious matter. To him, the war was of deadly interest.

Stewart's mood seemed to change to match the boy's. "We all need divine guidance." he looked far away through a window. "It's sad business, Major."

Marion nodded. "But to discuss it is not my mission here today. This is Bill's expedition. I will wait below."

"I would rather have you stay, sir." Bill flushed an apology for asking the favor.

"So? Then I'll stay." Marion sat down as though he had nothing in the world to do except oblige a boy.

Stewart glanced at the flat table clock and urged, "Well, young man?"

This was the moment Bill had hoped for and dreaded long before he left New York. He held back more since meeting Stewart, for, while the Tory was a model of civility, he was officially an enemy and it took courage to ask his help. He glanced at Marion, received an encouraging nod, and made the plunge.

"I am the son of Thomas Barlow," he began.

"Eh?" Stewart leaned forward. "Drop me down! Not my friend, the New York merchant?"

"Yes, sir."

"Well, well! Well, well!" Stewart slapped both hands on his fat knees and looked hard at Bill. "You *do* favor him. Yes, you *do*. How is he?"

"He died last winter."

"No, no, no!" Stewart leaned backward. "A long illness, I presume. I haven't seen him for — let me think — for five years."

"It was a tropical disease."

"Damn the tropics! Don't like the tropics and never did. Bugs, snakes and sickness. White men shouldn't go there. Let the natives have it."

"Father was taken there as a prisoner."

"Prisoner!" Stewart sat up straight. "You said prisoner?"

"Yes, sir. He was captured by pirates."

"Pirates! Drop me down! Pirates! The scum of the earth and the stinking froth of the seven seas! Give us the tale, boy. Eh, Marion?"

"If he wishes to," the major said.

"Of course, of course, if you wish to, William," Stewart amended hastily.

"I do, sir," Bill told him. "I came here for that purpose."

"Our ears are itching." Stewart's face was eager as a boy's.

Bill thought a moment, arranging his facts, then said, "A year after his last trip to Charles Town my father sailed again to trade with you."

"One of my best customers," the merchant explained to Marion. "Bought heavily of rice, indigo, lumber and tar. Continue, William."

"He took ten thousand pounds in gold and — "

"And the blasted pirates got it all!" Stewart interrupted vehemently.

"No, sir. They chased his ship and drove it into an inlet. He buried his gold on a small island during a fog. When the fog lifted, the pirates captured his ship. Most of the men were killed in the fighting. The others were carried off to a pirates' island in the West Indies and forced to work as slaves. All except my father died within two years. He escaped and came home, but he was stricken with his last illness soon afterward."

"And the gold was recovered?" Stewart poured himself a glass of wine and spilled part of it, for he was excited.

"Not that we know of, sir."

"Ten thousand pounds! Drop me down! A deuce of a lot of money, Marion, a *deuce* of a lot."

"A deuce of a lot," the major agreed.

Bill took a long breath and came to the point. "My father told me to ask your help, sir, in trying to recover it."

"'In *trying* to recover it.' I like the way you put it." Stewart jumped up nimbly for a man of his size. "You have a map?"

"No, sir."

"Thunder and blazes! He buried all that treasure and made no map?"

"He made one, but he was obliged to destroy it to keep it from the pirates."

"I see, I see. How deuced unfortunate! Damn the pirates! But perhaps he could tell you the location."

"All he could tell me was that it is under a big cypress on a point on an island up the coast from Charles Town. There are three small islands in a group and this is the middle one."

"There are ten thousand big cypresses on a hundred islands up the coast from here!" Marion cried.

"We'll find it! We'll find it!" Stewart's eyes snapped. "I'll take a ship and — " He stopped. "But I'm not at liberty. I am a prisoner in my own house. Oh, blast this war!"

"As for that," Marion said, "all Tories will soon be released."

"Hooray!" Stewart tossed an imaginary hat in the air, a ridiculously sprightly gesture for so solid a gentleman. "When I'm my own master, William, we'll go a-treasure hunting."

"But, sir," Bill protested, "everything has changed since I left home. I can't ask you to help me in these times."

"That's just why I want to go, boy, just why. I've been cooped up here till I feel like a stuffed fowl. I need action. Come back when I am my own man again and we'll lay our plans. No! Don't come back — stay here. I insist that you be my guest. Eh, Marion?"

"Bill is free to choose," the major answered. "He is welcome in the fort, but I daresay he will be more comfortable here."

"He must stay," Stewart puffed. "Blast it, he's going to stay. There's much to talk about. I must know more of your father's story, William. Aye, you must stay!"

Bill preferred the fort and the men he had fought beside, but under the circumstances he could not refuse his father's friend.

"I shall be happy to accept your hospitality, sir," he said.

As he turned to say good-bye to Marion he noticed the door was open a crack into the room where Graves the secretary had disappeared.

CHAPTER IV

AFTER Marion left, Stewart kept Bill in conversation for a while and the talk returned to pirates. The merchant searched his writing table for a chart of the coast in an attempt to form some idea of where the island lay.

"When I did my own work I could find things," he sputtered. "Blast all secretaries! They cause more confusion than a typhoon." He raised his voice and threw it over his shoulder: "Graves! Graves, I want you." There was no reply from the adjoining room. He glanced at the door, which was now closed, then went over and opened it. "Gone!" he rumbled. "A secretary's room should have only one entrance, like a cage. Then when you put 'em in, there you've got 'em. But there should be none of the creatures in the first place. Blast all secretaries!" He slammed the door and added, "Especially that one."

"May I fetch him for you, sir?" Bill offered, without stopping to think he did not know his way about the house.

"No, he's out for a strut. He'll reappear at mealtime. By the way," he glanced at the clock, "dinner will be served in an hour." He yanked the tasseled handle on a bell and went on fuming. "Has that boy gone too? I suppose so. Negro servants are as bad as indentured whites. I've tried both. All worthless. I'll skin that boy when he does come. So help me, I'll skin him!"

"Yes, suh." A Negro houseboy stood grinning in the doorway.

"Ham, you rascal, show this gentleman to his room."

"Yes, suh. Please yo' to foller me, suh."

They went along the hall that was lighted by candles in sconces, giving off a faint perfume of juniper. The bedroom was also in candlelight, for the servant who tended the lights had just made his first round of the evening. Bill eyed the great bed with its tightly drawn curtains, then caught sight of himself in a mirror.

"Holy smoke!" he burst out. "Ham, I can't go to dinner in these clothes I wore in battle."

"Yo' wuz in de battle, suh?" The little Negro's eyes widened.

"Yes, and look at me — all dirt and powder stains and sweat."

"Ah'll fotch yore bag, suh, so yo' kin change."

"My bag is at the bottom of the ocean."

"De good Lawd! Yo' mus' been keerless, suh."

"Are there any clothes in the house I can borrow? Perhaps Mr. Stewart has a boy my size."

"No, suh, he completely boyless kaze he a bachler."

"What can I do, Ham?"

"Yo' go to bed, suh, an' Ah clean yore clo'es."

"I can't get into a clean bed when I'm black with powder smoke."

"Mabbe yo' lak to purify yo'se'f, suh. Yes, suh. I fotch de bathtub."

"Good! Double-quick so I won't be late."

In an astonishingly short time, considering how far it was to the kitchen, Ham was back with a wooden tub nearly full of warm water, a lump of soap and three towels.

"Peel de duds offen yo'se'f an' see kin ole brudder Ham make 'em shine lak de angel wing," he said. And when Bill handed them to him he was off like a rabbit.

During the next half hour he did not transform the garments into angels' wings, but he performed a lesser miracle by getting them clean.

"You deserve a shilling for that job," Bill said admiringly, "but I haven't a penny. 'Thank you' is all I can pay at present."

"Dat las' longer'n money," Ham answered philosophically. "Now yo' dress yo 'se'f an' prommynade to dinnah. Massah John mighty fussy effen folkses is late."

Bill made it by an eyelash, meeting Stewart at the dining-room door as though by calculation, though it was pure luck. The table was set for three, but no one else was in sight.

"Where's Graves, Pansy?" Stewart asked the waitress.

"He gone out on business, suh. Let on as he'd be back soon."

"Slippery devil. Never know where he is. Why is he so full of business of a sudden?"

"He didn't 'spress hisse'f, suh."

"Nor do I care. Sit down, William, turtle soup waits for no man."

The soup was as smooth as a sea breeze and as tangy. It whetted Bill's appetite until his hands shook with eagerness and when the baked fish, stuffed ham, sweet potatoes and other dishes appeared he wished he was at a rough table where he could lay into them unawed by burnished silver and white damask. Stewart was a large and skillful diner who used his knives and forks and spoons gracefully, the while he talked steadily, the outbound tide of words never delaying the stowing of food.

"I presume you are a Whig," he remarked, as the meal was ending.

"I don't know much about politics," Bill evaded.

"Don't parry an honest question, boy. You know where you stand — for the king or against him."

"Against him," Bill answered stoutly. "I have already fought on the American side."

"Rubbish! Rubbish! There's no such thing as 'the American side.' We're all British — loyalists or rebels. Good fellows on both sides, but the rebels lack intelligence."

Bill said nothing, for he knew he could not hold his own in a political argument.

"Did you fight voluntarily or did they force you into it?" Stewart asked abruptly.

"I wanted to help Major Marion."

"An old family friend?"

"No, sir. I never heard of him till the night before the battle."

"Huh. Yet you offered to die for him, as they tell about."

"Not exactly that, sir. I like him, so when I saw he was in for trouble I wanted to help him."

"Drop me down!" The Tory wagged his head in puzzlement. "What is that man's power? Nothing to look at, never says much, no money to speak of, might be called a nondescript bachelor planter, but show me a man, woman or child, black or white, who doesn't think he made the earth and put a white picket fence around it."

A step sounded in the hall and the door opened.

"At last, Graves." Stewart was plainly displeased.

"Your pardon, sir." Humility cringed in the secretary's tone. "I went to the shop for ink and was delayed by the crowd."

"What crowd?"

"The rebels are arrogant enough to be celebrating."

"I don't blame 'em. Fact is, I'd blame 'em if they didn't kick up their heels. We would be doing the same thing if the shoe was on the other foot."

"Yes, sir."

"Sit down and eat," Stewart commanded impatiently.

"Your pardon, sir, if I refuse. To while away the delay at the shop I purchased sweet cakes and killed my appetite."

"A foolish choice, but your own. Wine?"

"A small glass, sir." Graves lowered his narrow black eyes virtuously and poured a drink.

"I suppose the Whigs are fifing and drumming fit to disturb all Britain," Stewart remarked.

"There is much marching and music, sir."

"Well, let 'em whoop. Let 'em, while they may. They'll change their tune before long. Pardon my opinion, William." The old Tory chuckled.

Graves rolled his eyes at Bill and then toward Stewart, smoothly, as though they turned in oil.

"If I may offer a suggestion, sir," he said, "I will gladly act as the young gentleman's guide, if he cares to see the sport."

"But does he?" Stewart smiled. "Having tasted the cream of adventure in battle, he may spurn the skim milk of parade. What say you, William?"

"I would like to see the fun," Bill answered. A veteran he might be, but he was still a boy who would rather be on the street at such a time than spending a sedate evening with an old gentleman.

"Then go." Stewart stood up. "Drop me down! I'd go myself if I weren't on parole. Blast this war! Blast it!"

"Thank you, sir." Bill rose to his feet as quickly as he thought respectful.

He and Graves went down the street at a fast clip, for the distant sound of martial music quickened their legs. It was dark along the way, where the houses were lighted only by candles and many of them were far back behind garden walls. Occasionally a slave came along, lighting his master's path with a torch or lantern, the master being on foot if he were vigorous, but in a sedan chair carried by four husky blacks if he were old and gout-ridden. Farther out in the street horsemen and people in vehicles clattered by in the gloom. Sometimes they collided and then, according to their mental habits, they apologized or cursed.

"May you have been in the city for long?" Graves asked.

"A few hours," Bill told him.

"Then it is unfamilar to you."

"Naturally." Somehow, Bill had no wish to be courteous to him.

"Does it please you?"

"So far."

"Ah, I love Charles Town!"

"Then why didn't you turn out and help defend it?" Bill could not help asking.

"Not I. The better class welcomes the British," Graves answered, with smooth, infuriating arrogance.

"Better class!" Bill bristled. "What do you call Colonel Moultrie and Major Marion and the rest of them?"

"Rabble."

"Well, by thunder!" Bill stopped in his tracks. "If that's the way you feel, we part company right now."

"I apologize," Graves said quickly, too quickly to be convincing. "I shall confine myself to being your physical, not your social, guide."

"You don't need to be either, you stinking prig!" Bill flared and turned abruptly down a pitch-dark street.

For all that he was a stranger in the city, his sense of direction told him he was headed toward the waterfront. That was where he wanted to go, for he guessed that boats would be plying to the fort during the evening and one of them would give him a lift across. He would sleep better with a stretch of water between himself and Graves. It might not be good manners to walk out on Stewart, but, unless signs were false, the old Tory would not take sides with his secretary. Neither by word nor implication had he called the patriots "rabble." He knew a man when he saw one, regardless of the color of his coat, and being a gentleman, he had no thought of advertising himself as one of the "better class." He would understand the boy's spleen against Graves.

Angry clear through, Bill went as fast as he could down the dark street, fleeing from Graves instinctively. There were occasional lights in windows and the buildings became smaller until they were mere shacks that looked like sailors' drinking places. Grog shops they would have been called in the North, but under any name they formed a tough quarter and the people abroad in it might well have stirred up qualms in anyone who sported a gold chain or a bulging pocket. But Bill had nothing to lose and so went straight through, following his nose toward the smell of salt water. Then of a sudden the night was full of stars that blazed and vanished in blackness.

He was half conscious again a moment later, for the blow on the back of his head had been a glancing one, but he could not move. He knew two people carried him into a building and upstairs to a dimly lighted room, where they laid him on a bed or bunk. Unable to think clearly at first, he was surprised and relieved when Graves' face floated into his field of vision. Much as he disliked him, here was an acquaintance who might help him back to Stewart's house or over to the fort. The face disappeared, but he could hear Graves talking. "The one I told you about" and "walked into it" were the only words he understood. Someone laughed and bottles clinked together.

After a while the numbness began to wear off. Bill moved

little by little, cautiously, for as his mind cleared he realized he might not be among friends. The pain in the back of his head was the result of no accident. He had been deliberately slugged, though by whom and for what reason he did not yet know. It didn't matter; the thing to do was to get away if he could.

He lay still on his back until he felt his muscles were ready for action, then turned slowly toward the light. Graves sat on a low stool beside a table on which stood two candles stuck in black bottles and two other bottles with the corks out. Across from him on another stool was a pirate, if there ever was one. Swarthy, heavy-set, with gold rings in his ears, a red kerchief on his head, sea boots reaching to short cotton trousers, a blue sash and a once-white shirt, he had all the markings of an unhanged rascal. By contrast, Graves, with his pasty face and neat, almost foppish, clothes looked weak and almost respectable.

The door to the stairs was closed and, for all Bill knew, locked. The only window was beyond the table. If he was quick enough to overturn the candles he might jump into the street. He drew up his knees and the rickety bed squealed like a pig. Both men turned and the light revealed a brace of silver-mounted pistols in the pirate's belt.

"So!" Graves smiled hatefully. "The young gentleman is himself once more."

Bill knew he must play for time, so he sat up slowly and rubbed his head.

"What happened to me?" he asked innocently. "Did I fall against a stone?"

"No, I hit you," Graves answered readily. "It seemed

the surest way to persuade you to stop and hold conversation with me and my friend, Master Bottle."

"Mr. Stewart will have something to say about this," Bill blustered, to cover the fear that was growing in him.

"Oh, unquestionably." Graves made a gesture of resignation. "But we shall have our say first."

Bill tried throwing a bluff straight at Bottle. "I don't know who you are," he said, "but if you harm me you'll answer to my officers, Colonel Moultrie and Major Marion."

"Nary heard o' th' gentlemen," Bottle answered in a voice that sounded as though it had rusted in sea water.

"Never heard of the commanders on Sullivan's Island?"

"Nope." He took a swig from one of the bottles. "Graves, I'm a busy sailorman with little time to fritter."

Graves acted on the suggestion. "William," he said pleasantly, "I know why you are in Charles Town."

Bill remembered the slyly opened door and shot back, with more spirit than tact, "You heard it while eavesdropping this afternoon."

Graves ignored the jab. "Ten thousand pounds is more money than a lad of your age needs. Captain Bottle and I have decided to share it with you."

"I haven't a pound of it," Bill protested.

"Oh, we will help you find it." Graves gave that hateful smile again. "Bottle has a ship. We will share equally."

"Well, of all the gall!" Bill fairly gasped.

"What's amiss with such a dicker?" Graves asked, as though he believed he was honest. "You came to Mr. Stewart asking aid. We offer it to you. I arrange the business details, Master Bottle supplies the ship, you produce the map, and away we merrily sail. When the gold is equally divided we put you safely ashore with your portion. Could anything be more honorable?"

"You'll find me an honest sailorman," Bottle put in modestly.

"What map do you mean?" Bill looked blankly at Graves.

"The one showing where the treasure is buried. What other?"

"Then you didn't open the door soon enough to hear me tell Mr. Stewart there is no map."

"Yes, indeed, but I'm not such a fool as to believe it."

"It's the truth, Graves."

"You didn't come from far-off New York without first knowing the exact lay of the island."

"Yes, I did."

"Oh, no, you didn't."

"I tell you I did."

"You're a liar!" Graves' pale face colored.

"I am not!" Bill stood up.

So did Graves. "Give me that map or I'll kill you!"

"There is no map."

"Take you choice — and take it quick."

"I can't give you what doesn't exist." Bill looked at Bottle. "Don't you believe me, Captain?"

"Nope." Bottle took another nipper. "We're a wastin' val'able time, Graves."

Without another word Graves sprang across the floor and drove his fist into Bill's face. The boy fell back on the bed and Graves pinned him down, smashing him again and again until the blows slipped in blood and lost some of their force.

"Will you talk now?" he panted.

"There is — no — map," Bill repeated faintly.

"Easy, mate." Bottle pulled Graves away. "There's nary profit in sendin' of him to th' bottom."

"I won't be blocked by the damn little rebel."

"Aye, but leave th' life in him. I knows a few tricks we use on th' Main to loosen tongues."

"Torture?" Graves asked hopefully.

"Oh, no, no, no!" Bottle sounded shocked. "Just a bit o' fire here, a gentle twist there an' first you know they're talkin' like a parrot on a yardarm."

"Then do it," Graves said. "There's gold in it for us both."

"Aye." Bottle clumped across the room.

HOURS later Bill lay unconscious on the bed, a pitiful sight.

"I'll kill him!" Graves raged.

"Nope," Bottle said placidly.

"What's it to you? You have failed."

"I've a notion th' lad told th' truth."

"Whether or not he did we can't let him live and talk. We must finish him or swing."

"I'm a hard-workin' sailorman as turns a honest shillin' when he can."

"But he must die — there's no other way out for us, you fool."

Bottle looked down at Bill appraisingly. "He'll mend an' I'll clear fifty pound on him," he said.

"Will I be clear of it?" Graves asked anxiously.

"Aye. And it's possible you may profit later."

They talked together for a few minutes, then rolled Bill in a blanket and carried him downstairs. He was in a stupor when they hoisted him from a small boat to the deck of a ship and still unconscious as the ship slipped down the harbor and out to sea.

CHAPTER V

BILL wished groggily that the wind would stop blowing and tossing him around in that treetop. He was sore from head to foot and hot and sick-feeling, so the constant motion was painful. He couldn't remember how he came to be in a tree or where the tree was, but probably he had been fishing in the Hudson and Cornelius Van Derber's red bull had put him up a tree. It had happened before, for that bull thought he owned all of Manhattan Island. Now he was bellowing.

"Praise de Lawd! Ah's gwine be free!"

That was no bull. They didn't speak English, especially Van Derber's bull that had been raised in a Dutch family.

"Moses done lead us outen de wilderness. Hallylulya!"

Another bull? Don't be such a fool. That was a man's voice, a Negro's. Of course, one of Van Derber's slaves come to fetch the bull.

"Hey!" Bill shouted. "Tell your master to keep his bull home or answer to the magistrate."

"I'll tell him, lad," a voice answered near at hand. Sounded like an Englishman. "Go to sleep for a bit."

"I can't sleep in this tree with the wind blowing."

"You can't fall. Take it easy, you are tired."

Yes, he was tired, dog-tired. If the fellow knew what he was talking about . . . and he couldn't fall . . . It would be a good idea to sleep . . . The wind . . . The bull . . .

When he awoke again his head was clear. It ached, as did the rest of his body, but he saw that he was in the hold of a small ship, lying on a pile of canvas not far from an open port. He moved experimentally and realized how sore his flesh was, then he remembered the beating and torturing Graves and Bottle had given him.

"If there's any justice on earth I'll settle that account," he said aloud.

"Yo' says what, suh?" A huge Negro came out of the gloom and stood in the light of the port. He wore only short cotton breeches and was the most magnificent physical specimen Bill had ever seen.

"Who are you?" the boy asked.

"Ah's Luke — a free man." The Negro did not smile, but his whole face lighted. It was an intelligent face, handsome even under those conditions. He repeated in a deep musical voice, "Ah's a free man!"

Bill continued his questioning: "What is this ship and where is it going?"

"Hit am Cap'n Bottle's ship, suh, gwine ter Africa."

"Bottle! That pirate?"

"Cap'n Bottle am a fine gen'man, suh. He lead us outen bondage lak Moses done de chil'en ob Izreel."

Bill made no comment. He knew that Bottle was no Moses, but this was not the time to argue about it. The mere thought of being on that ship gave him such a sick feeling that he closed his eyes.

He opened them when that quiet English voice inquired, "How is the lad this morning?" A bearded man was leaning over him, looking sharply with blue eyes.

"Who are you?" Bill asked, astonished at the sight of a gentleman in that place.

"Dr. Pardee, the ship's surgeon." A man of much practice, too, for he made no attempt to show off by pulse taking and chest thumping and question-asking antics.

"Then this is not Captain Bottle's ship?"

"Yes, it is."

"You don't look like that kind," Bill said bluntly.

It seemed to him that Dr. Pardee blushed above his beard and that his eyes winced. Before he could speak, Bottle himself dropped lightly through an open hatch, barefooted, stripped to the waist, but still wearing the gold earrings.

"Did I hear th' rebel frog a pipin'?" he asked good-humoredly, in his rusty voice.

Bill said nothing, for sight of the man sickened him, but Dr. Pardee answered, "He is coming round, Captain."

"Bully!" Bottle scratched his huge hairy chest. "Pleasured to know he's mendin'."

"You say that, when you tried to kill me!" Bill's strength returned with his anger.

"Now, now, now!" Bottle shook his head almost playfully. "Graves was pullin' fer that. I broke his oar. I'm an honest sailorman."

Bill felt the sweat pouring down his face. Dr. Pardee noticed it, and told Bottle, "Leave us now, Captain, if you please."

"Eh?" Bottle glared at him. "Do I take orders on my own ship?"

"You do if you want this lad to recover." Pardee looked him in the eye.

"Shrimp fish!" Bottle growled. But he went on deck.

"I don't understand things," Bill said, feeling weak again.

"Who does, lad?" Pardee smiled faintly and walked away.

Within a few days Bill was able to walk about. He had no broken bones and Dr. Pardee knew how to reduce soreness. More and more, as his strength returned, the boy wondered why such a seeming gentleman served with a man like Bottle. But he was learning not to ask personal questions. Though it was his first experience with such characters, he knew each one had a shady past and that, if he wanted to live, he must keep his suspicions to himself.

And he did want to live. Sometimes, when he realized he was only a boy, without friends, on a lawless ship bound for an unknown destination, it seemed hopeless to try to survive. He would feel that way for a while, especially just before dawn, then, as daylight strengthened, his courage would rise up and kick him for being a coward. Every man had once been a boy. Unlike himself, not all of them had been gently reared and shielded from the tough side of life, but whoever they were they had fought their youthful battles and survived them. Perhaps that was what strife — mental and spiritual and physical — was for, to weed out the quitters because they were of no earthly use. When it came, a fellow had his choice of folding up or meeting it like a man. It was his choice and he must make it alone, whether he was at home with his family or out here with cutthroats. What if Major Marion had squawked and gone down when he was shipwrecked as a lad? There was a man, but he would not be if he had quit as a boy. Quitters are never heard from when the roll of men is called.

When Bill was able to go on deck he was pleased to find that Bottle paid little attention to him. The captain was occupied with other things, particularly the wind, which was so nearly absent that for hours at a time the ship scarcely moved. Bottle was forever cursing the weather and watching the horizon through a prospective glass. When they sighted another sail, as they did several times, he fell to berating the crew, but Bill could not decide whether those outbreaks of temper were because he wanted to overhaul the vessels or avoid them.

The ship was small and dirty. So was the crew, there being only ten members of it; all, except Pardee, looking like parts of a human mop used by a giant for swabbing out his kitchen. What kind of ship she was Bill did not know, for he was no sailor, but she had less cargo space than a merchantman and was armed with six fair-sized cannon, besides racks of muskets and cutlasses. Honest trader or pirate, she was a poor specimen of her class.

Her cargo was equally questionable, for as near as Bill could see, it consisted of some thirty Negroes. But she was not a slaver, as none of them were in chains. On the contrary, they were almost deliriously happy and spent most of their time singing and dancing in the hold, none of them being allowed on deck. Following up his first conversation with Luke, Bill learned they were all former slaves from the Carolinas, who had come aboard at Bottle's promise to carry them to Africa. Some of them had been born there and the others were only a generation or two removed, so to them it was still the land of home and freedom. In what they called an honest attempt to pay their passage they had brought along whatever they could take, liquor, silverware, Chinese silk, hams, jewelry, sweet potatoes, and Bottle only knew what else.

Bill was new to the ways of chicanery, but he was learning fast.

"We aren't going to Africa," he said to Dr. Pardee one day, when they were alone.

"One never knows where a voyage will end," the doctor answered vaguely.

"In the first place, we haven't a quarter enough supplies for such a trip."

"I haven't inquired."

"Nor have I, but I can see."

"Yes."

"And I heard Bottle say the water won't last three days."

"It may be true."

"And, too, he doesn't love the black people enough to risk his neck trying to set a few of them free."

"I don't know his heart."

"I've had a glimpse of it."

"Take my advice, lad" — The doctor lowered his voice — "don't seek the origin of evil smells. It is unhealthy business."

"I'm not an idle noser," Bill said shortly, "but I'm mighty concerned about where we are bound, because Bottle is taking me there against my will."

"So?" Pardee gave him a quick look. "I gathered he rescued you from an enemy in Charles Town."

"How do you make that out?"

"I don't," Pardee said and walked away.

Bill was so worried and lonesome he fought to hold the tears back. He didn't ask anyone to fight his battles, but it would be a lot easier if there were a friend to talk with. But he mustn't cry. If he gave in and bawled he would be farther in spirit from men like Marion. Somehow, if you did as you thought they would have you do, they seemed nearer.

"Luke," he asked later, "what are you going to do when you get to Africa?"

"Preach religion to de heathens."

"Try to civilize them, you mean?"

"No, suh, jes' give 'em religion."

"But religion is part of civilization."

"Don' seem so to me, suh."

"Well, what do you call civilization?"

"Readin' an' writin' an' ridin' in a kerridge."

"And what is religion?"

"As Ah git hit, suh, religion is bein' friend wid ever'body. When ever'body's friend wid ever'body else ain't goin' be no fightin' an' thievin' an' cuttin' up sinful. Dat don' have no truck wid civ'lization."

"Perhaps religion boils down to friendliness, I don't know," Bill said. "I wish I had a few friends right now."

"Us is friends, suh."

"Are we, Luke?"

"Shore." The big fellow's sincerity was absolute.

"Shake hands on it."

"But, suh, whar Ah wuz fotch up white folkses don' shake hands wid us."

"And where I was raised a man gives his hand to a friend no matter what the color is."

So they shook hands.

Bill awoke the next morning before dawn, as usual. A breeze was coming through the porthole, bringing the smell of green things. He got up quickly, flinching as his sore muscles took hold, and looked out. Darkness fitted the ocean closely and on the southern horizon it was deeper, shutting out the lower stars in a great rough arc. From that direction came the sleepy conversation of birds that were not sea birds.

"Land on the port bow!" sang out a voice on deck and the ship came to life.

Within a few minutes the island was visible, stretching back from shore across open land to considerable mountains that looked timbered and rugged. The Negroes were wildly excited, for they believed it was Africa. As Bill moved toward the companionway he passed among knots of them, kneeling with their arms about each other, singing and shouting praise to Heaven.

On deck there was no commotion. Bottle himself had the wheel and the men were handling the sails as the mate ordered. Dr. Pardee leaned with his elbows on the rail, an open flask of brandy in one hand.

"What land is that?" Bill asked him.

"Nameless." Pardee offered the bottle without turning his head.

"No, thank you."

"Show your gratitude for a voyage safely made."

"It's only partly made."

"Possibly."

"Do we stop long here?"

"Who knows? A man might do worse than hole up here forever, the world being what it is."

"I'd make almost any kind of a change to get away from Bottle."

"Um." Pardee drank from the bottle and coughed.

"Honestly, don't you know the name of that island, Doctor?"

"No."

"Where is it?"

"Yonder."

"You know what I mean."

"Lad" — Pardee moved close to Bill and spoke guardedly — "you ask too many questions. Hark ye, yonder is one of the West Indies. It is of considerable extent and is monopolized by an Englishman known as Lord Bob. There's royal blood in his veins and he's not molested by British or French because of court politics. That is all I know about it and, if you're as astute as I judge you to be, you'll not try to learn more." He corked the bottle and walked away.

Bill went as far as he could into the stern and sat on a coil of rope to wait for what might happen next. The ship was raising the island steadily and he could now make out a small wharf with a few buildings behind it. In tropical fashion, they were sprawled at random under the palm trees and farther back were fields that might be sugar cane or sweet potatoes. Beyond those fields the wooded fields rolled away in the distance. It was a peaceful-looking scene, but the boy had been through so much lately he had developed a sixth sense that now warned him of trouble approaching.

The visible symbol of it was a small boat that put out from shore and came to the ship. It was rowed by eight black slaves and in the stern squatted a huge white man.

"Ahoy, Lord Bob!" Bottle roared from the rail.

The man raised his hand and stood up in the boat with the ease of an old sailor. He was immense in all his lines, looking to be seven feet tall, with the girth of a hogshead. Dressed in white, he seemed like a cloud drifting in and when he came up the ladder over the side his round red face suggested the sun rising out of the sea. He and Bottle went directly to the cabin, leaving the wheel to the mate, and after a few minutes Dr. Pardee was called to join them.

By clever handling, the ship was brought to the wharf within an hour and made fast by slaves working under a mulatto boss. There was no excited welcome from shore; even the dockhands were silent and only an occasional Negro woman or child peeped from behind the trees. Plainly enough, they had seen this crew before and were not happy at its reappearance.

In that strange silence a loud laugh boomed and Lord Bob rolled out of the cabin. "Joy to the world!" he blared. "Up hatches, Bottle, me lad, and let freedom reign."

The captain, grinning all over his evil face, raised a hatch cover, and shouted down, "Shake a leg, brothers and sisters! All ashore for Africa!"

The Negroes came up, singing and crying, their faces radiant. Bottle dropped to the dock and they followed him like sheep up a path to a low heavily timbered building. He stopped and motioned them inside through an open door. When the last one was in he closed the door and fastened it with a chain and padlock.

Not until that moment did Bill understand what had happened: Bottle had lured those unfortunate people away from their former owners, with promises of freedom, and then sold them to Lord Bob. The boy accepted Negro slavery as a matter of fact, but such betrayal of childlike trust made him boil. And he was as helpless to do anything about it as were the slaves themselves.

Bottle came back over the rail and joined Lord Bob on deck, both roaring with laughter.

"I sold 'em too cheap," Bottle said, hitching up his cotton breeches, which was the only garment he wore.

"Cheap my eye!" The Englishman puffed his fat cheeks in protest. "You sucked me dry."

"No, no, no! I'm an honest sailorman." Bottle grinned. "Too cheap, I say, but to play such a jest was worth somethin'."

"Africa and freedom!" Lord Bob slapped his huge thigh.

"They're a extry stout well-fed lot," Bottle said. "You may have trouble when they wake up."

"I've handled black cattle before," Lord Bob answered confidently. "Now where's the cockerel you mentioned?"

"Yonder."

When Bill saw them walking toward him his spine tingled and his mouth went dry. He hated them both and he feared them with all his heart. What they had in store for him he could not guess, but surely it would not be good.

"William," Bottle sang out, in as genial a tone as his rusty voice could manage, "I give you th' honor o' meetin' Lord Bob himself."

The boy said nothing, but bowed civilly.

"Not so unlikely to look at." The giant cocked his great round head appraisingly.

"You can read an' write an' figure, can't you, William?" Bottle asked.

"I can," Bill answered, wondering what difference that made.

"They're better l'arnt in th' north colonies," Bottle explained to Lord Bob. "They're healthier too, less fevers an' such."

"Twenty pound," Lord Bob said.

"Nope."

"How much?"

"Twenty-five."

"Robber!"

"Now, now, now!" Bottle looked hurt. "I make you a honest price, as one friend to another, an' you call me that name!"

"Twenty-two."

"Nope."

"Thief! Twenty-three."

"Nope."

"Twenty-four, you whelp."

"Nope. I'm a poor sailorman as needs his honest money."

"Liar! I'll take him." Lord Bob rumbled in his throat like a bull.

Bill realized with horror and anger that they had bought and sold him — like a bale of merchandise.

"Hold on!" He took a step toward them. "I am free and white. You can't sell me."

"Now be a good lad, William." Bottle's wheedling tone was ridiculous under the circumstances.

"I am told you are a prisoner of war," Lord Bob said. He had a smooth voice, as though it had gathered oil in passing between his fat lips.

"I am not a prisoner of war," Bill denied.

"You fit th' king's men at Sullivan's Island," Bottle reminded him.

"I did, but I wasn't made prisoner."

"Later you was captured."

"Later I was slugged by Graves."

"Don't make no dif'rence." Bottle gave him a hard look. "You're a rebel, you was took prisoner by a loyal British subjeck an' it's legal to sell you as a prisoner o' war."

"Quite right," Lord Bob said blandly. "It is common practice to sell such prisoners. Naturally, they ain't treated on a level with slaves. Heavens no! We use 'em like our own people."

"But you buy and sell them," Bill threw at him.

"Oh, yes, a mere formality. You will be my secretary. Then I'll make you an overseer. These mulatto overseers are stupid devils. And when you're of age and know the ropes I may take you into partnership."

"That doesn't tempt me," Bill answered. He turned to Bottle. "I say you have no right to sell me, but if money is what you want I will pay you twice what you ask this man if you will set me ashore in Charles Town or New York."

"I don't run no passenger ship. You're sold to Lord Bob." Bottle swung around and strode up the deck.

"You are free to leap into the sea," Lord Bob said, with utter indifference. "The sharks will welcome you. Or you are free to go ashore and make the best of the fortunes of war. If you were black I would use physical persuasion, but one is restrained by one's color." He followed Bottle into the cabin.

Bill stared after him, almost numb with dismay. Shipwreck, battle, torture, and now slavery! Short of death, was there anything else that could happen to him?

" 'The world is too much with us,' eh, lad?" Dr. Pardee appeared from nowhere.

"I have been sold as a slave!"

"I knew you would be."

"Why didn't you warn me?"

"To what end? There is no escape."

"But they can't sell a white man, Doctor."

"They can do anything out here."

"I won't work for that — that lump."

"Harkee, lad." Pardee glanced about and spoke softly. "At present your body is not your own — but your mind is. Use it. Go ashore with me and wait your time."

"With you? Are you a slave too?"

"No. Lord Bob employs me. His slaves are sick and he is losing money on them. I may stay for a year," he looked away for a moment, "or I may find the peace I want and stay forever."

Something about the strange little doctor calmed the tumult in Bill's brain. "It's the island or the sharks. I'll try the island first," he said, and tried to smile.

CHAPTER VI

TO the end of his days Bill never knew the name or exact location of that island. It was large enough to be of considerable value, yet no flag flew over it. The only inkling to the situation came from Lord Bob himself when, after bending his elbow excessively, he sometimes boasted that the law would never trouble him because of his influence at court. "I may be a skunk," was his inelegant way of putting it, "fact is, I am a skunk, but for the sake of their fastidious noses they won't stir me up."

It was more than six months before Bill knew much about the gigantic planter, who had apparently decided to give the boy time to cool off and resign himself. During that time Bill was never admitted to the sprawling, ramshackle house of pink-coral blocks where Lord Bob spent most of his days. When they landed he and Dr. Pardee were assigned to a cottage of palm logs that was staffed by an old Negro cook and a boy-of-all-work. There the two whites lived in comparative isolation as far as society went. There was a strange unfriendliness in the island's atmosphere, not open fear but a sort of sullen suspicion, that kept people apart.

Dr. Pardee, whom Bill found more likable and mysterious every day, went directly to his business of mending native health. He was gone all of every day and returned at night pale and weary.

"I have made the rounds at last," he said one evening. "Inspected every hide."

"How many?" Bill asked.

"One hundred and eighty-two Negro adults of working age, ninety-three children, all in varying stages of ill health."

"What's the cause of it?"

"Abuse and neglect, mostly."

"Are they all slaves?"

"Except for a dozen mixed-blood overseers who own themselves, if such ownership means anything."

"Am I classed as a slave?" The word rang in Bill's ears after he spoke it.

"Lord Bob bought you from Bottle."

"Bottle couldn't sell what he didn't own."

"He sells anything he can carry off."

"I won't stand it!" Bill jumped up. "I'm strong enough now to demand my rights from Lord Bob."

"Lad," Pardee said earnestly, "if you irritate Lord Bob he will shoot you as he would a bothersome dog. We are helpless for the present."

" 'We?' " Bill picked up the word. "Then you are a slave?"

"A slave of my own folly." Pardee drew in his breath as though trying to take back what he had said. Then he went on hurriedly, "I am hired by Lord Bob to minister to his livestock. They have been dying at an unprofitable rate. Now that I have taken inventory the real work begins. You can help me when you are able."

"I'm able now. Give me something to do, Doctor. I'll go daft just thinking."

"Tomorrow then."

It was not pleasant work, but better than sitting and fussing. The Negroes were in pitiful physical condition and their mental state was worse. Fear seemed to be the only emotion they had left. Hope no longer existed for them and they sullenly rejected any attention that might prolong their lives. Those who had come on the ship with Bottle were the worst of all, for their few days of elation made their present despair deeper. The mighty Luke, who might have been a man of real worth, was now a battered animal, but not yet beaten, for he still held up his head in the chain gang where they had set him to cutting timber.

"We will get out of this some time," Bill whispered to him at the first opportunity.

"No chance fo' slave."

"Yes, there is."

"Git away, fool! De Lawd done fo'sook dis islan' an' hits folkses."

Truly, Bill thought as he saw more of it, the place was devoid of all good. Despite its tropical beauty, it stank of evil. As he made the rounds with Pardee, day after day, it became a nightmare to him. Undernourishment, unset broken bones, flesh that had been beaten and left to fester — such sights built up within him a burning hatred of Lord Bob.

"I could kill that man," he said to the doctor.

"Doubtless."

"He deserves it."

"Yes."

"How can you be so calm about it?"

"I am no Galahad to crusade against every iniquity I see."

"I don't know who Galahad may be, but I say no man has a right to abuse people this way."

The doctor answered placidly, "Tyrants great and small are natural growths on the body of mankind."

"That doesn't mean they are necessary."

"Nature has always seen fit to create monarchs and lesser autocrats and, as a rule, power brings out the worst in a man."

"In America we don't believe kings are necessary." Bill stuck out his chin. "We are fighting to prove it."

"A very interesting experiment," the doctor said, in a tone that closed the conversation.

In a narrow personal sense, Bill had no quarrel with Lord Bob at first. The man was his master, but he seldom saw him and never suffered directly at his hands. At the same time, his present discomfort was due to the strange creature. The boy loathed him and all his works and gave every spare moment to planning escape from him.

As they traveled about the island, dosing, lancing and mending slaves, Bill kept his eyes open for a means of getting away. It would have been easy to slip into the woods, but that could give only temporary freedom for, as far as he could learn, there was not a boat on the place larger than a canoe. Nor was there any lumber with which to build one secretly. Some of the Negroes worked at cutting mahogany timber, but the logs were piled near the dock to be loaded on ships. Other slaves raised tobacco, rice and indigo, and a few tended the half-wild cattle that were kept to supply dried meat and hides for export. Twice during his first year on the island Bill saw mean-looking vessels take on cargo, but he never was near enough for a good look at them.

"Are they pirates or smugglers?" he asked Pardee.

"Why not honest merchantmen?" The doctor's eyes twinkled.

"That kind don't call here."

"It's not all bad, Bill."

"The man-made part is."

"You and I have done worthy work here the past year. The slaves are in a better way."

"To what purpose? So they can work harder for that ogre."

"I am a physician, lad, not a priest to decide under what conditions life is worth living."

"Your everlasting calmness maddens me!" Bill flung away.

Outside the house the tropical night was sultry and still. The boy looked away at the dark ocean and beyond it toward where he knew America lay. Were they still fighting for liberty over there? As an answer he saw in memory the small, tense figure of Francis Marion outlined against the sky and heard his passionate words: "I can not turn back. I must go on. There is no choice. Give me the strength and courage and faith to meet what is before me, and though I be denied all else, may I not fail my country." Yes, they were still fighting, if they had not already won. Those men would never quit. And because he had known them, even for a little while, he could go on.

Perhaps Dr. Pardee complained to headquarters that his assistant's quick temper and disrespectful attitude were hard to bear. At any rate, within a few days, Bill was transfered to Lord Bob's counting room. "Counting room" was what its owner called it, but Bill could see little there to count except the swarming insects. It was located near the middle of the gangling house and around and through it milled slovenly Negresses, naked children, and more of those yellow overseers Bill had learned to detest. The master himself occasionally rolled in and overflowed a huge wicker chair in one corner. Though he wore enough white cloth to sail a ship, he seemed only half dressed and his immense red face looked like something that was about to melt and run over the floor.

"Boy," he asked, with no preliminary remarks, "how do you fancy my island?"

"Little enough," Bill answered straight out.

Lord Bob gave a chuckle. "I have allowed you a year to recover your health, yet you are still ungrateful."

"You have no right to keep me here," Bill retorted. "I should be free."

"It is the fortune of war, my lad, the fortune of war."

"But, sir, I was never a prisoner of war. I was the victim — "

"A prisoner of war in the technical sense," Lord Bob interrupted. "I bought your services — at a profit, if the war continues long enough."

"Do you mean I shall be freed when the war ends?"

"Surely, surely, such is the law of nations."

Bill smiled to himself at the thought of any law being applied to this island. Then he asked, "Do you know how the war is going, sir?"

"As a whole yes, at the moment no. It is only a matter of time before that bounder Washington and his fellow rebels are hanged."

Bill covered his resentment with another question: "Is there news from the South, from Moultrie and Marion?"

"Never heard of the rascals."

"They were the heroes of Charles Town when I was there," Bill answered proudly.

"Doubtless they've been hanged by now." Lord Bob brushed the subject away with a motion of his fat white hands. "Do you wield a pen easily?"

"Yes, sir."

"And do accounts?"

"Yes, sir."

"I need a white clerk. These black-and-tan numbskulls can't be taught the difference between A B C and 1 2 3. Sit up to the table and sharpen your quills."

In a manner of speaking, Bill sat there for eighteen months. For reasons unexplained, Lord Bob saw fit to keep records of the business transacted on the island. Whether he could not or would not do the work himself, he had not. There were stacks of notes and figures for the past two years — number of logs cut, weight of different crops, hours of slave labor — to be sorted and entered in ledgers. Among the slave records Bill found four notations "died from flogging" and two "died from shark bites." He asked no questions.

The work itself was not difficult, but the surroundings were. In time Bill grew accustomed to the constant yelling of women and children, but his aversion to Lord Bob never lessened. The man was drunk three-quarters of the time, and in his sober intervals, he abused everyone except Bill and Pardee, whom he pretended to respect because of their color. There was a blood-stained whipping post behind the pink-coral house and the slaves hinted at other tortures.

"He is the devil himself," Bill said to Pardee one day, when they had been working over a slave Lord Bob had knocked senseless because she upset a chair.

"All of that," the doctor agreed. He looked sick.

"Why do you stay here?"

"Where can one go to escape the weaknesses of mankind?"

"Good Lord, any place is better than this! Why don't you clear out to Europe or Asia or Africa?"

"I have been to those places, lad." Pardee's voice was flat and even, as though held in leash. "I found tyrants everywhere. I hate tyranny."

"Then why don't you go to America and fight for liberty?"

"I lack courage." The doctor's lips barely moved when he said it. "It is easier to take Lord Bob's shilling."

A strange man. All was strange in that place. The whole setup was fantastic to the boy who, less than three years before, had regarded the crossing of the Hudson River as a voyage of adventure. What he had endured since then!

And he was still alive, more alive than he had ever been. When the pressure of circumstances became almost intolerable he kept going by remembering Francis Marion out there on the sand dune praying not for mercy but for strength to meet what lay ahead. The greatest force in the world, the inspiration of hero worship, carried him on.

Outwardly, Bill appeared resigned to his lot. He worked in the counting room and, as far as he was able, kept the muddled accounts in some kind of order. Lord Bob ignored him for weeks at a time, then talked to him for days. At such times they visited outlying parts of the island and the man outlined vague plans for its improvement. On those trips Bill occasionally saw Luke, who was usually in the chain gang rolling logs, for he still fought his captivity. Bill was also fighting to keep sane until he saw a chance to escape or until freedom came with the end of the war.

The war teased his thoughts more and more, perhaps because he had no way of learning its progress. At intervals of three or four months ships stopped at the island for cargo, but Bill was not allowed to speak to the crews. At such times he was flatly given the choice of staying at Pardee's house or being locked in a storeroom. He chose the first for, though he had given up trying to fathom the doctor, he enjoyed his company. Whether the man was a sort of missionary, a criminal in hiding, or a plain ne'er-do-well, he was no fool.

"Won't you ask the sailors how the war is faring?" Bill begged him again and again.

And always he got the same answer, "I am not interested."

"But don't you care if the new nation lives or dies?" Bill shouted at him one day.

"Not a penny's worth," Pardee answered calmly. "If it dies it is unimportant. If it lives it can thrive only on its neighbors' blood. Such is human nature. The intelligence of mankind is below that of shellfish, who are content to live at peace with one another."

"If I were to stow away on one of those ships," Bill thought aloud.

"I would shoot you first, if I knew it."

"You would! What would it be to you?"

"Lord Bob searches every ship before it sails. What he does to stowaways — " Pardee left the sentence unfinished.

So Bill hung on, working, hoping, growing tougher in body and mind, until July of the year 1779.

"Boy," Lord Bob said one day, with his usual abruptness, "I'm satisfied you're a good feller."

"Why, thank you, sir." Bill looked up in amazement.

"A good feller," Lord Bob repeated, and nodded so sharply that drops of sweat flew from his round red face. "An excellent feller. The kind of a feller I want for a partner."

Bill waited, speechless.

"I said partner."

"I heard you."

"Young blood, white blood, brains, ambition. I'll teach you the business and turn it over to you."

Bill pulled himself together. "Thank you for the offer, sir, but I don't want to stay here all my days."

"Don't want to?" Lord Bob looked amazed.

"No. I want to go home."

"Nonsense! You won't be staying as a slave — or even as an employee. You'll be my partner, then I'll make you my heir and some day you'll own it all. Of course you want to stay."

"But I tell you — "

"Stop!" The word exploded from Lord Bob's fat lips. "Roll it over in your mind for a while before you answer."

Bill stared at the dazzling harbor that looked lifeless except where a shark's fin sliced the surface. Sharks were always out there, beating about the wharf until the slaves screamed with terror. Lord Bob liked them and fed them whole quarters of beef and occasionally a live dog. The partner of such a man? More honorable to be his slave. But a partner would be able to get away from the island, so far he would never come back. That possibility was worth a large temporary price.

A screech ended such thoughts. The door flew open and two overseers dragged a Negro girl into the room. She was bloody from a beating and terrified almost beyond human resemblance.

"So you caught the little cat," Lord Bob remarked casually.

"Yes suh." One of the guards grinned. "De dogs kotch her in de woods."

"This is the third time she has run away?"

"Yes suh."

"See it doesn't happen again." Lord Bob motioned toward the harbor.

"Yes suh."

The guards started to take the girl away, but she pulled free and dropped on her knees at Lord Bob's feet.

"Not de sharks, massah! Not de sharks!" She clasped her bruised hands together frantically. "Whip me, burn me, massah, but not de sharks! In de Lawd's name, not de sharks!"

He eyed her a moment, then shot out a foot and kicked her flat. The guards picked her up and carried her away, down to the harbor and onto the dock. They swung her high and tossed her far out. Her long scream ended when the cutting fins converged where she fell.

Bill watched, too horrified to move. When it was over he lost his head.

"You damnable brute!" he raged. "Ask me to be your partner! I'd rather be in partnership with the devil!"

Foolishly, he turned his back to leave the room. Like a huge cat Lord Bob was upon him.

CHAPTER VII

LORD Bob's peculiar fancy was pleased to be gentle with Bill. The boy was husky for his age, but in those great soft hands he was helpless.

"So!" the giant puffed. "I have given you upwards of two years of loving care and you repay me thus. Such ingratitude!"

"Two years of torment," Bill retorted, for he was through saying one thing and meaning another. Anyhow, he had gone too far to expect to live.

Lord Bob held him by the shoulders and gazed at him with sadness that was ludicrous under the circumstances.

"I rescued you from the clutches of a villain," he continued piously. "I employed a doctor to restore your health. I kept you safe from war. I welcomed you to my bosom and would have made you my heir. How did you react?"

"Too slowly," Bill answered defiantly. "I should have killed you."

Lord Bob sighed, a vast sound like wind blowing through a cave.

"You refuse to be my son," he said, "therefore you shall be my slave. I can't afford to lose money on you."

Bill caught at the words, which did not suggest the immediate death he had expected. Worse might come of it, yet there was always hope while life lasted. Even when two of the hated overseers came in and handcuffed him, he felt cheerful.

"William," Lord Bob almost sobbed, "it staggers my faith in humanity to see so promising a future as yours deliberately blighted. But such is your choice. You get no second trial."

The two guards marched him through the tobacco fields and up the mountain toward the logging camp where the chain gang worked. The way was hard and the sun was hot, but they refused to let him drink from any of the streams they crossed. Ambitious fellows, those lesser devils, always alert for ways to employ their talents.

Toward dark they came to the camp. Slaves, chained in pairs, were carrying logs on their shoulders from the forest and piling them in a clearing to be hauled down to the dock by oxen. The last in line was working alone, carrying double and being encouraged by a guard with a bullwhip. The Negro was gigantic and for all his misery he walked with a trace of pride. Bill recognized Luke, but neither made a sign. Luke threw his log on the pile and straightened up, his back muscles quivering.

"Tired, black dog?" the guard jeered.

"Yes."

"Beg fo' mercy yo' kin res'."

"Not beg effen Ah die."

"Smart is yo'? I tie yo' up wid dis white man, see is yo' tired."

"Don' do dat!" Luke rolled his eyes in protest. "Ah cain't lug him an' ma load."

"Yo' kin else I riddle yo' hide." The guard cracked his whip. "Ho dar! Fetch de white man dis way."

They chained Luke and Bill together and were vastly pleased with the arrangement. Obviously they were out to break Luke's spirit; to give him a weakling for a team-mate was one way to do it. The other slaves took an unusual interest, for having a white degraded to their own level raised their self-esteem, a new experiences for the poor wretches. They were almost happy as they sat about in the gloom, eating their supper of yams and half-cooked beef.

After the meal they were all locked together in a string and made to lie down for the night.

"I'll do my share, Luke," Bill whispered.

A big hand found his shoulder and squeezed it gently. "De Lawd hain't fo'sook us, suh," Luke breathed. "Ah knowed hit when Ah seed yo' comin'. He gwine fotch us outen Egyp' yet."

During the ensuing weeks it was Luke's simple unshakable faith that kept Bill alive. Life, or rather existence, in the logging camp was brutal. Under the best conditions the work would have been hard, but hampered by chains, tormented by heat and insects, and driven by sadistic overseers, the slaves were hopeless denizens of a living hell. All except Luke. He endured more than any of the others, for the yellow fiends were resolved to break him, but his immense strength and courage kept his chin up. He had laid hold of a trust in God that might have shamed men of culture.

His faith was not hollow but soundly timbered with works. His words would have put heart into the Negroes, if such a thing had been possible, and, numb as they were to emotion, his example subconsciously stimulated them. Being his teammate, Bill profited most. When he reeled with exhaustion the giant not only lifted the whole log they were carrying but held him on his feet by keeping the chain taut. And at night Luke's big hands massaged the boy's pain-knotted muscles and brought sleep.

But for all that, there came a morning when Bill could not rise. The guard kicked him in the ribs and yanked on the chain.

"Kill me and be done," Bill mumbled. "I don't want to live."

"Pull him up," the man snapped at Luke.

Luke raised him gently and caught him when he swayed.

"I'm finished." Bill leaned against the slave.

The guard cursed. Luke looked him in the eye and said meaningly, "He white. He die de big massah feed yo' to de shark."

"He die, he die."

"Not effen yo' fotch Dr. Pardee."

It was pure bluff, but it worked. The guard was shrewd enough to see he could pass the buck to Pardee and his fear of Lord Bob urged him to do it. He whispered with the other guards, then took a key from his belt and unlocked Bill from Luke. It was plain the boy lacked strength to escape, so he left him in the shade and brought a bucket of water.

"Yo' res', suh," Luke said, as the gang moved away.

" 'Member Dan'l done come outen de lion den a livin' man."

But Bill was not interested in Daniel. His only thought was to drink and drink and drink without spilling a drop of the precious water, for fever was burning him up.

He had forgotten about Pardee before the doctor came.

"You'll keep afloat, lad," he said, after an examination. "It's not the fatal fever." His voice sounded more weary than usual.

"I don't want to live," Bill groaned.

"It is Lord Bob's will that you do."

"He sent me here to kill me by inches."

"No, to discipline you. You will be a better partner for it."

"I'll never be his partner — so help me God! If I get free I'll kill him."

"Lad," Pardee gave him a long look, "use your head. Take his bounty and wait."

"You fool!" Bill opened his eyes wide. "Do you call this torture bounty? Get away from me!"

Pardee sat back on his heels and opened his wallet.

"Chew these leaves at your leisure," he said, laying a packet by the water bucket. "If you need sleep take a few drops of this in a gourdful of water." He held up a metal phial. "It won't kill you if you take it all, but you would sleep uncommon long."

"Thank you," Bill said grudgingly.

"You're a good lad." The doctor smiled. "A bit hasty, but well meaning."

When Pardee went away Bill ate some of the leaves and after a while found it easier to lie quiet. He slipped the phial inside his shirt and fell to thinking. Luke bathed him in cool water that night and he slept by snatches. In the morning he felt better, perhaps because of the rest, but he feigned to be worse.

In the afternoon, as he sat propped against a tree, he saw Dr. Pardee coming up the hill and with him was Bottle, earrings, sea boots and all.

"Ahoy!" The pirate's voice, even when he tried to sound genial, had the same rusty rasp as before.

"I fetched a friend to pay his respects," Pardee said.

"A friend!" Bill watched them through half-closed eyes.

"Aye, a friend," Bottle said. "I heard you're in th' sick bay."

"I am here thanks to you."

"Now, now!" Bottle mopped his face with a red kerchief. "I'm a busy sailorman, but I ain't forgot you, lad."

"Nor I you."

Under pretext of taking his pulse Pardee came close and muttered, "Be civil. It's to your profit."

Bill drew up his knees and asked casually, "How goes the war, Captain?"

"I know little about it." Bottle sat down on the grass. "I've not touched the mainland for two years. Too busy."

"Then it's not finished?"

"Oh, no, no, no! And won't be for many a day. Th' Frenchies're in now."

"On our side?" Bill forgot his illness.

"Aye, if by our side you mean th' colonies."

"France has really joined us!"

Bottle nodded. "I'll tell you somethin' that'll gripe th' gizzard of old King George: a French fleet an' army're makin' ready in th' Indies to sail for th' Colonies."

"Is that mere rumor, Bottle?" Pardee put in.

"Rumor me boots! I seed 'em with me own eyes, I did."

Bill sat up straight. "That news is better than your medicine, Doctor," he cried. "It has cured my sickness."

"The captain steals my thunder." Pardee smiled.

"Steal nothin' I don't!" Bottle denied, missing the inference. "I'm a honest sailorman an' one as remembers his friends, which is what brings me here."

"Just to see me?" Bill asked sarcastically.

"To gab with you." Bottle leaned forward in a confidential pose. "I've not forgot th' buried treasure you mentioned."

"You mean that Graves mentioned," Bill retorted. "By the way, is that polecat still unhanged?"

"No doubt he's servin' his king."

"The more such servants the king has the better."

"But th' treasure, lad, th' treasure. I've no time for many words."

"Well, what about it?"

"This is my offer an' a fair one it is, as you'd expect. Tell me where th' treasure is hid. When I find it I'll buy you from Lord Bob an' set you down in th' Colonies."

"Yes," Bill said bitterly, "as you set the escaped slaves down in Africa!"

"Oh, now, now, now!" Bottle wagged his head. "They was only cattle, but I give you my word as one white man to another."

"And I give you my word I don't know where the treasure is," Bill told him. "But if I did know I wouldn't tell you."

"In exchange for yore freedom? Think well, lad."

"I wouldn't get my freedom, only a knife in the back."

"Oh, no, no, no!" Bottle made a wide gesture of innocence. "Such a suspicion ain't right. You shouldn't have no such thoughts."

"You taught them to me."

"Oh, no, no, no!" Bottle sounded horrified. Then he went into his most persuasive manner. "To prove me good faith an' prove as I'm yore friend, I'll steal you away from Lord Bob an' we'll treasure hunt together on equal shares."

"That's the point I had in mind, lad," Pardee said softly.

Bill was beginning to feel too tired to search for polite language. The sickness was returning to his bones and with it the old black sense of futility.

"Doctor," he flung out, "I've been tortured by this brute and I've seen him torture others. I know what to expect. If we found the gold he would steal it and murder me. There's nothing to choose between him and Lord Bob, so I'll stay right here and deny him the pleasure of a chance at the treasure."

Bottle drew one of his silver-mounted pistols and jumped to his feet, cursing.

"Take care." Pardee raised a hand. "The lad is Lord Bob's property."

Bottle's face was ferocious. "I've a mind to give you th' first shot, Pardee," he roared.

"If you do, save one for yourself and use it before Lord

Bob gets a hand on you." The doctor looked him in the eye. "I mean it, Captain."

"Damn you landlubbers!" Bottle put the pistol back. "A man's not master unless he has his own ship under him." He swung on his heel and stomped away, his earrings bobbing up and down.

"A delightful person," Pardee remarked. "And one to bear watching." He too went down the path.

Exhausted by the scene, Bill slept for a while and awoke with a feeling of new strength. He stretched his muscles and looked toward the woods. No one was in sight and it would be easy to make a break, for he was still unchained. He brushed the flies from food that had been left within reach and ate with a good stomach, then went to sleep again. When the guards returned he was twisting and muttering and his wide-open eyes were fixed on nothing.

Darkness came and he moaned as incessantly as the wind in the trees, but he was watching every move about him. The camp routine proceeded as usual. Three of the guards had withdrawn for the night to higher ground where the mosquitoes were less bothersome, leaving one man beside a smudge pot to keep an eye on the slaves. He would sleep about two hours, then wake up, take a long drink from the rum bottle beside him, listen for unusual noises, take another drink and sleep until dawn. It was always the same, night after night.

Bill waited until he could hear the fellow snore before he began crawling toward him. There were few dry twigs in that tropical growth, but to be safe he felt out every inch of ground before crossing it. The smudge pot gave off enough glow for him to see the guard asleep on his back. There was a knife in his belt, but Bill was not tempted by it. His eyes were on the rum bottle and finally he reached it. A slip now would ruin everything and he had to fight to keep his hands steady as he took the phial of medicine from his shirt and poured it into the bottle. Then he crawled back into the shadows and waited.

It seemed as though the fellow would never wake up, but he did finally and, true to habit, took a pull at the bottle. He yawned, listened a moment to the night and emptied the bottle. Bill sat still until the snoring was resumed and held back for what he judged to be half an hour before he touched the man's face lightly with a long stick. There was no response; he was unconscious. Bill put the knife in his own belt, for, much as he hated the guard, he could not kill him while he lay helpless. So he took the keys and walked over to the chain gang. Five minutes later the chains were empty.

"Scatter," Bill told the slaves. "They will have the dogs after us tomorrow and we must leave as many trails as possible. If they close in on you, try to reach the highest peak on the island. We will make a stand there together."

The men faded into the night. Bill found Luke beside him and shook his hand.

"Good-bye," he whispered. "We'll meet somewhere again."

"Ah gwine wid yo', suh," Luke answered.

"Our chances are better alone."

"Ah gwine wid yo'."

"There's no time to argue." Bill tried to sound displeased, though inwardly he was thankful. "Come on, Luke."

CHAPTER VIII

THEY detoured the other sleeping guards and picked up two axes at the log pile. "What next?" Bill asked, suddenly aware that he had planned no farther than this.

"Steal boat," Luke suggested.

"I haven't seen one on the island bigger than a canoe."

"Build big one."

"With these tools?"

"Mebbe."

"If we had time. But we haven't. The dogs will be out by midday. Lord Bob will be sure to pick my trail first."

"Yes." Luke grinned. "He mad 'cause yo' fox him."

"Leave me, Luke, and strike out for yourself. It's your best chance."

"No." There was no question about his determination. "Dis what us do, suh, res' hyar till sunup, den mak log trap."

"Log trap?"

"Yes. Ma papa teach me how he mak 'em in Africa to catch big animal."

"I don't know what you mean," Bill said, "but it's sensible to stay here. We can't get off the island tonight so why waste our strength running round in the dark?"

He lay down and tried to relax, but the instinct of a hunted animal urged him to be up and away. Where? In the darkness one part of the forest was as good as another. He began to wonder if he had not been a fool for not lying to Bottle about the gold. If he had kept his head he might at least have exchanged his place on the island for a no more uncomfortable one on the pirate's ship. When it came to a choice of masters Bottle was no better than Lord Bob, but with him the chances of escape would have been better. However, regrets were useless now.

At the first touch of dawn they moved on into the forest until Luke found a place that suited him. He was only one step away from his ancestral jungle and overnight he had reverted to its ways. In a ravine, whose sides were about a dozen feet apart and so overhung with vines that it was a green tunnel, they built a log deadfall, weighting it with enough stones to crush anything that might enter it.

"But they hunt with dogs on leash," Bill objected. "You'll never get a man in there."

"Jes' want to catch dog, suh."

"But don't you see? The men won't let the dogs go in."

"Yo' res', suh. Ole man Luke show yo' a trick."

He did. With the skill and patience of an artist and with materials ranging from grass blades to small trees, Luke camouflaged the trap in a way that would have deceived a hawk, if such a bird had been interested. Bill forgot his troubles as he watched the creation grow. It was more fascinating than the work of a landscape painter he had once seen put the Palisades on a piece of canvas.

Luke viewed the job from various angles and distances, added a leaf here, shifted a branch there.

"Mighty well done," Bill praised him. "How did you do it?"

"De Lawd help me, suh. Yo' shirt now."

"My shirt? What for?"

"Dog smellum."

"Oh, I see."

Luke laid the shirt in the deadfall, well tied to an innocent-looking vine that ran back to the trigger. To make doubly sure, he strung another vine behind a log, where he sat down ax in hand. Bill's battle station was a few yards away behind a screen of bushes.

It was past midday when they heard the long wail of a hound in the valley. Bill's scalp prickled and the palms of his hands were damp and cold. It was the first time he had been hunted and his animal nature told him to run for his life. His brain fought for control and won, but the struggle left him trembling.

"Think they're on the trail, Luke?" he called softly across the ravine.

"Hope so, suh. Dis ax say, 'Gimme blood to drink.' "

Two dogs were baying now in the direction of the log pile. There was a pause, then they were nearer.

"Dey come!" Luke sang out. "De Lawd deliver 'em inter our han's lak He done de headen folkses to ole man Joshua."

Bill clutched his ax helve and sat there shaking. The baying approached, one voice higher pitched than the other, echoing among the trees in an eerie duet. One moment they were sounds, the next they were shapes crossing a little wild meadow at the foot of the hill. Each hound was tugging one of the guards at the end of a leash, four other guards followed armed with muskets and behind them — Bill blinked — was Dr. Pardee. A pretended friend, he was among the first to join the hunt.

It seemed an age before the troop climbed the hill and appeared close at hand. The hounds were yelping excitedly as the scent thickened, pulling the men after them in long strides. The guards were peering ahead apprehensively, yet eager for the fun to begin. Only Pardee seemed unmoved; his thin face was paler than usual and he looked to be thinking hard. Bill held his breath as the dogs entered the trap. They were so near he could hear them panting. Both saw the shirt at the same moment and leaped for it, dragging the two guards with them. Then the roof of the forest caved in.

As the rocks crashed down there was a mingled yelping and screaming. Out of the underbrush rose a black demon, roaring strange words and swinging an ax. Before Bill could join in the fight he saw one guard's head split like a melon. Muskets thundered. A man lunged at him with a long knife. He sidestepped and struck with his ax, a down blow that caught the fellow squarely in the chest. He dropped, but the blade stuck and pulled the helve from Bill's hand. As he reached for it he saw another guard level a pistol at him. With the flash someone stepped in front of it and fell backward upon him.

Bill fought himself free. Blood blinded him. He brushed it from his eyes and gasped. Pardee lay at his feet and close by were the mangled bodies of four guards. Luke was wiping the blade of his ax and talking to it.

"Look lak ole man Samson been argufyin' at de Philisteens wid de jawbone ob a jackass." He grinned at Bill.

Bill bent over Pardee and found him shot through the chest but still conscious.

"You saved my life, Doctor," he said in a tight voice.

"Lad," Pardee wasted no words, "Lord Bob has hired Bottle and his crew to hunt you. Their ship is unguarded. Slip through the line tonight. Provision the long boat. Take the small compass from the cabin. Blow up the ship. Sail straight north to the French Indies."

"We will take you with us," Bill said.

"Won't be here then." Pardee began coughing and Bill raised him in his arms.

"Tell me what to do for you, Doctor."

"Join the fight for freedom in America. Follow that man Marion you've told me about. Glorious cause. I lacked the courage to take a hand in it. I've always been weak."

"You're a — a hero, sir," Bill said unsteadily.

"Nonsense, lad." He coughed again, for the last time.

A few minutes later Bill said, "We should bury him, Luke."

"No time, suh."

"He deserves it."

"He want fo' us ter git away."

"Yes, he died to help us get away."

"Den we bes' git, suh. Don' want his hant pesterin' us."

"I don't believe in such things, but I do believe in taking good advice. We'll go."

They each took a musket and two pistols with ammunition and set out. With infinite caution they skirted the deserted logging camp and worked down the path to the lowlands. Twice at a distance they saw parties of armed men, one led by Bottle himself, fanning out toward the hills.

"De sailormens git los' up dar." Luke grinned.

"Lord Bob must have posted a big reward to make them venture out. They take it for granted we will go as far as possible."

"Dem fool slaves is up dar."

"We should have kept them with us."

"Don' yo' fuss yore haid 'bout dem, suh. If de Lawd figure dey wuth savin' He do hit Hisse'f."

Their first plan was to work in as near the wharf as possible and wait for darkness. From the edge of the woods they scouted the fields without seeing a person. Obviously Lord Bob, the ship's crew and the overseers were in the interior, and the slaves had taken to cover until the storm was over. Even the women and children had disappeared, indicating that their master was in a high temper.

"When dat big man see de mess we make up yender he gwine bus' hisse'f all up." Luke chuckled.

Bill made no comment. He was thinking, his eyes on Bottle's ship that rubbed lazily against the wharf like a black hog scratching its side.

"Luke," he said after a while, "why do we wait till night? Now is the time to get away in the small boat."

"Effen yo' sez so, suh."

"Shake a leg."

With their muskets ready, they crept to the row of storehouses, then along it to the edge of the dock. There was no sound except the lapping of the water. They crossed the planking and went on deck.

"Look in the hold," Bill whispered. "I'll see what's in the cabin."

He had taken about six steps when he heard a click and in the cabin door stood Lord Bob with a drawn pistol. Bill's musket missed fire. The pistol cracked but the bullet went wild, for the instant before the shot something flashed across the cabin through the open window opposite. Lord Bob pitched forward on his face with a knife handle protruding between his shoulder blades. It had touched the spinal cord and he lay motionless except that his head was rolling from side to side.

"Back, eh, partner." He could still fight with his wits. "All is forgiven."

"Not on my side of the question." Bill reloaded and looked down at him.

"No bad blood between us, lad. No, no no! Help me off the ship and we'll draw the partnership papers."

"I have no authority to remove cargo from Captain Bottle's ship." Bill was wondering if he could kill the helpless giant.

"The ship is mine. Bottle doesn't own the boots he stands in."

Luke came around the corner of the cabin and asked quietly, "What we do wid him, suh?"

"He's your game, you winged him."

"Send for Pardee." Lord Bob's eyes bulged as he struggled and failed to move a finger.

"Dr. Pardee is dead," Bill told him.

"Oh, no!" It was a frightened tone.

"He took a bullet you ordered for me."

"No, lad, no! It was all a mistake."

"You lie!" Bill snapped in disgust. "Keep an eye on him while I look around, Luke. Nice work with the knife."

"Good ole knife!" Luke grinned wickedly.

Bill was at the other end of the ship when he heard Lord Bob's voice ring out in mortal fear: "No! You black devil — no!"

Bill wheeled to see Luke lifting the huge white man and balancing him on the rail.

"The sharks!" Lord Bob screamed.

Luke gave a push. The scales of justice balanced.

They worked swiftly, loading a small boat with what supplies they could find. Neither was a seaman in the real sense, but they had a general understanding of handling sail and Bill could read the compass. Given fair luck, they should reach the French Indies that Pardee had mentioned. How far it was they could not guess. They lowered the boat over the side and Bill stood thinking.

"We must sink the ship so they can't follow us, Luke."

"Punch a hole in de bottom."

"Too slow. Bottle may show up any time. We'll blow her up. Did you ever lay a powder train?"

"No, suh, but Ah knows gunpowdah am a fas' stepper."

Bill experimented with pieces of twisted tow until he

found the correct length to burn for five minutes, then he cut a piece six times as long. He opened the magazine and ran a trail of loose powder from a keg across the floor to the foot of the companionway, piling it around one end of the piece of tow. Luke made sure the boat was cast off and shouted that all was ready. Bill lighted the other end of the tow and ran. They threw all they had onto the oars until they were at a safe distance, then hoisted sail and made out to sea.

It seemed more than half an hour before a sheet of flame rose from the edge of the island, outlining the palm trees for a moment in the twilight. A deep roar hurried across the water and silence took its place. Bill turned his face to the north, where his future lay.

CHAPTER IX

THE thumb of circumstance that had pressed down on them for so long relaxed, and they sailed quietly for four days and nights. It was a blessed time for Bill, the longest interval of peace he had known since he sighted the coast of South Carolina more than three years before.

He was still a boy in years, but he felt himself to be a man. And rightly so. The successive blows of fate had forced him to mature rapidly or die. The grim process of living had toughened him in body and mind more than an ordinary lifetime might have done and had brought out latent resources of courage and self-reliance beyond the usual measure. Above all, it had taught him two things: to save his life one must not be afraid of losing it, and to make it worth saving one must be free. Freedom was every man's right, the only thing he was always justified in fighting for, and helping others to fight for. Through all the darkness of the island days Francis Marion's words had shone before his eyes — "Though I be denied all else, may I not fail my country." Since he had first appreciated their truth other things had seemed cheap by comparison. Even the buried gold, that once loomed so large in his plans, occupied his thoughts only now and then.

The fifth day at dawn Bill was asleep in the stern when Luke sang out, "Sail stickin' up yender, suh."

She was a small fast ship and was bearing across their bow to the southeast. As they watched, she came about toward them. Within half an hour they made out her flag — French. When they were within hailing distance a fussy officer in a cocked hat and long-tailed coat shouted through a trumpet a string of words that made no more sense than the cackling of a hen.

"Americans," Bill answered, making a guess at what was wanted.

"Ho! Les Anglais?"

"No — Americans! United Colonies of America. George Washington. Charles Town. New York. Get any of that?"

Sailors ran about the deck as though preparing for a major engagement. The officer waved his trumpet and appeared to be calling on high heaven to witness his heroic efforts. Bill didn't know what to expect, perhaps a broadside. Finally a slim officer came to the rail, exchanged bows with the cocked hat, and received the trumpet as though it were a scepter.

He aimed it at the little boat and bellowed, "Attensheon! Eet ees require to identi-fy."

"Americans!" Bill repeated.

"From what place you come, monsieur?"

"I don't know. We are escaped prisoners of war bound for the French Indies."

"Aha!" The trumpet leaned forward dangerously. "Monsieur have frien' in ze islan'?"

"The French are our allies, aren't they?"

"Oui, yes, oui, oui, oui! Vive la France! Vive les Americaines!"

"Never mind the flumadiddles," Bill said aside. Then he shouted, "May we come aboard?"

"Oui. Ze sheep ees honeur, zhentlemens. Oui, oui, oui!"

After enough talk and gesturing to last a Yankee crew a lifetime the Frenchmen got their guests over the rail. In the course of time Bill learned that the ship was bound from Savannah, Georgia, to the Indies with despatches and would soon return to that port, which was being besieged by a French fleet and an allied army. Thanks to the superlative bravery of the French, the British were on their last legs and the war was as good as over.

"How about the American army?" Bill asked.

"Sauvages!" The interpreter threw out his hands. "Ze mens fight behin' trees, ze hofficer dance like peasant."

"Still," Bill reminded him, "they have held out against the British for four years, the same British who licked the French in the French war."

"So much monsieur does not honderstan'," the man answered pityingly.

But when, six weeks later, on returning from the Indies, they sighted Savannah, even a stupid American could understand that the British were still there. Not a sign was left of the allied army or the glorious French fleet. Dodging enemy patrols, the ship slipped down to within sight of Charles Town and got an eyeful: the city was closely invested by a British army and fleet.

"The French are not as conspicuous as I was led to believe," Bill remarked.

"Eet ees ze strate-gy, ze gran' plan." The interpreter looked very knowing. "Monsieur will honderstan' w'en we return to ze islan'."

"But monsieur is not returning to the islands," Bill told him.

"No?"

"I am going ashore here."

"For why?"

"To help my people fight."

"You one fool, monsieur. Zey haf no money, no king, no glory to fight for."

"But they have something better."

"Eh?"

"They have the love of freedom."

"But, monsieur, I t'ink — "

"Never mind what you think. Luke and I are going ashore tonight if we have to swim."

The Frenchmen were not unhappy to part with their guests. After so much boasting about the glory of French arms it was embarrassing to find no visible French army or navy. And the American was impolite enough to remind them of it. So when darkness came they put Bill and Luke ashore in a secluded bay and satisfaction was mutual.

Bill felt the earth under his feet and stooped to touch it with his hands.

"We're home, Luke!" he cried. "We're home!"

"Ah don' want to go home, suh," Luke said plaintively.

"You mean back to your master?"

"Yes."

"We'll fix that up when we find the American army."

"Whar yo' figger dat army at, suh?"

"Defending Charles Town. We saw the smoke and heard the guns." Bill looked around in the darkness. "Do you know the way there?"

"Come day we kin fin' hit. We bes' git oursef's a dry spot an' sleep. No sense bus'in' our haids in de dark."

By luck they found such a place, a pine knoll in the swamp, and lay down. Bill dug his fingers into the soil of his country, drew a long breath and fell asleep.

In the morning it took them two hours to work their way out of the swamp to a brush fence that bordered a sort of bridle path. It was probably called a road, for it bore hoof-prints, and roads always lead somewhere, so they followed it. After a while they heard a horse galloping behind them.

"If he's a Britisher we'll pick him up," Bill whispered. "Grab his horse if he tries to get away."

"Yes, suh."

The horseman came around a bend, a tall young fellow in a blue cloak, who sat his saddle as though he had grown out of it. To show goodwill, Bill grounded his musket and held up a hand. The rider shot glances into the bushes, searching for an ambush, then pulled up, the hand under the cloak resting on a pistol.

"Your indulgence, sir," Bill said. "Can you tell me where I am?"

"Square in the middle of the road." The other grinned boyishly.

Bill liked the grin, but he said severely, "I am not jesting."

"Nor am I. You're square in the middle of the road that leads from Charles Town to St. John's Parish."

"Which way is Charles Town?"

The rider jerked a thumb over his shoulder. "I've just come from there."

Bill took an eager step toward him. "What's the fighting there, sir?"

"What's the fighting?" The man stared at him. "Pray where have you been holed up for the past few years not to know there's a war?"

"I do know there's a war, but I've spent nigh three years in the Indies. Just landed here."

Before he could wink, Bill was looking into the muzzle of a very large pistol.

"Whig or Tory?" the horseman snapped.

"Whig." Bill met the sharp blue eyes. "What are you?"

"Whig."

"Then put up that gun. We have no quarrel."

"Any identification papers on you?"

"Not a scrap."

"Any friends hereabouts?"

"I don't know where they are now. I used to know John Stewart, the Tory merchant in Charles Town, and Major Marion of the South Carolina Militia."

"Yes?" The pistol did not move. "I need more than a stranger's word for it."

"I have nothing else to give you."

"Walk ahead of me in the road. You too, black boy."

"We gwine mess him up, suh?" Luke looked at Bill.

"Not at present." Bill slipped his musket into the hollow of his arm and sauntered down the road without looking back. It was a glorious morning, the robins were singing their heads off, his country was round about him, and he began to whistle.

"Stop that noise," the horseman ordered.

"Don't like music?"

"Try to signal your friends and you get a bullet."

"It might be worth it if I could find a friend."

An hour brought them to thinner woods, then to cleared land. Not far away a rooster crowed vigorously. Another turn in the road showed a plantation house, not a pretentious mansion but a comfortable-looking place.

"Turn in there," the rider commanded.

They went down a driveway between double rows of trees and swung toward the portico. Bill noticed that the lawn was unkempt and the whole place showed lack of care. A man stood on the top step leaning on a cane.

"Major Marion!" Bill stopped, checked an impulse to run forward, and saluted sharply.

Marion looked even smaller and thinner than ever, but his black eyes were none the less bright.

"Who is this fellow, MacDonald?" he asked coolly.

"I picked him up on the swamp road, sir. He claims to be your friend."

"I fail to recognize him." Marion looked Bill up and down. "Your name, if you please."

"William Barlow, sir."

"It means nothing to me." Marion's tone was cold.

"I spotted him as a spy, sir," the young soldier said in a pleased voice.

"But, Major Marion!" Bill protested.

"Address him as colonel," MacDonald growled.

"Your pardon, Colonel. I had not heard of your promotion since the battle of Fort Moultrie."

"Fort Moultrie?" Marion gave him a sharp look. "Were you there?"

"Yes, sir. Perhaps you remember the boy from New York who came ashore the night before the battle."

"Jove, yes! I turned him over to John Stewart and he disappeared. But you are not that lad. He was slight and gentle."

"Three years as a slave doesn't beautify a man, Colonel," Bill said.

"You are that lad!" Marion snapped his fingers with excitement in that old way of his. "It comes back to me. MacDonald, you did a rare good deed in fetching him here." He shifted his cane to his left hand and held out his right. "Welcome, Bill, welcome!"

CHAPTER X

BILL stretched himself in a chair on the porch, feeling he was home, though he had never been there before. He was free and with his countrymen. More, he was with the man who had stirred him to hero worship, the one he had dreamed of following into the great fight for liberty. Now that dream might be realized. At the risk of being impolite he closed his eyes for a few moments and hardly breathed.

The French had been his friends in an official sense only. Their politeness had seemed artificial and their talk, such of it as was translated to him, had been shot through with threats against the British and condescension for the Americans. But here were men he could understand and trust, who spoke his language even when nothing was said. The soft-spoken little colonel and the strapping red-headed soldier neither boasted nor posed. Being a bachelor and having no women in his family, Marion's home lacked gentleness and color, a deficiency that his absence during the war years had emphasized. The place was in disrepair, yet the spirit of hospitality flourished.

After a while a servant showed him to an upstairs room and brought in a tub of hot water. It was Bill's first real bath since the one in John Stewart's house so long ago. What had become of Stewart and his sneaking secretary Harold Graves? It didn't matter right then. The present was an orgy of hot soapsuds. The French had not bathed on shipboard, and on the island the fear of sharks had kept Bill out of the water. He shuddered at the memory of those sharks.

The servant returned with an outfit of clothing that looked about his size. Probably some relative of the colonel's had left it there. A sensible fellow, too, by the feel of the soft material and the easy cut of it. MacDonald knocked on the door and came in, appearing two sizes bigger indoors. He was not clumsy either, all lithe muscle which, with his red hair, would make him a good partner in a fight.

"You look less like a spy now." He grinned. "I was tempted to shoot you on sight."

"I felt the same about you."

"But I had the draw on you."

"The one of us you didn't get would have finished you."

"I knew it — hence the bluff."

"Luke would say you are an angel in disguise to bring me here."

"Well disguised."

"Are you the colonel's aide?"

"Sort of, since his injury."

"A battle wound?"

"No, that's the toughest part of it. Fell from a window and broke his ankle. He's well-nigh wild to be out of the fight so long."

"Was he at Savannah?"

"Was he! You should have seen him leading the charge up the breastworks."

"I can imagine. I saw him in action at Fort Moultrie."

"Wish I'd been there."

"What has become of Colonel Moultrie?"

"He's the general in command of Militia at Charles Town. He won't have a chance because Lincoln, the Continental, is over him. Lincoln is slow and takes everybody's advice. If nothing happens to him we'll lose the city."

"And I knew another grand fellow, a Sergeant Jasper."

"He was killed carrying the colors at Savannah."

"Oh! Savannah was a mess, I take it."

"Awful! If the French had helped us attack when they first landed the place would have fallen in five hours. But the idiots wanted to besiege it and they talked Lincoln over to their side. Our South Carolinians most blew up. I thought one time Marion was going to paste Lincoln in the nose — I sure did!"

So they talked, as young men will, and the more they talked the better they liked each other.

"You'll be enlisting with us, won't you?" MacDonald asked earnestly.

Bill told him that he had enlisted years ago.

"Continental or militia?"

"Militia. I want to be identified with Moultrie and Marion."

"That's the ticket! We — " A bell sounded in the hall below. "If you happen to be hungry we'll go down."

"If I happen to be!" Bill was through the door. At the top of the stairs he said, "I suppose I must walk, but I'd rather slide down the banister."

"Do so, by all means," Marion shouted up. "One — two — three!"

Bill shot down the rail, closely followed by MacDonald. An old servant, who happened to be in the hall, hurried to the kitchen and told the cook there was life in the army yet. It may have been an omen.

During the meal Marion lost himself in the story of Bill's adventures. He sat on the edge of his chair like a boy, his pale cheeks flushed. MacDonald's red hair fairly bristled at some of the episodes and Bill felt secretly important to hold so much attention.

"That despicable Bottle!" the colonel burst out. "In these times a man may find an excuse even for piracy, but never is there justification for breaking faith as he did with those Negroes."

"Will it be possible to give Luke his freedom now?" Bill asked. "He has earned it."

"Do you know the name of his master?"

"Thomas or Thompson, a Tory planter."

"A Tory? Ho, ho!" Marion's eyes snapped. "Then Luke is your property as spoils of war."

"Does that give me the authority to free him, sir?"

"Certainly. In the presence of two witnesses, which you have here."

"May I bring him in now, sir?"

"Yes, do. I'll send for him." he called a servant.

Luke came in, stepping lightly as usual, his head high.

"Black royalty," MacDonald muttered admiringly.

"And how he can fight!" Bill added.

"Luke," Marion said, "I thank you for bringing Mr. Barlow back to us."

"He done fotch me back, suh," Luke answered.

"Then you are his property."

"Yes, suh."

Marion nodded to Bill, who said, "That being the case, Luke, I give you your freedom."

"Yo' means Ah's a free man, suh?"

"Yes. And perhaps I can help you get to Africa."

"Ah don' hanker to go right presen'ly, suh."

"You are free to do as you wish. What do you want to do?"

Luke gave him a steady look. "Ah wants ter help yo' git free frum ole King Jawdge same's yo' git me free frum ole man Bottle an' ole man Lord Bob."

"You mean you want to join the American army?"

"Jest so's Ah kin help yo', suh."

"You're a brick, Luke!" Bill cried. Then he added thoughtfully, "But I can't promise you wages."

"Yo' don' talk money when yo' unlock ma chains, suh."

"All right, Luke." Bill felt embarrassed. "We'll hang together."

"Yes, suh." Luke turned and went out. When he got through the doorway they heard him say to himself, "Ah's free dis time — oh, Lawdy Lawd!"

So the whirligig of life made another turn. And it kept turning. During the weeks of spring that followed, Bill served in the South Carolina Militia as aide to Colonel

Marion along with MacDonald. They were busy between the plantation and the city, for while the colonel had an active part in the councils of those who defended Charles Town, his slowly mending ankle kept him at home. The British under Clinton closed in on all sides, while Lincoln pondered and Moultrie fumed.

Bill rode in one afternoon, so weary he was not sure whether his horse staggered or he reeled in the saddle. Marion sat on the portico, his swollen foot in a chair, talking with a small Negro boy who was picking nervously at the grass with his bare toes.

"Tell Aunty Midge I will go to her," Bill heard the colonel say, as he rode past to the stable.

"Yes sah." The boy was off toward the woods like a rabbit.

When Bill came back Marion motioned him to stretch out on the grass, knowing how his muscles ached for relaxation.

"The same story today?"

"Yes, sir. Mac will fetch your letters after dark. The patrols are farther out and more numerous. I dodged three."

Marion nodded. "They have been seen on the road two miles from here. You and Mac be alert until I return tomorrow. I am going into the swamp."

"But, sir, your ankle!" Bill could not help saying.

"I will go by canoe."

"Your pardon, Colonel," Bill sat up, "but can't I go in your place."

"No, it's a matter of personal friendship."

"Oh."

Marion eased his foot to the floor. "I once had two people, Uncle Dan and Aunty Midge. When they grew old I gave them their freedom and they went to live with their kinsfolk on an island in the swamp. Uncle Dan died this morning. Aunty Midge wants to give him Christian burial, but none of her people can read the Scriptures, so she has sent for me. I can't refuse."

Bill stood up. "May I go with you, sir?"

"As nursemaid?" The colonel smiled.

"No, for the frisk of it."

"Ho! You are still a lad, for all your size and adventures. Why, yes, come with me if you wish. We will eat first."

It was nearly dark when they left for the creek that ran along the edge of the clearing. Marion leaned on a crutch, carried a rifle in the other hand, and had a Bible in a bullet pouch slung over one shoulder. As Bill was untying the dugout a Negro stepped out of the woods, wearing a single muddy garment of deerskin with the hair outside.

"Massa Francis," he said, in the thick accent of the swamp people, "redcoats camp on Big Fo'd."

"How many?" Marion asked.

The man thrust out his ten fingers and backed into the woods.

"I suppose that boy took his life in his hands to warn me," the colonel remarked.

"Then we don't go farther?" Bill sounded relieved in spite of himself.

"Certainly we do. It's only a patrol. Swing the canoe around."

"Yes, sir," Bill said. But he thought, patrol or whatever,

they are ten men who would be happy to drill us. Taking that chance to please an old woman!

Marion sat awkwardly in the canoe because of his ankle, but for all that, he paddled with a dexterity that amazed Bill. The creek was crooked as a snake, but the little boat followed it like an otter. Darkness brought neither uncertainty nor decrease in speed for the colonel had every turn and every tree mapped in his mind. Bill remembered hearing someone say back in Fort Moultrie that Dan Boone of Kentucky, who evidently had made a name for himself, was no better in the woods than Francis Marion.

A light winked among the leaves and the canoe slowed up as it slid into the clearing at the ford, which was illuminated by two fires close to the water and another farther back.

"Halt!" a soldier barked. "Who goes there?"

"Huntin' folkses," the colonel answered in a soft drawl. "Ah got a busted laig."

"Pull over here," the soldier ordered. By his voice, he was a more or less local Tory. The half dozen other soldiers visible were British dragoons.

"Hit don't pleasure me to gab," Marion grumbled, as he paddled in toward shore.

"Which leg is it?" the Tory asked.

Marion raised his bandaged ankle above the side of the canoe, then put it back gingerly.

"Wish we had a surgeon to mend it for you," the Tory remarked sympathetically.

"Mammy Killbain'll fix hit." Marion picked up his paddle. "Evenin' to yo' gen'mens."

They had just reached the shadow downstream when a voice farther up the bank roared, "Halt! Colonel Marion, halt I say! Damn it! Fire!"

The dugout disappeared as the muskets blazed. Bill thought the colonel was hit, for he was turning the canoe so it almost pivoted on its stern. When it was headed upstream he snatched his rifle and fired, then emptied both pistols. Bill got the idea and followed suit so quickly that the six shots made an evenly spaced string of sounds. Marion swung the canoe and they made off in the darkness.

A few minutes later, as they pulled up to reload, the colonel chuckled, "Probably no damage done. Merely an exchange of compliments."

"A tight squeak," Bill commented.

"Always snap back at 'em," Marion said. "Though you must run, keep your brush up."

They reached the island before midnight and found a score of Negroes wailing and singing in a palmetto hut that sheltered the earthly last of Uncle Dan. Some of the mourners faded out, for they were runaway slaves, but most of them only made room for the white men.

"De Lawd fotch yo'!" an old woman shouted, jumping up from beside the head of the slab coffin.

Marion took her hands and answered gently, "I came because you sent for me, Aunty Midge."

"Ah want Dan buried by de Book."

"He shall be."

"Hallylulya! Den he go plumb-smack to glory 'thout messin' wid no questions at de gate."

"I have brought the Book," Marion said. "Is there some special part you want me to read?"

" 'Bout de New Jeeruslum." The old woman's eyes shone. "Ah wants all dese folkses to hyar de trufe 'bout Dan struttin' hisse'f 'mongst all dat gol' an' diments."

"I will read that part," Marion promised gravely. "When is the burial?"

"Come sunup."

"Very well."

"Dar's b'ar meat an' yams aplenty."

"Thank you."

Later, Bill asked, "Should I sleep, if I can?"

"Best not," Marion said. "Can you sing?"

"Not a note."

"Then shout or wail — anything to keep the evil spirits away. The people will appreciate our efforts."

"And the spirits?"

"They won't notice us in this hubbub." Marion smiled with one corner of his mouth and broke into a folk song his parents had brought from France.

When the sun rose Uncle Dan was buried, it might almost be said, with a flourish of Scripture. The swamp people were vastly impressed, Aunty Midge's prestige soared and everyone was happy. Marion took leave of her as though she were a queen and, in turn, she sent half a dozen boys to tow his canoe several miles up the creek. From there the colonel and Bill paddled quietly home.

"Get some sleep, lad," Marion said, when they reached the house. "You are nigh to scraping the bottom of that barrel."

"May I help you upstairs, sir?" Bill offered, for Marion was bending hard on his crutch.

"Oh, no." The colonel turned toward his library. "Despatches to read — letters to write." He made a little gesture of resignation and hobbled away.

Once more Bill marveled almost reverently. The country this man loved more than life was threatened by disaster, the enemy was at his very door, yet to oblige an old servant he could spend a day and night skirmishing and laboring through swamps, then without sleep return cheerfully to work. Such physical, mental and spiritual endurance was the stuff of heroes. Give this little colonel a chance, even the slimmest fighting chance, and he would do the impossible. Just give him a chance!

On the eleventh of May Bill dodged Tarleton's cavalry for, it seemed, the thousandth time and delivered letters to headquarters. As he turned down a side street in Charles Town to feed his horse MacDonald overtook him. His face was almost as red as his hair and his big hands shook.

"The jig is up," he said abruptly.

"Surrender?" It had been in the air for days.

"Yes — tomorrow. I've heard the terms." MacDonald glanced helplessly at the cloud of smoke that was always visible of late. "The Continentals will be made prisoner, the Militia paroled and sent home, the big guns — over three hundred of 'em — and all supplies given up." He ground his teeth.

"In other words, Mac, all our military force in the South will be wiped out."

"Not by a jugful!" MacDonald's eyes flashed. "There are a lot of us who won't surrender."

"Well," Bill felt and sounded hopeless, "well, let's go back to the plantation while we can."

They rode out of the city and worked their way back to Marion. He took the news quietly and sat on the porch the rest of the day, moving only his hands. He looked sick, yet to the two young soldiers he was a powerful figure.

During the next few days they slipped in and out, bringing him even worse news of the collapse of the country. South Carolina was being treated as conquered territory. Looting was not only sanctioned by the enemy but encouraged. Every kind of crime against the Whigs went unpunished. Their money was worthless. Only a few patriots, those rare souls whose faith was beyond defeat, could see a glimmer of hope in the future. To all others the American cause was as dead as Nebuchadnezzar.

When Charles Town was wrung dry, Clinton sent Cornwallis and Tarleton to ravage the adjoining countryside.

"They will be here in the morning, sir," Mac said, as he slid from his horse and leaned against the portico. He looked ten years older.

"The slaves have already taken to the woods," Bill told him. "It's got around that the British are shipping Negroes to the Indies."

"They are," Mac said, "and white prisoners too."

"Luke is the only one left here."

Marion stood up and sniffed the air that was heavy with smoke from the burning homes of his neighbors.

"Lads," he said quietly, "tonight I shall take to the swamp."

"But, sir, you can't ride a horse," Bill protested.

"Yes, I can, if someone will give me a hand up. I am not" — he paused and again Bill saw that strange, almost fanatical, look sweep over his face — "I am not running away, I am retreating. I shall fight in another place and I shall return here some day."

The boys exchanged glances silently.

"Lads," Marion said slowly, "you have seen the battle lanterns by the guns in night engagements. It is dark where we are fighting now; we must keep our battle lanterns burning brightly."

CHAPTER XI

THEY were busy until dark helping Marion prepare to leave. Mac stood guard on the highway, he and his horse restless as racers before the start. The colonel was not wealthy in the traditional manner of Southern planters, for his Huguenot ancestors had escaped from France with only a few possessions. He collected half a dozen chestsful of silver, glass, china and family portraits, which Bill and Luke buried under the stable floor. Another chest lined with silk and filled with documents was taken to the woods and planted under a blazed tree that marked a corner of the boundary line. Several score bottles of old wine were let down a dry well in baskets and covered with rubbish.

Marion leaned against the house to rest his ankle and smiled faintly. "In fireside tales money is always buried in the garden, isn't it, Bill?"

"I have heard of such things." Bill picked up a spade. "Shall I dig a hole, Colonel?"

The smile twisted ruefully. "I haven't seen a piece of hard money in months and Continental isn't worth burying." He wagged his head. "My poor country! Without cash or credit, how much longer can you fight mighty Britain?"

"It would help some if we could find my buried gold," Bill said.

"I fear that is a fantastic hope."

"Mr. Stewart thought it might be done."

"Without a map?"

"It's one of three islands not a great ways north of Charles Town. He and I would have tried if nothing had happened."

"Perhaps he has."

"If he has found it he will give it to me, even if he is a Tory."

"Politics don't tarnish Stewart's honesty," Marion said. "And don't get it into your head that all Tories are villains. They are quite as good as we are."

"I couldn't find Mr. Stewart in the city during the siege."

"He moved out early." Marion raised his head and listened as he spoke. "He couldn't stand the way some of the British officers treated his Whig friends, and he couldn't decide to turn Whig himself. So he moved to a plantation he owns up Georgetown way."

Mac came cantering down the driveway, riding easily but with a hard look on his face. "They are burning the next place up the road, sir," he reported.

"Regulars or Tories?" Marion asked.

"Regulars. Tarleton's I think."

"He is the eighth plague." Marion shut his lips tightly and sniffed the air. "I have three horses left in the stable. Will you go with us, Luke?"

"Yes, suh, effen Ah has to walk afoot."

"Get the horses ready while I collect some food."

A few minutes later they rode north into the woods single

file. Marion led the way and did not turn for a last look at the place he loved above all others. Watching him, Bill partly realized how heavy his heart must be. The little man, so full of physical pain and mental anguish, rode away quietly and without flinching.

They took a swamp path, for Marion was at home there. His life had been spent in the lowlands of South Carolina and from them he drew his strength. He loved their soft silences inasmuch as he was given to solitary thinking. From childhood, when his puny body was not expected to survive a dozen years, he had hunted and fished and ridden and paddled every corner of a wilderness that was unknown to most white men. It had given him health in abundance, not the exuberant kind that Mac enjoyed, but an amazing reserve of endurance. In the Cherokee wars he had won a reputation as scout and rifleman, honors he never mentioned because he loathed fighting. Still, when red men or white invaded his land he was ready to throw all he had at them — every dollar, every drop of blood, every thought of his active mind.

Darkness closed in, but the colonel gave no sign of stopping. Bullfrogs challenged them, their voices twanging like a giant jew's-harp. Now and then a barred owl shouted the wild spirit of the swamp in a Whoo-ah! Whoo-ah! the last syllable dropping in a way that stirred the blood like a war whoop. The heavy smell of warm muddy water suggested great age, perhaps going back through aeons to the time when much of the earth was a swamp, and man was one of its creatures fleeing through the night to escape from his own kind, as at present. He was still at it, fighting and plundering and, for the most part, unashamed that he was still a beast.

"Tired, Mac?" Marion called back in a cheery voice.

"No, sir," Mac lied, for he was dead weary of this snail's pace. If they were going somewhere, why not find a good road and gallop? That was his idea of traveling.

"And you, Bill?"

"Fresh as a daisy, Colonel," Bill answered, with the mental reserve that all daisies wilt sooner or later.

"Is Luke still with us?"

"Yes, suh, de tail end ob dis percession am still a-waggin'."

Marion chuckled, for his spirits always rose in the swamp. "A mile from here," he said, "the trace forks. We camp not far beyond."

Bill wondered silently how the colonel could tell in which direction they were going, not to mention where they actually were. Perhaps he only thought he did. And that was the last time the boy was fool enough to question Francis Marion's sense of direction.

They turned right in due course and crossed a small bridge. A quarter of a mile or so beyond it Marion gave the word to halt.

"There is better pasture on the other side of the creek," he told them, "but a bridge gives warning of pursuit."

"Do you think we are being followed, sir?" Bill asked uneasily.

"I am sure we are not, but we must form the habit of

vigilance. Always, when possible, put a bridge between yourself and the enemy. The sound of his horses' hoofs on the planking may save your life. Give me a hand, please, this confounded ankle is tricky."

Luke, who could see in the dark like a fox, started a fire in a way that suggested magic. By its light they fed the horses and then themselves, sitting in the lee of the fire where there were fewer mosquitoes. They were only a minor affliction to the Southerners but Bill could never get used to the buzzing imps. Marion ate lightly as usual and lay back on his blanket to rest his leg. In a few minutes he was asleep. Luke covered him with his own blanket and went off to rub down the horses.

"Do you reckon that the army General Washington is sending to help us will turn back now Charles Town has fallen?" Bill asked.

"Don't see how it can," Mac answered. "They left Philadelphia the middle of April and must be almost here. They'd look silly marching all that way, then marching back without a fight."

"But our army ain't here to help them now."

"Two or three thousand Continentals with artillery can stand on their own feet. If we were half as many and half as well-equipped we wouldn't need any help."

"Who's this DeKalb in command of the Continentals?"

"Old Gates is in command, but he's too nice to travel with the army so he'll be along later, after DeKalb has done the dirty work."

"But who is DeKalb? I've been away so long I don't even know our officers' names."

"He's a German in the French army. They say he's good. Was with Washington at Brandywine and Germantown and Valley Forge."

"If he's Washington's friend, why isn't he in command instead of Gates?"

"Congress sent Gates."

"But I've heard Washington doesn't like him."

"That makes no difference. Gates is a politician and — "

"Well," interrupted Bill, "Gates must be something of a soldier to sew up Burgoyne at Saratoga the way he did."

"Huh!" Mac snapped a twig end-over-end into the fire. "From what I hear, Schuyler and Morgan and Arnold milked that cow, then Gates stepped in and skimmed the cream. Now he thinks he's a bigger man than Washington. Says so himself. That's the kind of a windbag they've sent to help us."

"Between officers of that kind and local Tories, I guess we'll need help," Bill said. "Though Colonel Marion thinks all Tories aren't bad."

"They ain't." Mac looked at a star through the branches and studied it for a while. "You know, Bill, my father is a Tory."

"No!"

"Don't let it fuss you. It's not one of those tragic things you hear about. Father and I are good friends."

"But how do you happen to be on opposite sides of the fence? If you don't mind my asking."

"Well, the governor feels he should stick by the king, while I say America is our country. And I'll tell you why. Our family was among the survivors of Culloden. You know the English not only licked the Scots that day but massacred all the helpless ones they could lay hands on."

"And your father is still loyal to the English king?"

"Yes, it's a habit with him. But not with me. You see, when our family and a lot of other Scots got away from the English, with barely the shirts on their backs, they came to America. Well, the Americans took 'em and gave 'em a new start over here. They didn't want charity, but they did want sympathy and an honest chance. They got it and they shouldn't forget it. But the governor believes English rule is best for the colonies. I don't. I was born here and I am an American."

"Me too, suh," Luke spoke out of the darkness.

"What is an American?" Bill looked into the fire. "Your people came from Scotland, Luke's from Africa, the colonel's from France, mine from England — yet we are all Americans."

"And all sleepy." Mac yawned.

"Americans are red-flannel hash," Bill said, as though he had found the answer in the fire.

"What's red flannel hash?" Mac stood up.

"Something they make up North out of corned beef and potatoes and salt pork and onions. Each part has its own flavor and they blend for a common purpose."

"That fits the picture." Mac stretched his arms over his head. "So long as it is ourselves and not the British who make hash of us. Turn in, gentlemen, tomorrow will soon be knocking on the front door."

It was raining in the morning, a warm drizzle that was a pleasure to be out in. Before they mounted, Marion rested a hand on his horse's mane and took a long look around.

"If anything happens," he said, "if we become separated, our point of rendezvous is Charlotte, North Carolina. The Continental Army should march that way within two weeks."

"Why couldn't they have started a month earlier and saved Charles Town!" Bill said bitterly.

"Regrets are useless." The colonel swung his lame foot impatiently.

"Congress had to play politics with Gates," Mac growled.

"Hush!" Marion said sternly. "General Gates may soon be our commander."

"Your pardon, sir," Mac said, "but we are South Carolina Militia, not Continentals."

"Perhaps we are the South Carolina Militia." Marion's lips twisted. "I wonder if any others are left. But come, come! We must march. Give me a hand up, Luke."

"Yes, suh. Set yo' in de saddle?"

"No, just ease the weight on that foot."

"Yes, suh."

"Now!" He swung his leg over. "Thank you, Luke. With a horse between my knees I am as good as new."

They started down the trace, rolling their shoulders and hitching up their breeches as they settled down comfortably for the long ride. Marion rode ahead, sniffing the swamp air like a fox. His shoulders were squared and there was a defiant tilt to his head that disclaimed any thought of defeat. Bill watched him and recalled his words that night in the canoe: "Though you must run, keep your brush up." Here was a man to follow, to fight for, to die for if necessary. The boy had dreamed those things many times on the island and now they were realities. He shivered nervously.

Mac's horse was an old hunter that knew better than to step into a muskrat's hole, but they had not gone a mile when he did just that. To make it worse, the hole was between two buried logs so that when his weight threw him forward his leg was held fast. There was a sickening snap and the horse reared, coming down on three legs and holding the other loosely in the air.

"The devil! It's broken!" Mac jumped off and steadied the horse by the bridle.

Marion swung around and winced at the sight. He knew what a broken bone meant and his first thought was of the animal's pain.

"He'll be suffering bad in a few minutes." He looked into the frightened eyes. "Unsaddle him, Luke. Ease me down, Bill."

"If you want me to shoot him, sir — "

"No, I'll do it. There's a spot close behind the ear. He won't know what hit him. Lead him into the woods, Mac."

Marion hobbled after the horse, there was a pistol shot and he reappeared, followed by Mac with an empty bridle.

"I am to blame." Mac stopped beside his saddle. "I should have watched his footing."

"Nonsense." Marion stood thinking.

"I will replace him, sir."

"Nonsense again. The difficulty is, we are a considerable distance from friends who will oblige us with a horse."

"They are all Tories around here?" Bill asked.

"Yes, intense Tories. Davey, back beyond the fork, is bragging that he will establish a dukedom from our confiscated land."

"Thief!" Bill commented.

"Colonel," Mac asked suddenly, "may I borrow Luke's horse for an hour?"

"Yes" — Marion saw the big fellow's eyes dancing with an idea — "providing it is for a legitimate purpose."

"It's for the glory of our cause, Colonel."

"Then go. We will wait here." He was considerate enough not to ask embarrassing questions.

"Are volunteers accepted, Mac?" Bill asked.

"One, if he is brave and handsome."

"That's me."

They mounted. "On to glory!" Mac shouted and galloped up the road, with Bill pelting after him.

They crossed the bridge and took the turn they had avoided the night before. There they stopped and made their plans, then went on for half a mile until they sighted a luxurious plantation house.

"That must be where old Davey roosts," Bill said.

"Yep. Pull your riding cloak up to your chin," Mac said, as they swung into the avenue. "It will protect your precious carcass from the rain and also conceal your lack of uniform."

They trotted sharply up to the big house and Mac hailed a Negro who was picking roses in the yard.

"Is your master home, Ebenezer?"

The boy glanced at them and answered, as a door latch clicked, "Dat him, Cap'n."

A small, rotund, pink-faced man strutted to the edge of the porch and stopped, as though on the verge of making a speech. He looked like one who could talk for hours without releasing anything heavier than sound.

Mac saluted smartly and announced, "The compliments of Colonel Tarleton to Mr. Davey."

"Colonel Tarleton! Colonel Tarleton, sir?" The queue of the man's white wig trembled with excitement. "Is Colonel Tarleton in the vicinity?"

"He is en route from Monk's Corners, sir, to sweep the country clean of the insolent rebels."

"Bully! Bully!" Mr. Davey smote his pudgy hands together. "Were I ten years younger I would be by his side. My greatest desire, sir, my greatest desire is to serve my king."

"Colonel Tarleton is aware of your loyalty, sir," Mac said gravely. "It will not be forgotten in the hour of victory."

"Oh, that I might hasten that hour!" The dreamed-of dukedom seemed to be coming up fast and Mr. Davey stood on his toes to reach for it. "So my loyalty is appreciated, eh?"

"Indeed it is, sir, and highly spoken of in influential circles." Mac laid it on thick. "You are known far and wide as a good friend of his majesty."

"God bless his sweet majesty George the Third!" Mr. Davey cried with all his heart, hoping that somehow the words would carry clear to the throne. "My most fervent prayer, sir, my most fervent prayer is that I may contribute to his glorious cause."

"If you could spare a horse, sir, it would be — "

"A horse, sir?" Mr. Davey interrupted. "Who wants a horse?"

"Colonel Tarleton is very busy chasing rebels. A fresh mount would be appreciated."

"Why didn't you say so in the first place? A horse for Tarleton to chase rebels with! Bully! Bully! The best horse in my stable too!"

"Colonel Tarleton does not wish to ask too much from you, sir."

"Too much! Nothing is too much for those who serve the king." Mr. Davey leaned over the side of the porch and shouted as he imagined a duke would shout, "Ho there, Dick! Come forth!" And when Dick did not come forth he continued in less regal language, "Where the devil is that son of a lop-eared donkey?"

"Hyar, suh." A Negro groom showed up.

"Awake, are you? Answer me, are you awake?"

"Yes, suh."

"Then fetch out Selim."

"Selim, suh?" The groom's eyes opened wide.

"I said Selim and, dammit, I meant Selim."

"Yes, suh." The boy moved off.

"Selim is an Arabian, sir," Mr. Davey explained to Mac. "The finest horse I ever owned — and I've had some beauties in my day. But I've no work worthy of him. That is, no work half so worthy as chasing rebels. Dammit, sir, on that horse Tarleton can run down any rebel in South Carolina."

"A magnificent gift, sir, and one that shall not be forgotten," Mac murmured, genuinely stirred. Bill coughed.

It was a magnificent gift, for Selim was a horse in ten

thousand. And to give it all the proper touch, the dukely gesture, Mr. Davey added a new saddle, bridle and pair of silver-mounted pistols. Tartleton would be impressed — and obligated. Being a gentleman, he would not fail to pay off his obligations when the time came. Considering the stakes, it was a small investment, and Mr. Davey was pleased with himself as he watched the two supposed British aides ride back up the avenue.

As they reached the road half a dozen dragoons — Tory cavalrymen by their uniforms — galloped toward them around a bend.

"Bluff 'em," Bill said out of the corner of his mouth.

"Or fight 'em if they won't bluff," Mac answered.

They pulled to the side of the road and stared haughtily at the troopers.

"Halt!" The lieutenant in command pulled up. "Who are you?"

"Despatch riders from Georgetown to Charles Town," Bill told him.

"In that garb?"

"We are in enemy territory, my friend."

"What are you doing with a third horse?"

"He was, shall I say contributed, by a native." Mac laughed and rode past.

"Hold on!" The lieutenant looked hard at Bill. "Where have I seen you before?"

"I have not the honor of your friendship." Bill bowed stiffly and rode after Mac. "Get out of here!" he whispered. "That is Harold Graves."

"Who?"

"Graves, the one who sold me to Bottle."

"We'll go back and cut his throat." Mac pulled up.

"We've got to stick by the colonel, Mac."

"Yes, we must. Did Graves recognize you?"

"He couldn't place me, but it will come to him."

"When it does he will try to fetch some friends to call on us."

"I hope I will be there to receive him," Bill answered grimly.

CHAPTER XII

WHEN they rejoined Marion and told their story his eyes danced with merriment, but he confined his remarks to comments about the horse Selim. His sense of justice was so acute that even under the stress of war he deplored seizing another man's property, but it was legal and, in the present instance, necessary. A horse was vital to them, and their combined purses could not have bought the shoes for one, so, regardless of how Mac came by it, criticism was not in order. And Selim was a magnificent animal, broad between the eyes, tall and powerful, an ideal mount for the big trooper. It was too happy a combination to invite interference.

They kept to the forest paths that day. It was a sweet country, heavy with the fragrance of jessamine, smilax and sweet bay. And a soft country, as is the case where foliage is always green. The horses' hoofs padded on the ground without clatter and the squeaking and tinkling of equipment was hushed by a curtain of gray moss. In the midst of war here was peace, yet Bill the Northerner was oppressed by it. To him it was languid and gloomy like the aimless streams that were stained black by acid from the cypress roots. He longed for sparkling trout brooks and the vigor of maple trees. Even the flocks of snowy herons and the exquisite music of mockingbirds were too dreamlike to suit his homesick fancy. He wanted to hear a partridge drum and see snowbirds wheeling before a storm.

It was strange, he mused, that a nation could be so different in its parts and yet be one. The people of the North and South were as far apart in some ways as maple sugar and sweet potatoes, yet they saw eye to eye on questions of liberty. The same emotions had blazed up at the same time throughout the colonies. The men at Ticonderoga, Lexington, Fort Moultrie and other places had played the same tune from the first and were still playing it. That was the wonder of it, that they had never quit. But men worth their salt would not walk out on leaders like Washington and Marion. Bill pondered what he knew of those two; born in the same year, farmers by choice, soldiers by necessity, early trained in Indian warfare, volunteers in the present struggle on which they had staked their lives and fortunes.

Late in the afternoon Marion shot a turkey gobbler and they camped early to roast it. To hungry men it was tantalizing to watch the spit turn slowly in Luke's hands, but they had to wait because their corn bread and bacon were gone.

Squatting on his heels, Luke cocked an eye at the treetops and wished aloud, "Effen Ah had a fishhook Ah'd catch some fishes we'd eat fustest."

"You would try to catch 'em," Mac amended.

"Dey shore bite now, suh. De ole folkses say, 'Effen de win' come from de wes' dey bite de bes'.' "

"A pig's eye!" Mac snorted.

"Kunnel, hain't hit de trufe?" Luke appealed.

"Beyond question," Marion said, as though he believed it. " 'If the wind comes from the east they bite the least.' " He nodded at Mac. "Based on observation, you know. A good thing for us to remember if we are to live off the land."

"When we join the Continentals we will eat beef," Mac said.

"I wonder where it will come from."

"The commissary," Mac answered glibly.

Marion wagged his head. "There is food enough in these swamps to feed an army. If we are scattered we need not starve."

"Scattered, sir?" Bill picked up the suggestion.

"Always a possibility. Should it become a reality our friends the bears, deer, rabbits and others would have a chance to die for the cause." A whimsical thought, but one to be recalled later.

The next day in order to bear northwest they were obliged to leave the swamp. As they approached the highway a Negro woman and two children scuttled across the path and fled into the woods.

Marion watched them dodging like rabbits. "They look too terrified to talk. Something has happened around here."

A few rods farther along, Selim threw up his head and snorted.

"He smells redcoats," Mac said.

Marion sniffed the air and said, "I smell the work of redcoats."

Then the others got it, the acrid odor of wet ashes. Where the woods fell away in a clearing they stopped in a knot, the horses with their ears pricked forward, the men tense in their saddles. In the field a blackened chimney was knee-deep in the remains of a burned house. Beyond it were heaps that had been outbuildings and a once pretty garden was a mass of trampled azaleas, wisteria and camellia japonica.

"God's mercy!" Marion urged his snorting horse among the trees behind the chimmey. Two men, one of them old, had been hanged from the limb of an oak and their bodies lay where they had been cut down. Near by were the bodies of a woman and two children with their throats cut. The riders stared in horror. This was the work of so-called civilized white men, not savage Indians.

"Oh, Lawdy Lawd!" Luke groaned. "De pore folkses! De pore daid folkses!"

"Loyal supporters of his Christian majesty George the Third!" Mac struck his saddle with his fist. "Here, Luke, hold Selim."

He dismounted and started searching the ground like a great angry dog. Bill joined him. They found nothing to show there had been a fight. Even if the men had tried to defend their home, there could have been no excuse for such slaughter. The thought angered Bill as nothing had before.

When they returned, Marion was sitting in the same place, his face set like iron and his eyes blazing. But he spoke quietly:

"These people and others like them will do more for liberty than ten times their number of soldiers."

"They didn't have a chance to strike a blow." Bill choked.

"Their chance will come. And they will go on striking as long as humanity lives. They fight with the silent rustless weapons of outraged innocence. Every decent man will turn against their murderers."

"I'd like to lead a hundred thousand troopers through the heart of England!" Mac cried.

"You are wrong there, Mac," the colonel said. "The little people of England wouldn't have done this. They don't want this war. But the big ones — a few of the big ones who happen to be in power — do, so they send out butchers like Clinton and Cornwallis and Tarleton to carry it on."

"They think they can scare us to our knees," Bill snorted.

"Yes. But they will win the war for us."

"I want a hand in the winning." Mac wheeled Selim impatiently.

Marion spoke slowly, with tremendous force behind every word: "The colonies were loyal to the core and would have remained so if they had been treated wisely. But they weren't. The politicians think we are slaves and the military think we are curs. Good! Lay on! Burn, pillage, murder! The more the better, for every blow of that kind will bring down ten honest ones on your heads."

"Should us bury de pore folkses, suh?" Luke asked.

"No." Marion turned away. "Don't cover such deeds quickly. Leave them open a while to the sight of all. Come, lads." Before he rode off he drew his sword and saluted his fallen comrades in arms.

They cantered up the road, trying vainly to pick up the trail of the redcoats that had been washed out by the rain. But from the top of a hill they saw half a dozen horsemen approaching.

"I hope they're Tories." Mac loosened his pistols in the holsters.

The little troop stopped at the foot of the hill and bunched up, then came on in open order, each man with a long rifle in his hands.

"Who be you?" Their leader came on a few steps and pulled up. He was a thin, nervous man who wore rough clothes and a round leather cap.

"Colonel Marion of the Militia. And you, sir?"

"Ed Simms. See what happened a ways up the road?"

"Yes. Who did it?"

" 'Bout a hundred an' fifty Britishers. We're after 'em."

"Only you six?"

"We cain't wait fer more. We're fightin' mad an' we're goin' to fight."

"Aren't you heading the wrong way?"

"No. They're at the Bixby plantation. Hit's a big place an' hit'll take some time to plunder. We're cuttin' round the woods so's to come at 'em from the west."

"We will go with you," Marion said casually, as though ten men against a hundred and fifty was no problem.

"Glad to have you." Simms looked back at his men and added, "Hain't we, boys?"

The five rifles were still ready and one man asked flatly, "Shore they hain't fixin' to fox us?"

"Gawd pity 'em effen they be!" another said.

"You know how hit is these times." Simms looked Marion in the eye. "Us has heerd of Colonel Marion, but we don't know him by sight."

"I can only say that I am he." Marion returned the look.

"I guess you'll do," Simms decided.

"Then let's be off."

Simms rode ahead and his men deliberately closed in around the Marion party, for it might cost a man his life to trust a stranger. Bill noticed that in addition to their rifles they carried long clumsy sabers.

"Where did you come by that blade?" he asked the man next him.

"Made her from a mill saw."

"How does it handle?"

"Hit'll cut a feather or fell a bull."

"Mind if I heft it?" Mac asked.

The man shifted his rifle before he answered, "Dunno's I do," and handed it over.

Mac handled it curiously at first, then with enthusiasm, circling, thrusting and parrying. In his powerful hand it seemed light as lath.

"I'll give you my blade for it," he offered and held out his fine English saber.

"You mean that, Mister?"

"Sure."

The man took it almost reverently, for he had never touched such beautiful workmanship. He was a small fellow and it suited his strength better than the larger sword.

"I'll swap you," he said and unbuckled his cowhide scabbard.

Mac clapped it against his thigh and laughed aloud. "Now give me some British timber to saw."

They cut around the woods and back by a sheep path,

trotting in single file. Beyond the pasture was a field of knee-high corn which they crossed and, as they were farmers, they were careful to keep between the rows. Another pasture gave into more woods. Simms pulled up at a brush fence and raised his hand. In the distance ahead they heard confused shouting.

"I aimed to scout the place but thar hain't time. They're at it now." His teeth clicked over the words like hedge shears.

He raised his horse over the fence and the others followed. The woods were open and within five minutes the big white house could be seen. A few rods farther and they made out the yard full of horses, mostly with empty saddles. Redcoats were all over the place, even in the chamber windows.

"They hain't fired hit yit," Simms whispered.

"Looting," Marion said. "We can double the surprise if we attack from two sides. I will take my men to the rear of the barn. When you see us round the corner you charge."

"We will, Colonel."

Marion led his troop of three to the right, behind a hedgerow that lay along the edge of the forest. He had forgotten his sore ankle and rode lightly, his eyes snapping. Bill remembered that was the way he looked when things were going badly at Fort Moultrie. The odds were heavier against them this time.

"Effen dem Philisteens don' run fasser'n us dey's gwine t'ink ole man Samson done come back wid de jackass jawbone," Luke whispered.

"Keep an eye on the colonel," Bill said behind his hand. "Cover him if he goes down."

"Yes, suh."

As they came out of the woods behind the barn Marion swung his horse around and told them, "Give your pistols to their horses first and set them plunging. Then at 'em with sabers. Don't stand and fight — keep moving. And yell like all hell was loose."

"A bit of it will be." Mac spat on his palm and grasped the big sword.

"Look to your priming." They examined their pistols. "Come on, boys!"

They swept around the corner of the barn in a column of four as though leading a regiment. Bill had never heard a man, and a small man at that, make as much noise as the colonel did. At the other end of the line Luke was screeching a battle cry brought from Africa by his father, and it had not been dulled in transit. Nor did Mac's vocal efforts fall short as he stood in his stirrups, swinging the great sword over his head.

They gave the bunched horses a volley that set them rearing and thrashing. Some broke away from the soldiers who were holding them and stampeded across the lawn, bowling over a knot of troopers busy smashing open chests they had brought from the house. Velvet coats, linen sheets, London hats and ball gowns were scrambled on the grass under a cloud of goose feathers from a tick. Five mounted officers came from the rear of the house to see what was going on. Selim hit them first. With mouth wide open, teeth flashing and eyes blazing, he put terror into the leading horse. As it reared and wheeled, Mac leaned far over and emptied the saddle at one sweep. Marion, Bill and Luke fanned out and closed in, thinking to shatter the line and be off.

But the Britishers were not stuffed shirts. Their swords flashed and with spur and rein they held their horses to the shock. Over a tossing mane Bill struck straight at a smooth red face. Lightning flickered along his own sword and he turned it with a snap of the wrist. His horse stumbled over the fallen man and the other's saber, aimed at the throat, missed by a hair and ripped his collar. He struck the arm, felt it give way and saw it drop, gushing a red stream. The officer drew a pistol with his other hand and fired at the same instant Bill's horse threw up its head to pull itself back on balance. It caught the bullet squarely and dropped in its tracks. Bill had no time to jump, but he saved his legs by kicking backward as he went down.

He came up surrounded by plunging horses, for dragoons were closing in on all sides. Three of them, momentarily in each other's way, were swinging at Marion. Bill made a lunging upthrust and got one of them under the arm. The soldier fell over his horse's neck as the horse backed away. Then Selim charged the other two, Mac standing straight and swinging his sword in circles. Empty saddles followed the strokes as stubble follows a scythe.

Bill caught a riderless horse and snapped into the saddle. Marion, spattered with blood, was heading back into the melee. His dander was up and he had forgotten his order not to stand and fight. Luke needed help, for he was hemmed in against one side of the house and was fighting desperately.

He had lost his sword and replaced it with a club that looked like a wagon tongue. Swinging it with both hands, he had swept the troopers clear on three sides of him. Blood was running down his face from a bullet scratch on his forehead and one bare foot was dripping red from a flesh wound in the thigh. The soldiers, furious at finding a Negro who dared fight back, were gathering for a rush, hoping to take him alive and make an example of him to local slaves.

But the rush backfired. As Marion's unit hit one side of the crowd Simms and his men, who had handled a skirmish of their own behind the house, hit the other side. Ten men who yell and fight like fiends can appear to be many times that number. The troopers believed they were surrounded. They were also a little drunk and confused, all of which added up to a desire to get away fast. Their horses were of the same mind and in three minutes there was not an able-bodied redcoat on the field.

The Americans looked at one another, mentally counting noses. No one was missing, but several were wounded. Four dragoons looked to be dead and half a dozen others were writhing on the grass. A quiet, black-bearded man, whose base of supplies was two saddlebags, was working over them with bottles and bandages.

"Who are you, sir?" Marion demanded.

"The regimental surgeon." The man did not look up.

"Is Colonel Tarleton in command of this raid?"

"He was not present here."

"Was he present at the place up the road?"

"He was."

"You are ashamed of what happened there, aren't you?"

"Yes, sir, I am." The doctor looked up honestly. "But I suppose the colonel had his orders."

"That doesn't excuse him."

"Not a bit."

"Will you treat my wounded?"

"Naturally."

"Thank you, sir." Marion turned to Simms. "Keep an eye on things. Mac, you and Luke see that King George contributes what weapons and ammunition those fellows left behind. With me, Bill."

They went through the house and found no one, for the family had escaped. It was a beautiful place, with the air of gracious living, but wantonly looted and wrecked.

"What folly war is!" Marion cried, as they passed the fragments of furniture. "Why can't disputes be settled by the best rather than by the worst elements of human nature?"

"We've got to fight, sir." Bill picked up a silk dress that had been ripped to rags. "We can't reason with people who do these things."

"We never could reason with them." Marion knocked a broken chair out of the way. "They think we are savages."

"What do they think they are?"

"Gentlemen, Bill, gentlemen." Marion smiled bitterly.

When they returned to the lawn they found Mac and Luke playing with the small arms they had collected.

"Hit jes' bus' ma heart to t'ink what ole King Jawdge say when he hear dis," Luke grinned.

"Luke thinks the war is over," Mac explained.

The British doctor interrupted to ask, "Will you and your servant have your wounds dressed, sir?"

"Thank you, no," Marion said. "We are only scratched. How are my men?"

"Able to travel."

"I have no money to offer for your services, but you have my deepest thanks."

"That is sufficient." The doctor bowed. "It is a pleasure to be of service."

"To an enemy?"

"The medical profession is not a political body, sir."

"What a boon to society if doctors formed a majority of the population!"

"Colonel," Simms put in, "what are we goin' to do with their wounded?"

"Leave them. There is nothing else to do with them."

"We might hang 'em."

"Do you want to be tarred with Tarleton's brush?"

"Well — no. But the redcoats'll come back and burn this place."

"We have neither the men nor the time to defend it."

A bugle sounded in the distance.

"They're comin' now!" Simms cried.

"Saddles!" Marion ordered. "To the woods."

They trotted away in the direction they had come. It was the only sensible thing to do, for it would be suicide to stand against the re-formed dragoons who outnumbered them more than ten to one. A smart blow had been struck, but its value would be lost by foolhardy resistance.

Back on the highway, Simms pulled up. "Colonel," he asked, "mind tellin' me whar you're goin'?"

"We are on our way to join the Continental Army."

"Can I go too?"

"Certainly."

"I mean, I'd like to serve under you."

"Delighted to have you." Marion was obviously pleased.

"Me too," another man said, and a third reined his horse over to join them.

"Boys," Marion said gravely, "I can promise you no money, no uniforms — nothing."

"All we're lookin' fer is a chance to fight the redcoats," Simms answered for the three.

"I can promise you that." Marion smiled the smile that made men follow him anywhere.

"We'll fetch our own hosses an' shootin' tools," Simms said.

"Thank you, boys." Marion's eyes lighted with pleasure. "A few men like you will become a thorn in the flesh of the British lion."

CHAPTER XIII

THE trip north was not a march in a military sense, though it was made by members of the militia. Rather, it was the journey of a handful of farmers who had been driven from their homes and were in search of a rallying point where they could organize against the authors of their troubles.

At the end of a week Marion was leading upwards of twenty men, all victims of British and Tory persecution. He had met them on the road and talked with them, and they had followed him. They were sick of politicians in uniform, who rode through the country, promising this and that and playing both ends against the middle. This quiet little man promised nothing except an opportunity to fight the enemy, but his sincerity was balm to those wounded by trickery. They looked at him and trusted him. He was quality, that is, he was a planter who could read and write as easily as a Charles Town judge, yet, like themselves, he had only half a blanket and not a coin in his pocket. His courage had been tested and his discipline was just and rigid. He was someone to tie to in these days of sad confusion.

The pitiful condition of the state spread before them as

they rode. With the fall of Charles Town the British considered South Carolina to be helpless, a conquered province to be plundered down to the last grain of rice. The army was sent out to live off the country during the summer, a sort of vacation of pillage and lust, which officers like Clinton and Cornwallis encouraged, to their everlasting shame. Companies roamed at large, burning, looting and murdering a people too disorganized to resist. Three or four thousand redcoats, superbly armed and trained, had terrified fifteen times their number of Carolinians who had only hunting pieces, homemade ammunition and negligible military science. In addition, they were discouraged by defeat, impoverished by violence, and threatened with extinction if they continued to resist.

Naturally, many of them turned their coats. It was treason, but in most cases the patriot leaders recognized it as a last desperate attempt at self-preservation. Marion even welcomed some of it as a means of saving part of the population for postwar work. Likewise, he was cheered by every enemy atrocity, for he knew such tactics must be fatal to those who employed them. He never lost faith that, bitter as it was, the medicine would cure the affliction.

Soon after crossing the North Carolina line they came upon Major Peter Horry eating corn bread and cold sweet potatoes in a grubby tavern.

"Well, well, well! If it's not Pete!" Marion cried from the doorway.

"Francis! You old original sinner!" Horry jumped up and met him in the middle of the floor. "But why the limp?"

"A broken ankle. Mending fast."

"And where are you going?"

"To join Gates and the Continentals."

"So am I. What luck to bump into you! Is that your command outside?"

"Volunteers. We are traveling together. Here, Bill!" He motioned with his finger. "You recall this lad, Bill Barlow, Pete. He was with us at Fort Moultrie and since has had enough adventures to fill a book."

Horry squinted one eye and regarded Bill.

"Not the little duffer who was shipwrecked!"

"Yes, sir." Bill tingled at being remembered.

"You must be my guests at dinner." Horry waved toward the puncheon table. "The food is as may be, but we will wax fat on news."

"First I must arrange for baiting the men and horses," Marion said. "Hello there, landlord!"

"I'm comin', I'm comin'." A barefooted man in grease-spattered clothing padded through the doorway. "But don't expect nary bite ner drop till ye show th' color o' yore money."

"Sir," the colonel explained, "I am a member of the South Carolina Militia."

"I don't keer effen you're Washin'ton hisself, ye git no credit." The man braced his feet wide apart, toes out.

"I haven't a penny in my pocket."

"Nor I." Horry shrugged and grinned.

"But, landlord, I must have food for my men and horses."

"Not on tick. No sir-eee!"

"I will give you my personal note to be redeemed at the earliest moment."

"I won't take it."

"I'll sign with him," Horry offered.

"I won't take it," the landlord repeated flatly.

"Look here," Marion's eyes narrowed, "we are fighting your battles and we expect consideration from you."

"Nobody fights my battles," the man retorted. "I'm runned over by both sides, I be. The British robs me one day, the colonists robs me the next."

That was probably true, as Marion knew. "I deplore such a situation," he said, "but we must have food. I can't do more than pledge my word to pay you. Accept it or we help ourselves."

"Can I live on paper?" The landlord fished in his pocket. "See this." He held up a leaf from a notebook. "Yistiddy a Tory officer paid me his bill with it. Today ye try to play the same dirty trick."

Horry caught him by the shoulders and shook him so sharply that the paper fell to the floor.

"Today we take what is left," the major roared. "That is war, my friend, war. I've lost my plantation but I'm not going to see my friends go hungry. I'll entertain our host, Francis, while you and the boys serve the meal."

"Easy, Pete," Marion cautioned. "Avoid the appearance of extortion."

Bill picked up the paper and glanced at it, then looked again.

"Landlord," he asked sharply, "did you see the Tory who signed this?"

"Shore I did."

"Yellowish skin, black eyes close together, too well dressed?"

"That's him. Said his name's Cap'n Graves."

"He signed it that way."

"I cain't read, bein' a poor man."

"Friend of yours, Bill?" Horry asked.

"Anything but that!" Bill followed Marion out.

The thought of Graves always burned him up. His first impulse was to take Luke and give chase as he would to a chicken thief, then he remembered he was in the army and soldiers don't run out on their officers without permission.

"Colonel," he asked, "may I try to run down Graves? He can't be far off."

"No." Marion did not pause in his stride. "We are engaged in a national, not a private, war."

Bill dropped back, his face burning. He knew he had been put in his place, rightly so, and he had sense enough not to resent it. Even in that ragtag military unit there must be discipline. And Marion played no favorites. He and his men ate from the same dish but, for all that, they took orders from him.

During the afternoon they saw two more samples of enemy work, which Bill charged up to Graves. In one place a house had been burned, and in another a flock of butchered sheep were bloating in the sun.

"Look at 'em!" Horry pounded his saddle in fury. "Killed and left there to rot so women and children will be without warm clothing next winter. That ain't war, Francis."

"Yes, it is." Marion shifted his hat, which had lost part of its brim. "It is the worst part of war. Battles are infrequent and soon over, but the country suffers without respite and will suffer long after the shooting stops."

"If it does."

"It will, Pete, and we will fire the last shot."

Horry looked gloomily at the ruined farm they were passing.

"It will take a divine miracle to restore this country. Look at it—brush and weeds everywhere. South Carolina is worse, yet only five years ago our rice and indigo crops were worth a million pounds sterling. Not to mention the trade in lumber, tar and cattle."

Marion nodded. "Three thousand wagons came into Charles Town every year from the highlands loaded with wheat, corn and fur."

"Francis, what a fool the human race is to create with one hand and destroy with the other."

"We show the same intelligence as a man who, having work to do, first bleeds himself white."

"One tenth of the effort and expense that have gone into this war would have averted it, if applied in the right direction."

"And we have learned nothing from it, Pete. We are training our young men to follow in our tracks, and when they promise to be as stupid as ourselves, we promote them." He smiled wryly. "When we join the Continentals I shall see that Bill and Mac become lieutenants."

Horry shook his head in puzzlement. "If, in spite of itself, the human race continues to survive it proves that the Almighty has future use for it."

"Then why didn't He endow it with horse sense in the first place?"

"You forget, Francis, He was restricted by the fact that He was creating the human race." Horry laughed and cantered on ahead of the column.

"Did you hear that?" Mac whispered. "We're to be looies."

"I don't see much advantage in that," Bill said. "The colonel himself gets no salary, no uniform, no rations."

"It's the honor, my boy, the honor."

"Each of us can do only one man's work no matter what his rank is."

"But it will give our grandchildren something to brag about."

"Maybe." Bill shrugged. "If what we are doing now lets them live free and peaceful lives we are the ones who should do the bragging."

"You sound sick of war, Bill."

"I hate it."

"I don't. It's a whale of a lot of excitement."

"Yes, but — Oh, I don't know. I just hate it."

"Not going to quit?"

"If I thought you meant that I'd beat the life out of you."

"You couldn't do it; I have red hair."

"It will be white before — "

"Hey, look!" Mac stood in his stirrups. "Here comes Major Horry like a scared cat."

Horry galloped up waving his hat, for he was always excitable except in battle.

"The Continentals are camped in the valley!" he shouted. "It's a sight to make your heart dance."

The men swung their leather caps in the air and pelted to the brow of the hill for a look. Off to the north was the encampment, laid out in precise rows of tents like a picture. An artillery park was here and baggage wagons were there, with long double strings of horses between. A troop of cavalry was coming up from the river and falling out in a grove.

"That is De Kalb's work!" Marion's eyes shone with soldierly pride. "He learned his trade in France."

"Sounds like a German name," Horry said.

"He is German, but he has spent a lifetime soldiering for the king of France."

"Spit and polish," Horry said contemptuously.

"No! Don't be so provincial, Pete. Washington thinks highly of De Kalb."

"I wonder what he thinks of the French since Savannah."

They rode down the hill in a crowd, talking, and pointing out things to each other. Two snappy blue-coated sentinels halted them on the bridge.

"Who goes there?" one demanded in a northern accent.

"South Carolina Militia," Marion told him.

"Soldiers?" Both sentries looked at the ragged horsemen and laughed ouright.

"Yes, soldiers!" Marion snapped. "You are addressing Colonel Marion." His voice had an edge that brought the sentries up, saluting. "Where may I find your commander?"

"General De Kalb's tent is under them trees, sir."

Marion clattered over the bridge. As the men followed him one sentry remarked to the other, "Soldiers! No wonder they sent north for help."

Mac's open palm shot out and the fellow did a neat backward dive into the river. The troop passed on in silence, except for Luke, who gloated joyfully, "Oh, Lawdy Lawd! Dat boy needs hisse'f a tooth dentis' to pull loose dat kiss."

They rode up the hill, occasionally meeting soldiers who wore the professional air of owning the world. They were openly scornful of the bumpkins in homespun and made remarks which the South Carolinians swore to pay back with interest.

At the top of the hill they turned toward the nicely spaced tents. A smart young officer, wearing high boots and enormous spurs, strode importantly out of the first one.

"Back, rustics!" He gestured with a riding whip. "This is a military camp."

Marion gave him a look. "Direct me to Baron De Kalb's headquarters and be quick about it."

"General De Kalb is not at the back and call of idle sightseers."

"Young man," Marion said patiently, "Colonel Marion is not an idle sightseer."

The officer stiffened, trying to bluff his way out of a bad mistake. "The name is unfamiliar, sir," he said, "but I will present it to General De Kalb."

He turned toward the tent and stepped nimbly aside as a soldier emerged from it. He was a powerfully built man with white hair, a ruddy face and sharp blue eyes.

"Colonel Marion!" He ignored his aide and took two long strides, his hand outstretched. "I have heard favorably of you from General Washington." He spoke with an indescribable Franco-German accent.

"Baron De Kalb!" Marion, who had dismounted, took the hand heartily. "In behalf of South Carolina I have come to welcome you to our state."

"Good!" De Kalb looked thoughtfully at the silent, ragged men in the background. He had seen similar Americans, only worse, at Valley Forge and was not deceived by their appearance. "You are the first I have met from that state. We shall serve together with honor."

"I am sure we shall, sir." Marion bowed. "May I present my second in command, Major Horry."

"I am pleased, Major Horry."

"I, sir, am honored." Likc everyone else, Horry fell hard for the old soldier at first sight. Impulsive and careless formality as always, he spun around and tossed his hat in the air, as he whooped, "Three cheers for the general, boys!"

The troop roared a mighty yell and finished it off with a round of gunfire. Officers popped out of their tents, clutching their sidearms, soldiers came running, Marion was red with embarrassment, but De Kalb was beaming.

"Thank you, soldiers!" he boomed. "A spontaneous salute touches the heart more than twenty-one guns fired by command. Forty-two years have I been a soldier but never did guns make me so happy."

"May you win battles as completely as you win hearts," Marion said honestly.

"Ah, Colonel, may the good God permit me to help you brave Americans win your battles. But we will talk of war later. Now you and Major Horry must dine with me." He nodded to a pudgy Continental. "Captain Pike, assign this command rations and quarters."

"Yes, sir." The captain turned to Bill, thinking he was an officer. "This way, sir." He led them back toward a bend in the river where there was a small meadow edged with trees. "Here is grass and water," he said. "Where is your baggage train?"

"We have none," Bill told him.

"Pardon."

"I said we have no baggage."

"No tents?"

"None."

"What do you do when it rains?"

"We let it rain."

"Each of us has a piece of blanket large enough to cover his head," Mac explained cheerfully.

"Mine comes down to my shoulders," Simms said. "I want to sell part of it."

Captain Pike's eyes widened. "Gosh!" he cried, forgetting his rank. "You men must want to fight!"

"Is there any other way to win honorable peace?" Bill asked.

"No. You are right. But, it seems to me, your privations are — are excessive."

"Don't you worry 'bout us, Mister," Simms put in. "We wuz raised fightin' Injuns an' varmints, so Britishers're jest one more pest to git rid of. But, effen hit hain't askin' too much, we'd like some corn meal so we can fix us some hoe-cake."

"You shall have it." Pike hurried away.

Bill looked after him and beyond at the tents that housed three thousand troops. It was a heartening sight.

CHAPTER XIV

NEXT day, July 25th, General Gates arrived in camp. He had many fatuous ideas, the two outstanding ones being that he was a better man than George Washington and that he was handsome. Strutting the title "hero of Saratoga," which battle had been won for him by Benedict Arnold, he was one of the most vain, conceited, double-crossers that ever wore an American uniform. It was a flawless uniform of buff and blue. His weak face was velvet smooth and, it might be, touched with rouge, and every hair of his white wig was in its proper place. He rode a race-horse to give the impression of urgency to his actions and he was forever having councils with his officers in which he asked their advice and then ignored it. The fact that he held any position at all in the army was due to the politics played by himself and his friends.

He ordered the troops paraded and rode down the line without drawing a cheer. His attitude was cold and critical, but he was favorably impressed by the regiments because De Kalb had drilled them to a fine point and they were doing their best for him.

When Gates came to Marion's company he stopped short.

"Baron," he asked in a shocked tone, "what is this exhibit?"

"South Carolina Militia," De Kalb answered. "Arrived yesterday. Fine men."

"In rags! Fine in what way, pray?"

"In spirit, sir. They have ridden from near Charles Town to offer their services."

"Did you accept them?"

"I did, sir, with pleasure."

"My God!" Gates wheeled his horse, ignoring the salutes of Marion and Horry.

Horry swore with gusto and raged under his breath, "Is that what Washington sent us!"

"No, Pete" — the colonel was breathing hard — "that is what Congress sent us despite Washington's protest."

"The yellow-bellied polecats!"

"Silence!" Marion said sternly. "We are out to fight the British, not Horatio Gates."

"Right." Horry made a gesture of resignation. "But, Francis, it would be a joy to beat the fog out of that pink-faced doll!"

That evening Bill and Luke went fishing in the river to supplement the poor beef and corn meal that had been issued to them. For all its fine appearance, the army was grumbling loudly about its rations. Horry reported that even on De Kalb's table there had been only a slab of skinny pork and a few sweet potatoes. At the review Gates had promised plenty of rum and food, but the men were waiting to be shown. They were mostly from Maryland and Delaware where the farms were fat, and this part of the

South, never too good and now depleted by war, was not reassuring.

The mosquitoes finally drove Bill back from the river and up the hill. As he went toward camp, crossing near headquarters, he heard General Gates' high-pitched voice in one of the tents.

"I tell you I have decided to march to Camden by the shortest route."

"It is so," De Kalb's heavy voice answered. "But I object to the plan."

"What is it to you? The responsibility is mine."

"Sir, as an old soldier, I think of my men. They will suffer if you lead them through the pine-barren country. It is half desert and, at most, can offer you only lean cattle and green corn. The inhabitants are Tories. But take the route through the fertile and friendly counties of Rowan and Mecklenburg and you will be well fed."

"I shall seize what food I need irrespective of the owners."

"But, General Gates, I repeat there is no food to seize in the pine-barren country. So it is, I know."

"On whose authority do you make that statement, Baron?"

"On the word of Colonel Marion, who knows that section well."

"Oh, that rustic!"

"He is a fine officer, sir."

"Impossible. No fine officer would lead such a ragtag outfit. The memory of it makes me shudder."

"They are volunteers, General. They serve without pay and supply their own equipment."

"But their appearance, Baron, their appearance! Those caps and homespuns!"

"After six years of war they have nothing better."

"Then they should have stayed in their cornfields to frighten the birds."

"Good God, General Gates, these men are fighting for liberty, not putting on a dress parade!"

"They are a disgrace to the Continental Army and I shall be rid of them."

"No, no General! They are superb scouts. We need them."

"For a time, perhaps, but at the earliest moment they must return to their dens."

"Your attitude will antagonize the Carolinas, sir."

"Baron De Kalb," Gates shouted in anger, "you will please refrain from criticizing your commander!"

"Yes, sir" — the old soldier's words were level and packed with meaning — "I shall leave that task for history."

"Hooray for you, Baron!" Bill whooped, and slipped away in the darkness.

The next day when Gates announced his plan of moving to Camden by way of the pine-barrens all his principal officers objected in a memorial which they presented to him. He ignored it and ordered the army to march immediately, promising again that they would meet their supply train within a day or two.

Almost at once they entered the barrens. The country itself was not unpleasant, being mostly an open forest of loblolly pine and yellow pine, with low-growing shrubs and little grass. But the soil was almost useless for raising crops and what few settlers existed were widely scattered and miserably poor. As Major Horry wrote, years later, "It was sufficient to have starved a forlorn hope of caterpillars."

Although fully warned of all this, Gates led his army of over three thousand men and hundreds of horses squarely into the midst of it. They had little food at the start and the supplies he had promised never existed. The man was obsessed by the dream of winning a quick victory and dashing north to claim the prize he had set for himself, the command of all the American armies.

There could be only one result: at the end of two days his men were famished and the third day they were on the verge of mutiny. The only thing that held them together was the fact that their officers were no better off. Marion and his men, who had been assigned to scout duty, fared comparatively well as they moved in advance of the army and picked up enough food for themselves and horses.

Gates issued more promises about provisions and then called Marion to his tent. It was an hour before he appeared and the general was plainly vexed.

"Presumably there is reason for this delay," he said, looking up from his writing table.

"Yes, sir. I washed my only shirt and was obliged to wait for it to dry," Marion explained.

Gates smiled coldly. "What straits we are in! Have you found us food for tomorrow?"

"Very little, sir."

"Have you found any?"

"An indefinite amount of beef and corn has been promised at the settlement of May's Mills."

"Promised!" Gates flushed. "Don't rely on promises, Colonel. Promises don't fill bellies. If the settlers have food take it from them by force."

Marion squared his shoulders. "General Gates," he said, "the people of South Carolina believe you have come to aid them, not to rob them. If you seize the food on which their lives depend they will turn against you, something you can ill afford."

"I pay for what I take, sir," Gates snapped.

"But you well know, General, that Continental money isn't worth the paper it is printed on."

"It will be eventually."

"Nevertheless, as you just observed, promises do not fill bellies. These people are willing to cut their food stocks to the bone to aid the army, but they must live. Appeal to their loyalty and you will get pounds; use force and you will get ounces."

"Very well, very well." Gates dismissed the matter, as he always did when he was bested. "By the way, Colonel, how is your command making out?"

"Quite well, thank you."

"I wish you might arrange with your state government for an issue of uniforms."

"So do I, sir." Marion fingered his ragged hat brim. "But the fact is South Carolina is penniless."

"You should not have been sent on this campaign without equipment becoming soldiers."

"We weren't sent, General, we came voluntarily with what we had."

"If Cornwallis sights your men first what sort of an army will he think I command!"

Marion flushed hotly. "When we meet Cornwallis, sir, we will give him something to think about besides the cut of our breeches."

Gates laughed in a tolerant way. "Since the days of Caesar, and doubtless before, partisan troops have been difficult." He picked up his pen. "Good evening, Colonel, good evening!"

"Good night, sir." Marion walked out, snapping his fingers in anger at the insinuation his command was a disgrace to the army.

Late the next afternoon, when Gates led his starving Continentals into the tiny log settlement of May's Mills, he found a small herd of scrawny beef cattle in a pen and, farther on, the mill was turning out a stream of corn meal. That crisis was over, thanks to the way Marion had handled the natives, and the commander sat down to write Congress that a month at most would see the destruction of Cornwallis and the liberation of Charles Town.

The evening turned sultry and it began to rain. Gates and De Kalb ate together in the headquarters tent, beef and hoecake topped off with a bottle of peach brandy. While the baron smoked his porcelain pipe after the meal, the general placed his chair by the tent opening and sat looking out. Much as he disliked camp life and hankered for the atmosphere of cities, he found pleasure in the pine-scented darkness. It was a good place and a good time to dream of a laurel wreath that might become a crown. When the colonies were free they could not govern themselves; they must have a strong ruler, and who was stronger than Horatio Gates? Many a crowned head had once worn the hat of a field commander who laid his plans in the shelter of his tent. Yes, it was pleasant to sit there in the darkness, listening to the dripping trees and camp sounds, and watching a flicker of lantern light in a nearby pool of rainwater.

A troop of cavalry clattered across the bridge by the mill and came up the road, the mud sucking at the feet of the horses. As they topped the hill against the light of campfires he recognized Colonel Marion by his short stature. An insignificant little man and too honest for his own good. Not the kind worth considering as a cog in a political machine. The men were singing, though Heaven only knew why as none of them had money or the prospect of a career. That big Negro had a beautiful bass voice.

They were passing the tent without noticing the man in its shadow. But even if they had seen him probably the bumpkins would not have saluted. They were downright disrespectful as well as crude and dirty. And they had a habit of wandering all over the road in a way to disgust a good cavalryman. Now they were swinging this way with as little regard for the tent as for a cow pen. Suddenly a big horse broke out of line, reared, and came down with a mighty splash in the mud puddle. The troop rode on, singing.

General Gates did not join in the song. He was busy mopping his face with a cambric handkerchief and spitting out the evil taste of muddy water. When he stumbled back to the lantern by which De Kalb was smoking he found that considerable more such water had violated his dignity and bespattered his person from his white wig to his black boots. Baron De Kalb was irreverent enough to smile.

"Is it such a joke?" Gates raged. Then, remembering that a commander should never lose poise, he retreated to his private room at the end of the tent.

When he returned he was wearing a clean uniform and wig.

"Baron," he said, in a voice that suggested boiling water running under ice, "I have a mind to order every man in Marion's troop publicly flogged."

De Kalb looked across his pipe bowl. "General," he said calmly, "Colonel Marion is a very popular man."

"And, pray, does popularity license such action?"

"The colonel is not answerable for the mistake of a horse."

"In this case he is. He makes no attempt to regiment those ignorant troopers of his. They are a shame to any army. They have been an eyesore to me since the moment I saw them. They shall be dismissed."

"Do you mean to turn them out of the army?" De Kalb rested his pipe on his knee.

"Yes, and instruct them never to return while I am in command."

The baron's rugged old face hardened in the lantern light.

"General Gates," he said slowly, "such an act would alienate the whole South."

"You speak hastily," was all Gates said to that.

"Haste is necessary to avert such a move." De Kalb laid

down his words one at a time. "God knows that the climate, the barren lands, the British and the Tories are enough for us to struggle against without bringing the Whigs about our ears."

"Nevertheless, Baron, I will no longer be infuriated and humiliated by that loathsome rabble. They must go! I will endure them no longer."

"Then I beg you to be tactful in sending them away," De Kalb implored. "In this section murder is forgiven sooner than insult."

Gates smiled that tolerant smile again. "Pray, do not be alarmed, Baron. I was not born yesterday. I have no wish to displease the worthy colonel. On the contrary, it is my intention to honor him." He turned his head. "Ho there, orderly!"

"Yes, sir." A young soldier stepped into the tent and saluted.

"My respects to Colonel Marion and request his presence here immediately."

"Yes, sir."

De Kalb continued smoking and Gates leaned back and crossed his knees confidently. When Marion arrived he looked even less impressive than usual, for he had spent all day in the saddle, his leg painful, and his face was heavy with fatigue. His wet clothing clung to his small frame and water dripped through the hole in his hat brim.

"Sit down, Colonel," Gates invited cordially. "Wine?"

"No, thank you, sir."

"A cigar?"

"I prefer my pipe."

De Kalb held out his tobacco pouch without a word. There was a wealth of understanding in the gesture.

"Colonel Marion," Gates began, "the past few days have provided me with additional evidence as to the worth of your command."

"Thank you, General." Marion filled his pipe.

"By nature and training they are fitted for special duty."

"They are good at scouting." Marion lighted his pipe from a candle on the table.

"Admirable. For that reason I am sending them to the Santee River, in the rear of Cornwallis, to destroy every boat and canoe the British might use in their retreat to Charles Town."

Marion looked up quickly. "We are to have no part in the battle?"

"Your men will serve better in the capacity I have indicated."

"Very well, sir." Marion puffed his pipe. Gates' words of the day before came back to him: 'If Cornwallis sights your men first what sort of an army will he think I command?' "We will go at once, sir," he said softly.

"Colonel" — Gates leaned forward and smiled warmly — "I suggest that you turn your command over to Major Horry in order that you may remain with me as a staff officer."

Marion stood up. "Sir," he said stiffly, "I serve in the Militia of South Carolina which is under the command of President Rutledge."

"Oh!" Gates also rose. "I am sure Rutledge will not rob me of your services."

"Until I receive such an order from him I must refuse your offer. I prefer to stay with my men." He looked Gates in the eye and added very distinctly, "I am not ashamed of them. Good evening, gentlemen." He walked out.

As he reached the road De Kalb overtook him. "You are going, Colonel?" he asked.

"Yes, tonight, Baron."

"Of course. Let me say, in parting from you, that you and your men have the spirit, the only spirit, that will win this war. Like those I knew at Valley Forge."

"I — I don't know how to thank you for saying that, Baron."

"Don't thank me. It is my privilege to pay you my admiration."

"It is an honor to warrant it. I hope we meet again, sir."

"As an old soldier, I feel that we shall not. May God be with you, Colonel Marion, and with the cause for which you fight. Your hand, sir!"

They shook hands silently, for there were no more words to say.

CHAPTER XV

MARION led his troop from camp that night. He gave no reason for the move, fearing that if the word leaked out the men would make the most of their last opportunity to settle old scores. They could stir up plenty of trouble and no one knew where it might end. He was too big for revenge, but he was hurt and angry. He and his men, impoverished by war, serving without pay, and supplying their own equipment down to the last grain of powder, were being set at unimportant work because their rags distressed a foppish politician. So it was better to take to the woods and cool off for a while.

The rain stopped about midnight and they camped under the trees where a brook was busy binding the edge of grassland. In the morning Marion was calm enough to talk with Horry. The major let off a few fireworks, as expected, then gradually became his practical self.

"So the old popinjay is sending us to destroy the boats Cornwallis might use in retreat."

"Yes."

"Thinks the British are as good as licked."

"Yes."

"You know they ain't, Francis."

"Yes."

"Can't you say anything but yes?"

Marion smiled. "You are itching for an argument, Pete, but there's no cause for one on this point. Cornwallis is a good soldier, his army is strong, well fed and rested."

"Go on, say it."

"Say what?"

"Gates is an ass, his men are half-starved and dog-tired from being dragged through the barrens."

"After all, Pete, we must not forget military etiquette."

"Etiquette!" Horry threw up his hands. "Is this a ball or a war? Let the professional soldiers have their etiquette and their ribbons and their gold braid, but we are farmers fighting for our homes. Must we refrain from criticizing a man we believe — and General Washington believes — is unfit to lead us?"

"Our judgement may be faulty."

"I hope to Heaven it is!" Horry walked up and down for a moment, and then asked, "Are you going to destroy those boats?"

"Not immediately. We will collect them, but boats are too hard to replace these days to rob the settlers of them unless it is necessary."

"Gates said to destroy 'em." Horry grinned impishly.

"Yes," Marion said. "But in my opinion, while we are in the state, we serve under Rutledge. I have sent a courier to him in North Carolina asking him to clarify that point."

"Excellent idea."

"I also recommended commissions for Bill and Mac."

"They deserve it."

"Tell the men we will rest the horses today."

"The horses need it."

"How about rations?"

"Enough for two days, if we help ourselves to some roasting corn down the road."

They spent the next two weeks collecting boats on the Santee and placing them where they could be quickly destroyed if necessary. Marion was absent from his command much of the time, trying to unite the people against the enemy, especially the marauding bands that were terrorizing the country. These were mostly led by British officers and were composed of the worst Tory element and runaway slaves. To save their own skins only the most patriotic planters dared come out against them. Those who had few scruples, and no property to lose, made a better living by joining the looters. Morals and morale were at low ebb as a result of the long war, and it took a patriot of high degree to stick to his guns.

"The curse of this country is its lack of education," Marion said to Bill one evening. "In the North the children are taught to read, aren't they?"

"As a rule, yes."

"Here in the South there are no public schools. Those who can afford it have tutors for their children, the others grow up in complete ignorance of books. They have no unity of thought, no access to public opinion. They don't know what the war is about and they don't care so long as it keeps away from their cornfields. When it comes close they strike for the side that offers the most at the moment."

"At present that is the British."

"Yes. Unscrupulous men like Tarleton and Wemyss, backed by orders from Cornwallis, rouse all that is vicious in their followers. No crime is barred if it is directed against us. Old scores are settled and foul ambitions are realized. The past week I have seen the bodies of three Whigs who were hanged while their homes burned. They were stripped of their last rag and the rings were cut from their fingers. That was done to South Carolinians by South Carolinians." Marion made a gesture of despair.

"Brutes!" was all Bill said.

"And why are they brutes, Bill? Partly, I believe, because they can't read the great thoughts of great men. They have been kept in ignorance by those in power, both here and in England, who want their cotton and tobacco and other products at low prices."

"I have heard my father say something like that," Bill commented.

"Any thoughtful man knows it. Had those people of power been interested in human welfare the colonies would be solidly loyal today. But they weren't. They gave us the choice of slavery or war." Marion shook himself and smiled. "But this ranting is silly when we need sleep. We move downstream tomorrow. I have heard of a Tory who plays host to Tarleton. We must investigate."

The next morning he left the others to carry on the search for boats along the creeks and with Mac, Bill and Luke rode eastward for an hour. They passed a cabin where tow-headed children took to cover like quail.

"They should be in school," Marion said. "We must free them from the British and then, somehow, God knows when, free them from their own ignorance."

By another cabin a lanky woman was picking corn, wearing a ragged homespun dress and a London bonnet of lace and feathers.

"Jumping up man!" Mac whispered. "She's got what you might call a head start toward high society."

"Ole Queen ob Sheby in de cohn patch." Luke chuckled.

"Loot," Marion said under his breath. "But they aren't so much to blame."

"Your charity is beyond my grasp, sir," Mac said bluntly.

"We give these people no schools and few churches and we set them the example of war and violence. As a race, we reap what we sow." Marion galloped away, as though to leave the thought behind.

Finally they came to a clearing and stopped to look across a meadow at a long white house in a grove of oaks. It appeared to be a well-kept place but not a busy one, as though the owner's business was other than crop growing.

"Tories, sir?" Mac asked.

Marion nodded. "According to reliable sources, a stopping place for enemy troops."

"There's a ferry scow tied to the dock," Bill pointed out.

"Sink her," the colonel commanded. "We will take no chances here."

They walked their horses down to the river, unslung their hatchets and went to work.

"Storm comin', suh," Luke warned suddenly.

It broke as he spoke. "Drop me down!" roared a voice.

"Hold there! Hold I tell you! What the devil do you think you're doing? Noah! Ham! Fetch my pistols. That boat cost me seventy-five pounds!"

Marion swung around and stopped short. "John Stewart!"

"Well — drop me down! Francis Marion!" The Tory's round red face was momentarily blank with amazement.

"We haven't met since Charles Town days," the colonel said.

"Charles Town! A vile place these days. I moved up here to escape the blasted war and here it is on my doorstep. I hate the war, sir! I hate it!"

"So do I."

"Stop that, you vandal!" Stewart lunged toward Bill, who was knocking a hole in the bottom of the scow. "Hands off my property! Hands off!"

"I am sorry to displease a friend," Bill said, "but this boat is classed as part of the British navy."

"Friend! Don't use that word to me." Stewart shook both fists. "Your insolence is intolerable!"

"Perhaps you don't recognize me, Mr. Stewart. I am Bill Barlow."

"Eh? Barlow? Why — why, not Barlow from New York! Not that boy!"

"Yes, sir."

"Well, drop me down! You were a little lad and now — But tempus fugit. And I thought you were dead. What a day this is! Marion, stop those infernal men of yours." He waved toward Mac and Luke who were calmly destroying the boat.

"I am sorry, Stewart, but this is war," Marion declared. "We can't allow that ferry to be operated for the aid of the enemy."

The Tory resigned himself. "Go on, sink it," he said, without vehemence. "It cost me seventy-five pounds — but sink it. I am helpless. We are all helpless in the clutches of this devilish war. I say, William, how do you happen to be alive?"

"I often wonder," Bill answered.

"And so would you, if you heard his story," Marion put in.

"I'm puzzled." Stewart mopped his dripping face with a white handkerchief. "I'm deucedly puzzled about this business. Harold Graves said you fell off the dock that night. We searched for your body for days — and here you are."

"Harold Graves is a liar," Bill said. "He sold me to a pirate."

"To a pirate! Sold you!" Stewart threw up his hands. "Sold you?"

"Yes, sir."

"Graves could well do that!" Stewart snorted. "He is a stinker. Certainly he is. And I had the pleasure of telling him so when he left my employ. 'Master Graves,' said I, 'you are a stinker.' Those were my words."

"Do you know if he is still in the British army?" Bill inquired.

"Don't call that gang of cutthroats part of the British army!" Stewart roared. "Graves calls himself a captain of volunteers under that barbarian Wemyss. They're a disgrace to all honest men on our side. A disgrace to all honest men everywhere. What a state this is! What a country! What a world!"

"Why not join our cause?" Marion suggested quietly.

"Turn my coat!" Stewart gave him a sharp look. "Oh, no. *No!* Long ago — in the French war — I swore loyalty to my king, and my oath sticks." The boat sank as he spoke and he groaned. "Seventy-five pounds sunk in the mud! Are you going to burn my house, Marion?"

"Certainly not," Marion said indignantly. "We are only removing such boats as the enemy might use in retreat."

"Retreat? What retreat?"

"In case Gates breaks Cornwallis."

"Breaks Cornwallis! Breaks him! Man alive, haven't you heard about the battle? Don't you know what's happened?"

"What are you talking about?" Marion caught his breath.

"The battle at Camden. Why, man, Gates was licked to a turn — routed."

"Dear Lord!" Marion's face blanched.

"Yes, routed," Stewart repeated, trying not to gloat. "Sure, the Continental Army is destroyed. Two thousand killed or captured, along with all the artillery and baggage."

"And Gates himself?" Mac asked in half a voice.

"Gates — bah!" Stewart thrust out his tongue. "Sat there like a bump on a log — didn't give an order or raise a finger — till the line broke. Then he let out a yell and started north. Lit out like a rabbit. Officers tried to stop him. Don't know why, but they did. He fought 'em off.

Only fighting he did that day. Never stopped till he reached Charlotte, seventy miles away."

"And what of De Kalb?" Marion asked, his voice firm again.

"De Kalb?" Stewart's eyes snapped. "There was a soldier! Grand chap — grand! Fought on foot. Stood like a cypress till he went down under eleven wounds. Grand chap!"

"Is he dead?" Marion waited, dreading the answer.

"Aye, gloriously dead."

There was a long moment of silence, the kind of involuntary tribute the old soldier would have valued.

"Blast the war!" Stewart peered into the water at his sunken boat. "Thank God, it's nearly over."

"Thank God if it were nearly over," Marion corrected.

"But, man, the South is whipped. The North must fall."

"The South is not whipped!" Marion flashed back.

"My dear Colonel, who is left to defend her?"

"The Southern patriots, leaders like Davie and Sumter and Clarke and Williams. Back of them is every man, woman and child who loves liberty above all else."

"Grand spirit — admirable — but you are only a handful."

"You are misinformed, sir. There are hundreds of us in little bands here and there and as the enemy atrocities continue thousands will join us."

"Granted there is a fringe of gallant lads, you have no core. Gates' army doesn't exist."

"We never counted much on it. Congress was so long in sending it, we laid our plans without it."

"Now, now, now! Not sour grapes, Colonel."

"No, not sour grapes. As far as I know, there were only two men from South Carolina in Gates' army. Locally, we are as strong as ever, and Cornwallis is weaker. And our dander is up. Sir, the real fighting has just begun!"

"Drop me down!" Stewart blew his nose. "If I were young enough to ride I'd be with you — blast me if I wouldn't!" He suddenly slapped himself across the mouth. "I didn't say that! Of course I didn't say that. I gave my oath to the king and I'll keep it. Do you hear me? I'm right and you can't change my opinion. Do you hear me?"

"Distinctly, as you are shouting less than three feet from my ear." Marion smiled at him.

The old Tory stamped his feet and blew his nose again. "Blast you!" he raged. "Why don't you behave like an enemy? Why aren't you disagreeable so I can keep mum with a clear conscience?"

"Do you want us to beat you?" Marion laughed.

"That's it — laugh! Be genial instead of mean, as an enemy should be. And a defeated enemy, at that. You're stubborn, Francis Marion. You always were stubborn and the fault grows on you. You persist in treating me like a friend. Bah! You're a sneak to take unfair advantage of me that way. You make it impossible for me not to warn you that Colonel Tarleton and two hundred dragoons will be along here any moment. Get out of here, if you value your worthless Whig hide."

Marion laughed and held out his hand. "Thank you, sir. War brings out the best in some people."

"None of that." Stewart shook the hand warmly. "None of that palaver. We're enemies. Blast you!" He stopped and cocked his head as a bugle sounded faintly in the west. "That's Tarleton. Move!"

"We're off." Marion took the bridle reins from Luke.

Stewart turned toward the house, then swung around.

"William!" he shouted. "Did you find that buried treasure?"

"I haven't had time to hunt for it," Bill called back from the saddle.

"We'll take a crack at it together some day. Blast the war!"

They rode into the woods and waited until the column of British cavalry trotted up to the house.

"If we were forty instead of four," Mac said wistfully.

Marion shook his head. "We must be about our business," he said and led the way back.

They rode in silence for an hour. Marion's head was bowed in thought. He was not greatly surprised at what had happened to Gates, for it had been impossible to expect much from that stuffed shirt. Yet always there had been the possibility that Fate would put him out of the picture and give De Kalb a chance. That hope was gone. The tragedy had moved inexorably to its conclusion.

Bill interrupted his leader's thoughts to say, "Major Horry is approaching, sir."

"Eh?" Marion snapped out of his reverie. "So he is." He shook out his reins and trotted down the road to meet Horry. "What brings you here, Pete?"

"Tories." Horry swung his horse into line. "We heard that a gang was looting a farm on the swamp road, so we took a hand."

"What luck?"

"Potted three of 'em. And we've got five prisoners over there." He jerked a thumb toward some buildings across a field. "The boys are baiting their horses."

"I will have a word with them."

"What's amiss, Francis? You look bleached."

"Cornwallis has destroyed Gates at Camden."

Horry gasped. After a moment he asked hopefully, "Did they get Gates?"

"No, Pete, they got De Kalb."

They rode silently to the barn and gave their horses to Luke to feed. Around a corner men were talking and laughing, for they had not heard the news. Bill moved away and left the two officers sitting on the grass.

After a while Marion said, "Things don't look so bright, Pete. We are cut off from the rest of the colonies, and I wonder if we can do much for South Carolina."

"We could if the Tories didn't stab us in the back at every turn," Horry growled. "They should be rooted out wherever found like poison weeds."

"We have been too good to them, Pete. By and large, they — "

"Colonel Marion!" Bill came around the corner of the barn in long strides. "They are going to hang the prisoners."

"What!" Marion stood up in a single motion and was around the corner.

In the stable yard a man was kicking on the end of a rope that had been thrown over a gate beam. The colonel cut him down with a sword stroke and then wheeled on the men in a fury.

"Who gave you permission to do that?" he shouted, catching the nearest one by the collar.

"Why," the fellow did not struggle. "Why, nobody, sir."

"What do you mean by doing such a thing?"

"Why, Colonel, he's only a Tory."

"Suppose he is only a Tory? Tories are human beings and deserve humane treatment."

"Swear t' Gawd, sir, we didn't think you'd mind."

"Didn't think I would mind! What do you take me for? Hear this and pass it on: if another prisoner is mistreated the man who does it will pay in kind." He threw the man from him and limped back around the corner.

"Francis" — Horry grinned — "what about being good to Tories?"

"Go take a nap," Marion retorted and lay down on the grass.

THEY finished with the boats in two more days and rendezvoused in a swamp along the Santee. While his men cared for the horses Marion sat on a log thinking. His frayed hat was on one ragged knee and from time to time he rubbed his swollen ankle. One by one, the men came in, each carrying what few provisions he had found — a sweet potato, the carcass of a rabbit, a sack of corn meal. All were pooled on a hummock and Luke took charge, for he was recognized as chief cook.

Marion ran his fingers through his graying hair and stood up.

"Boys," he said, with no attempt at oratory, "you know the fix we are in. All our hopes from the North are at an end. We must stand on our own feet. The enemy is braving us up to our very firesides and altars. Personally, I shall fight, for I can see no other course. I urge you to come with me, but I acknowledge every man's right to obey his conscience. What do you say?"

Without exception they volunteered to stand by him.

"Thank you." He looked at each one of them in turn and his sharp black eyes were soft. "Draw your sabers," he ordered and set the example. "Form a circle to symbolize our eternal union. Point your blades toward Heaven and swear to Him who made us free you will never be slaves."

Mist blurred Bill's eyes as he pledged all he had to the cause and to Colonel Marion.

CHAPTER XVI

DURING the days that followed the disastrous battle of Camden it seemed to Bill that the war contracted not to the State of South Carolina, but to a small northeast section of it. He knew vaguely that after the victory Cornwallis was resting and waiting for reinforcements from Charles Town, after which he would move back to Virginia to begin another campaign. In the North was General Washington. No matter what happened, he was the rock foundation of hope. But he was so far away as to be almost legendary. So far as Bill Barlow was concerned, the vital, tangible part of the war centered on Colonel Marion.

Marion's field of activity, assigned to him by circumstance rather than by deliberate plan, was, roughly, between the Santee and Pee Dee rivers. It was strategic country, commanding the rivers and roads that led from the British base at Charles Town to George Town, Camden and lesser points. With a reasonably strong force he might have raised havoc with enemy communications, but he had only about thirty men, and they were outnumbered many times by the hostile Tory population and bands of roving British cavalry. Not only must the colonel fight a war of his own but he must raise and equip his troops.

He did not hesitate. Like other partisan leaders in the South, he had given up hope of aid from distant, dilatory Congress. South Carolina must be freed by South Carolinians. And soon. For a week he and his men were out of the saddle only when their horses needed rest, as they sifted the country for recruits. Somehow they raised their number to nearly a hundred, including such militia officers as Colonels Hugh Horry, John Erwin and John Baxter, and Majors John Vanderhorst and John James. All the men brought their own horses and every kind of firearm they could lay hands on. Few had sabers, so necessary to cavalry, but Marion, remembering the tip from Simms, stripped enough mills of their saws to equip the troop with passable swords.

Bill thought the colonel never slept or ate. At any hour of day or night he could be found awake and sharp-eyed, if he could be found at all, for often he disappeared into the swamps he knew and loved so well. He preferred to do his own scouting, when there was time for it, and the redcoats he met on the road did not suspect that the ragged little man was dangerous.

As fast as recruits joined up he set them to work according to their ability. Some scouted, some mended and made equipment, some hunted and fished for food, others went out to the plantations and cabins and forest hideouts to drum up more volunteers. To bluff the Tories around Port's Ferry they threw up a redoubt on the east bank of the Pee Dee and mounted two old fieldpieces. There was not enough powder to fire them half a dozen times, but they looked like a military setup.

Peter Horry was out with a scouting party and Marion was about to start on a similar mission when Mac galloped into camp. It was evening of a sultry August day and Selim was dripping sweat.

"Colonel," Mac leaned from his saddle, forgetting to dismount and salute, "a batch of about a hundred and fifty Continental prisoners with a guard of thirty British regulars are camped for the night at a house in the Great Savannah near Nelson's Ferry."

"Bound for Charles Town?" Marion jumped up from the log where he had been sitting.

"I judge so, sir."

"You saw them?"

"Yes, sir. I picked up their tracks in the road, then I trailed 'em about a mile and watched 'em make camp."

"Did they see you?"

"No, sir."

"Have they posted sentinels?"

"Yes, sir."

"Is that the house at Horse Creek ford?"

"Yes, sir."

"Good work, Mac." Marion's plan had kept pace with his questions. "At two in the morning you will guide Colonel Hugh Horry back there and take possession of the ford. The rest of us will circle and take them in the rear. Get some rest now."

For hours the camp hummed softly with preparations, then dozed until jumping-off time. When it came, men and horses slipped out and away without even disturbing the swamp owls. There was no shouting of orders, no nervous plunging of horses, no confusion. The troop moved smoothly down the path and out into the road, for every man and every horse knew his place.

A faint light was in the east when Horry and fifteen men rode softly along the sandy road and took position between the ford and the big house that sat in the shadow of the forest. They left the horses in charge of one man and crept along behind a brush fence to be ready to close in when Marion appeared in the rear of the place. Mac had located the fence that afternoon and figured how far they could safely go.

But he did not know that the sentry posts had been changed at dark. Suddenly a clump of wild rosebushes in the clearing spat fire and before the roar of the musket reached them a man standing between Bill and Mac threw up his hands and fell backward.

"You'll pay for that!" Mac roared.

He dropped his rifle and vaulted the fence. In immense quick strides he charged the bushes, drawing his sword. The sentry broke cover and dashed for the house, bawling the alarm. It was a short race.

"Even score!" Mac shouted and kept going.

Horry and his men were close behind, for they must strike quickly or wait for Marion. Delay might wreck the plan and they were taking no chances on failing to liberate the prisoners. Sentries at two or three other posts fired and fled. Somewhere behind the house a rooster crowed in defiance of disrupted routine.

"Seize those arms!" Horry shouted over his shoulder as he passed a stack of muskets on the lawn.

He leaped for the front door, it opened in his face and a soldier fired point-blank. It looked impossible to miss, but he did, and Horry dropped him with a pistol bullet. At the same moment Bill winged another at a side door and sent him back, yelling that the house was surrounded by an army. A hubbub broke out inside and then a white handkerchief fluttered from a window.

"Come out one at a time without arms," Horry ordered. "You are covered and will be instantly shot if you make a false move."

They obeyed quickly, one scared-looking little subaltern, two Tories and twenty-two regulars of the Sixty-third Regiment.

"Where is your commander?" Horry thundered.

"I — I don't know, sir," the little noncom squeaked.

"None of that!" Horry cocked a pistol.

"I really don't, sir, I really don't know. He was in the house, sir. Yes, sir, the house."

"Fetch him out, Bill," Horry ordered.

"I'll get him, Colonel," Bill promised.

He went in with Mac and Luke. Three rooms were empty, but in the kitchen Luke let out a chuckle and slapped his thigh.

"Gen'mens, come see de big boss sojer dat ole King Jawdge send ter whip us!" he shouted.

They found him in the middle of the kitchen floor, pointing at the chimney, which held the boots and part of the legs of an officer. Mac and Bill looked and whooped.

"I say, I am coming out," announced a muffled voice up the chimney.

"Stay where you are or we'll fill you full of holes." Bill slapped the boots sharply with his saber.

"Oh, come now," the boots pleaded. "A pound note if you won't tell my men. That's a good chap."

"Hold him, boys," Bill said and left the room.

He came back dragging the little subaltern, who was ready to cry and kept repeating, "I don't know where he is, sir. Really I don't, sir!"

Bill pointed at the boots and told the youngster, "Your military education won't be complete till you learn how to extract your commanding officer from an embarrassing position. Pull him out."

"But, sir — "

"Pull him out."

"Oh, no, sir!"

"This calf is too puny to raise anyway." Mac picked up a clothesline. "We'll string him up to that hook in the ceiling."

By the looks of the boy, he would about as soon be strung up as to face his company commander under such conditions.

"I am forced to do it, sir," he piped and tugged at the legs.

They came slowly and their owner with them. He was covered with soot and his face was red, but his bluff was undamaged.

"Quite all right," he said graciously to the noncom.

"Thank you, sir! Oh, thank you, sir!"

The captain turned grandly to the others. "I was merely trying to recover some papers that had blown up the chimney." He began dusting his uniform furiously. It was bad enough to be caught this way, but to be ridiculed by two rustics and a Negro was a bit too much.

"So you see, nipper," Mac said to the subaltern, "the parade-ground hero is a coward and a liar. Want to kick him?"

"Good Heavens, no, sir!"

"Some day you'll regret it, little man."

There was the sound of horses outside, and Luke called from a window, "De kunnel comin' rippity-snort."

"We must show him our prizes," Bill said. "Prisoners, march!"

"But I say, I must bathe." The captain looked at his sooty hands and down his long nose, which was also black.

"Can't allow it," Bill snapped. "We want Colonel Marion to see one of his majesty's warriors in war paint. March!"

The colonel had arrived too late for the action but he was in high spirits at the result. The thought of liberating a hundred and fifty of his countrymen warmed his heart. But the British captain was most unhappy, especially when he saw that he and his regulars had been terrified by a handful of crude militiamen. In spite of his ridiculous appearance, he surrendered his command with ponderous formality and handed over the key to the barn where the prisoners were confined.

"Tell them to come out slowly," Marion said to Horry, giving him the key. "They may think their freedom depends on speed."

The prisoners lounged through the open door almost reluctantly.

"You are free!" Marion shouted. His face beamed. "The fortunes of war have swung in your favor."

There was no cheering, nothing but sullen looks.

"What do we do now?" asked one, a short man with a big nose.

"Do?" Marion was staring hard at them. "Why, I suppose you will join us and take up the fight again."

"Fight? Well, I guess we ain't goin' to fight when all is lost," Big Nose said, and the others plainly agreed with him.

"All is not lost." The colonel's eyes narrowed.

"Ain't, eh? Mebbe you don't know what happened at Camden."

"Gates' army was not our only hope." Marion rode close to them. "We shall win without it."

"Well, we don't think so," another man growled. "We know when we're licked. We didn't want to come off down here no how. Now we ain't goin' to fight no more."

And a third one spoke up: "We've had more to eat since the British took us than we ever had in our army."

Marion began snapping his fingers. "Do I understand you resent being liberated?"

"We ain't goin' to help you fight, if that's what you mean," Big Nose said flatly.

The colonel rose in his stirrups. "I don't believe you are all ingrates!" he cried. "Those among you who still call yourselves men step forward."

Three young soldiers left the crowd and stood beside his horse.

Marion gave the others a long, cold look and remarked bitterly, "Now I understand why the battle of Camden was lost."

As he turned to ride away, Big Nose called out, "what you goin' to do with us? We ain't got no food and we're a long ways from home."

The colonel swung his horse around. "We haven't the powder to shoot you or the time to hang you," he hurled at them. "Shift for yourselves. But if you plunder as much as one ear of corn from the land you refuse to serve, you will get no mercy."

He rode to the edge of the forest and sat there alone, while his men went about the business of cleaning up. A mockingbird, his favorite songster, poured music over him but he did not raise his head. The ingratitude of the Continentals was a hard blow to him and, as always, he sought the companionship of trees to recover his balance.

The troop rode back to camp at Britton's Neck, where the men slept through the heat of the day. Marion resumed his seat on the log and hardly moved, hour after hour, except to drink from a bucket of water.

Bill could not sleep. The heat was intense, but there was more than that. He knew the colonel was deeply discouraged and he ached to be of help to him, but one nondescript soldier was so negligible in a war. He could fight, even die, but the tiny gap would close and he would never be missed. If he were a leader, or had something big to offer like ships or supplies or money, he wouldn't feel so insignificant.

These men he knew, men of means such as Marion, James and the Horry brothers, had thrown in all they had. Marion, he thought whimsically, had even contributed half of his last hat brim.

He studied the colonel's face at a distance and realized how its lines had deepened during the past month. For all his sturdy courage, the man was being eaten by worry, as any sensible person in his place would be. He was an optimist, but not one of the silly kind who think a grin is good taste on all occasions.

To Bill, who had grown to worship his commander, Marion's present sadness was unspeakably hard to look upon. He couldn't just stand and watch, so he started for the woods. Of a sudden he stopped and stood there so long that a rabbit hopped past without noticing him. He eyed the rabbit vacantly, then walked over to the colonel.

"Yes, Bill?" Marion looked up.

"Excuse me, sir, but I have been wondering — " He hesitated for words.

"Wondering, perhaps, as I have been, if this country is worth fighting for."

"I'm sure it is, Colonel."

"Of course it is! Of course it is! I shouldn't have made such a remark. The fact that a few refuse to fight any longer is no reason for doubting other men. Or these men. When they are rested they will doubtless change their minds. Our summer climate sometimes depresses Northerners. We must have charity. What were you saying?"

"I am wondering, Colonel, if we could find my buried treasure and — and use it for the war."

Marion gave him a long look that made his spine tingle. "Do you mean that, Bill?"

"Yes, sir."

"God bless you, lad! You have restored my faith. And at a time when it was sorely needed."

"Then you will accept the gold, sir, if we can find it?"

Marion studied the ground between his boot heels. "How much is there?"

"My father buried ten thousand pounds."

Marion whistled. "Enough to go a long way toward bolstering the credit of South Carolina." He looked away at the forest, then added, "But it is yours."

"The United States is my country, Colonel."

Marion blew his nose. "As I remember, you have no map showing where the money was buried."

"That's right, sir. Father destroyed the map to keep it from the pirates. All he knew was that the island is the largest of a group of three between Charles Town and George Town."

"The enemy has an air-tight blockade between those ports. To run that blockade we haven't so much as a canoe. At present, Bill, your plan seems impractical."

"I am sorry you think so, sir." Bill's face fell. "But please keep it in mind so we can act when the time comes."

"Could I forget such a magnificent offer!" Marion stood up.

Bill blushed and hated himself for it. He was glad to hear horses approaching and to recognize Selim, for the tireless Mac had been out scouting. He was followed by a boy on a small sweat-soaked horse, its ears flopping with fatigue.

Mac saluted. "A messenger for you, sir," he said and pulled to one side so the other could come up abreast of him.

"What is it, lad?" Marion asked.

The boy was shy and squirmed in his saddle, but his blue eyes were steady.

"My pa's name is Dixon Harris," he said. "He knowed you down Charles Town way, but now he's got a rice plantation on the Pee Dee."

"I remember him." Marion looked pleased. "He has sent me a message by you?"

"Yes suh. He wants you should know the Tories're bunchin' up nigh our place for a raid. He says can you hit 'em afore daylight you'll git fifty."

"A nice bag." Marion looked years younger. "How far is it to your home?"

"Mebbe forty mile."

"We will be there before sunrise. Now tell me where to find the Tories."

"Lend me a horse an' I'll guide you, suh."

"Eighty miles in twenty hours will break you in two."

"Shucks, suh." The boy threw out his chest. "It'll pleasure me to do it. Last week the Tories burnt our neighbors' house an' murdered seven folkses."

For a moment the colonel's lips set in a straight line, then he said, "Get some rest, lad. Bill, see that Luke feeds him."

"Yes, sir. Come along, son."

That night Marion led twenty men — that being the number of fresh horses they had — down the forty miles of dark swamp road. At daybreak they hit the Tory camp savagely and killed or captured thirty-nine. Fifty horses, as many stands of arms, and a quantity of precious powder were welcome booty. Marion's Men were getting into their stride. As the colonel cleaned his saber, for he always cared for his own weapons, Bill heard him humming a tune.

They returned to camp at a leisurely pace and in high spirits. News of the victory ran before them, sending Tories to the woods, and cheering Whigs to every crossroads they passed. A dozen men joined up and others promised to come as soon as they could make arrangements at home. They were still only a small band of ragged men, not even militiamen in the strict sense of the word, but they knew the glow of triumph. What was more, in routing the Tories they had struck a real blow in defense of their threatened homes. And the little dusty, weary colonel up front would lead them on and on.

Then the wheel spun in the opposite direction. Two days later Peter Horry led a scouting party of six squarely into the middle of fifty British regulars on their way up the Black River to Camden. They were camped in the barns of the Widow Windham, a friend of Marion's, and Horry was surrounded before he knew they were there. He cut his way out in a running fight, but he left three wounded behind. One of them was Bill, who had been clipped on the head with a musket butt.

When Bill came to, his ears roared like a waterfall, and the sun was cutting circles in the sky. After a while he decided it was a lantern, not the sun, he was looking at and that he was in a barn. He tried to sit up and everything disappeared. When he came to his senses again he lay still.

His head ached frightfully and in his middle there seemed to be a void the size of a haystack, but his mind was clear. Judging by bits of sound, there were four or five other wounded in the same room, part of them British. He dug his fingers into the blanket on which he lay and tried to figure a way out. Obviously he was in enemy hands, such an alarming thought that he fainted again.

The next thing he knew someone was feeling his head and the lantern revealed a sharp-featured middle-aged face above him.

"Who are you?" Bill asked.

"British army surgeon," the face rumbled.

"I am not one of your men."

"Wounded by us. Puts us in your debt."

"I swan!" Bill opened his eyes wide, for that was something new from a Britisher. "Who is in command here?"

"Major Muckleworth." The doctor stood up. "Remain quiet until morning. Good evening." He disappeared.

"I swan!" Bill repeated and lay staring at the rafters.

When daylight came again he got slowly on his feet and leaned against the wall. The other men in the room were worse wounded so he tiptoed through the door. There was no guard in sight, and as he stood wondering if he could make a break, the Widow Windham and a portly, tired-looking British officer came into the yard.

"And how did your poor men ever get so hurt, Major Muckleworth?" the old lady was saying.

The major, whose voice was as soft as a parson's, answered, "In a brush with your brave countryman, Colonel Marion, madam."

Bill leaned weakly against a gatepost and gawped at the phenomenon.

"A brave man the colonel is and sweet it is for you to say so, sir," Mrs. Windham said.

The major glanced at the sky. "I must be off now, but I am leaving a surgeon to care for the sick people, yours and ours. What is your bill for the trouble we have made you and for keeping the doctor and our men for perhaps a week longer?"

"Bill?" The widow stared at him. "Do you mean you will pay?"

"Certainly, madam."

"You pay your enemies, sir?"

"You are not my enemy." The major shook his head. "My king does not make war against widows."

"But your countrymen do," she said tartly. "Many's the place hereabouts that's been plundered and burned, not leaving the women and children a cover over their heads, a bit of bread for their mouths, nor a stitch of clothes for their backs."

"True, madam, true." Muckleworth moved uneasily. "But the king and the English people don't know it. If they did they would call those officers to account." His tone changed. "But come, I must be off. What is my bill?"

"That is for you to say, sir," the old lady answered.

"Here then." He counted out some guineas and put them in her hand. "If the doctor and the sick people cause you more trouble and expense than I expect, address me at general headquarters in Charles Town and I will send you the balance. Good-day, madam." He was away around a corner of the stable.

"Well, I'll be a gosling's uncle!" Bill burst out. "It was worth a crack on the head to meet such an Englishman."

Bill knew that Marion would even the score as fast as horse flesh could bring him, so he ate breakfast and then walked about the yard. His head was sore and if he moved it sharply the landscape began to dance, but on the whole he had mended fast. He was making for the barn to help the doctor with the wounded when the colonel came down the road with forty horsemen at his heels. Mrs. Windham met him before he could dismount and, with the gold in her hands and tears in her eyes, gave him the story of Major Muckleworth.

"So, Francis Marion, you must not harm that dear good gentleman." She thumped his knee with her fist as he sat in the saddle.

"Have you turned Tory?" His eyes twinkled.

"Shame on your tongue for that! But a gentleman is a gentleman whatever the color of his coat."

"Surely. A few officers like this Muckleworth would ruin our cause by winning the hearts of our people. Truth, there would have been no war if the best Englishmen had prevailed."

"But you'll not harm the major?" she insisted.

"I can't promise." Marion's face saddened. "This is war."

"Lawsy me, don't I know that! And a bitter business it is." She shook herself. "You'll feed your men and horses, Francis."

"We have baited, but," to send her away, "I'll have a

cup of tea with you." When she went to make it he said to Peter Horry, "Take our best horses and follow Muckleworth. I'll be after you as soon as I have had a word with the wounded boys."

A few minutes later he and the rest of his men were off up the Statesburgh road. Bill rode with him, his head thumping at every step, but in high spirits at being on the move again. Marion did not make a sound for an hour, then he groaned.

"Bill," he said, "I feel as I suppose I might if I were out to kill my own brother."

"There is no fun in chasing a fellow like Muckleworth," Bill agreed.

"Yet we must. It is our duty. Our duty to put an end to a very decent and worth-while life! And his duty to wipe us out if he can. He likes us, we like him, yet we must try to murder one another." He dropped into another long silence.

About mid-afternoon Horry caught up with Muckleworth at Singleton's Mills and firing broke out. The British were slowly retreating when Marion appeared and the first thing he saw was one of their captains, a handsome youngster, dead in a pool of blood.

"I can't stand it!" The colonel rose in his stirrups and waved his sword at his bugler. "Call off the troops! Call off the troops!" He sank back and said to Bill, "Ten righteous Lots would have saved Sodom. One generous Muckleworth shall save this handful. We will keep our powder for those who deserve it."

Such a generous action was its own reward, for a few days later scouts brought reports that three columns of British and Tories, heavily armed and numbering more than eight hundred men, were closing in from the east, west and south. Marion gathered his officers in council and proposed a temporary withdrawal over the line into North Carolina. They agreed with him. The men groaned aloud when they heard the verdict. Some could not obey for they dared not leave their families without protection, and others stayed behind to act as scouts and messengers. Only half the troop, less than sixty, followed Marion north.

It was a clever move, leading the enemy to believe that Marion's Men were scattered beyond recovery. With that comfortable belief in their heads the ruffians, led by Major Wemyss, set out to make an example of that part of the state that had dared to harbor the patriots.

The colonel and his men made their camp in White Swamp, North Carolina, to get a bit of rest and await developments. There, one afternoon in early September, Marion and Bill were watching a runway in the hope of getting a deer for supper. Now that his ankle had healed, the colonel took his turn with the others at hunting. Most of the men enjoyed that part of their work, but mosquitoes being what they were and snakes to be avoided at every turn, Bill got small fun out of it.

The titillating notes of a hunting horn sounded from the edge of the swamp and both men started for it. The troop used the horn instead of the bugle and it was always a call to be heeded. This time the cause of its summons was Major

John James, who stood beside a horse that was too tired to nibble grass.

"Tally-ho, John!" Marion stepped into the clearing, followed by Bill.

James waved his hand in a half salute and came to meet them.

"What brings you from South Carolina, John?" Marion inquired.

"The devil himself."

"Bad company."

"I'm not jesting, Colonel. The devil has taken the name of Wemyss and blasted a path along the Black River, Lynch's Creek and the Pee Dee."

"A raid, you mean?"

"More than a raid." James' tanned cheeks quivered. "The hellions have left a track seventy miles long and fifteen wide that is complete desolation and suffering."

"Did they meet resistance?"

"Only feebly from the families they attacked. They burned every building, slaughtered every head of stock, even burnt the church at Indian Town and made a special fire for the Bible and Psalm Book."

"And the people, John?" Marion asked tensely.

"Dozens were shot and hanged. Some escaped to the woods. Some are in Negro cabins. Most of the Negroes have been sent to George Town for shipment to the Indies. You remember Adam Cusack?"

"Yes, he helped us many times."

"They threw him into jail. His wife and children begged for his life on their knees before Wemyss. He was mounted and would have ridden them down if one of his officers hadn't stopped him. He ordered Cusack dragged out and hanged — and sat by while it was done."

Both officers fell silent, picturing such scenes to themselves.

"Your home is in that section, isn't it, Major?"

"Yes. It's all gone." James made a sweeping gesture. "I got my family away. Eighty of my sheep were bayonetted and left to rot. There, as everywhere else, the devils took pains to destroy the flocks and loom-houses to cut off our supply of food and clothing."

"John," Marion said quietly, "it is an awful price to pay, but a necessary one. It had to happen before the people would wake up and fight."

"They're awake — those who are left alive," James said grimly. "And they are begging you to come and lead them."

"They won't have long to wait," Marion promised.

CHAPTER XVII

MARION returned to South Carolina by a forced march. To the men who rode with him it was more like a prolonged steeplechase. They started out with two fieldpieces, of which they felt considerably proud, but after a few hours of tugging at their artillery they backed it into a swamp and galloped off. Never again did they attempt to carry anything that could not be strapped to their saddles, for the success of their kind of warfare depended on speed.

Sometimes on that ride south they followed roads and again they cut across country. They rode fast and almost without rest, as each man had two horses and changed every hour. The colonel was always ahead, riding quietly, saying little, and setting a stiff pace. He had a whole hat now, one Mac brought in from somewhere, and he also had a blanket and cavalry boots that had changed sides in the war since they left England. Between hat and boots he was still ragged, but the men had an eye out for a Tory who wore his size clothes.

On the fourteenth of September they reached Lynch's Creek and were joined by about forty men who had been gathering there. Every one of them had recently suffered at the hands of Wemyss and they were burning to hit back. While the recruits were being welcomed Major Horry, who had stayed in that vicinity to scout, rode in from another direction.

"Gad, Pete, it's good to see you!" Marion cried, as they shook hands on horseback.

"And you too, Francis!"

"You look well fed."

"British officers live well."

"What! Have you turned your coat?"

"Sure. I put on a red coat and persuaded a British teamster to follow me." Horry grinned. "In the wagon was wine, smoked meat, flour, sugar, spices — "

"Mercy, Pete! Spare us the torture."

"There's bigger game afoot." Horry turned serious. "Two hundred Tories are camped at Sheperd's Ferry on Black Mingo Creek."

"How far from here?"

"Fifteen miles."

"Is Wemyss with them?"

"No. He and his dragoons are in George Town."

"Two hundred, you said?"

"About that number. But we'll pick up reinforcements. The country is rising."

Marion rode over to his men. "Boys," he shouted, "shall we tackle two hundred Tories tonight or wait for help?"

They yelled to attack and kept on yelling until he raised a hand for silence.

"The ayes have it." He smiled with satisfaction. "We

will camp here until ten o'clock and then go on a 'coon hunt."

It was midnight when they approached the north side of the ferry over Black Mingo. The Tories held the south side in too great strength to attempt a crossing there, but a mile upstream was what Horry called "a sort of bridge."

"As I remember," Marion said, "the approach is through a swamp over a log road bed and the bridge itself is planked."

"Right," Horry agreed. "I saw it this afternoon. The road is narrow and the logs are slippery — an alligator roost."

"Double file at a walk," Marion ordered, and led the way up the road.

The night was heavy and still. A noiseless stream of air from the west carried the smoke of the Tory smudges up the creek and made some of the horses snort nervously. Distant sounds seemed near, and the swamp owls talked back and forth across the miles as though in a family circle. The last man in line heard Marion's horse splash in the mud when he came to the crossing and, as others moved in, the darkness was filled with the steady minor sound of slipping hoofs.

When the column gained the bridge the planks began to rumble like rolling drums. Marion leaned toward Horry and said, "We were fools not to cover the planking with our blankets."

"Too late now. But they may not hear us."

"Remember it in the future — blankets or hay."

They felt their way over the logs on the other side and

as they reached the comparative quiet of solid ground a shot rang out downstream.

Marion's voice cracked like a second shot: "Follow me! Gallop!"

They tore into the night full tilt. Riding knee to knee with Mac, Bill wondered how the colonel knew the way. But it was safe to bet he did for he had the instincts of a fox. Keep a tight rein, loosen your feet in the stirrups and lean toward the outside, ready to roll clear if your horse stumbles and goes down. Follow the little man up front, leave everything to him in wild, blind confidence that fills the moment with sweet danger and the glory of meeting the unknown with a laugh.

As they swung into the main road the word to halt was tossed back along the line. Three hundred yards away the Tory fires showed the camp and, dimly, a large house by the ferry. Marion ordered all but ten men to dismount. Captain Waties, leader of the latest recruits, was sent down the road to attack the house. Colonel Hugh Horry led two companies to the right, while Marion, Peter Horry and the mounted men moved to the left, ready to charge in where most needed.

Bill, Mac and Luke were with Hugh Horry. For all their eagerness, they walked deliberately toward the campfires. Not an enemy was in sight, but there was no reason to suppose they had fled. When Bill realized that the darkness held upwards of two hundred armed men waiting to blow the life out of him he felt cold and sick. He had been under fire so many times he had believed he was case-hardened, yet of a sudden the urge of self-preservation was threatening his reason. It would be easy to drop behind a tree and lie safe until the danger passed. Wouldn't it be wise? What possible good could he be if he were dead? Wasn't it sensible to make sure of life first and then, taking time to think calmly, do something worth while with that life? At a secure distance almost anyone would call those yellow thoughts, but set him down there in the darkness, facing ten score men who hankered for his blood, and see if he was so sure of himself.

The roar and flash of muskets almost in his face brought Bill to his senses. Instead of being in the house, the left of the Tory front was in a field opposite it, where they had waited until they calculated Horry's men were near enough. Only the blackness of the night prevented the ambush from becoming a massacre.

Someone fell violently against Bill and knocked him flat. He got to his knees and ran his hands over the body until he felt a beard, which showed the man was not Mac. A big hand closed on his shoulder from the other side and Luke shouted in his ear, "Dat yo', suh?"

"Yes. I'm all right."

"Praise de Lawd!"

"Are you hit?"

"Naw. Dem Philisteens couldn't hit a smokehouse do' effen dey wuz inside hit."

Confusion was all around. Rifles began cracking, but no one saw what he shot at or what he hit. The Tories sent in another volley and the Whigs began falling back toward the trees, for by instinct they were woods fighters. No one touched him, yet Bill felt himself drawn backward. He thought: You're running away from the fight. You're a heck of a soldier, you are!

"Hold the line, lads!" Horry shouted. By the direction of his voice he had not retreated a step. "They're shooting high. Keep down till you can use your sabers. Come on now! Follow me!"

The tide turned and started back, roaring as it gathered force. On the left of the Tory line a light flickered, then shot upward in a burst of flame, revealing itself feeding on a haystack. The Tories stood out plainly in the light and Horry's men found the target. As Bill looked down his rifle barrel he saw a huge man swinging a huge sword come around the burning stack and fall on the enemy's rear single-handed.

"That's Mac, Luke!" Bill shouted. "He needs us!"

The two of them raced toward the light and the blazing muskets. Then men appeared everywhere. Waties' company hit the Tory front. With a whoop and a yell Marion and his horsemen came out of the darkness and smashed the center. On the left came Horry and his men.

Bill ceased being an individual and became part of a surging, slashing, yelling mass. He could grasp only fragments of what was happening: Marion leaning over his horse's neck to strike off a hand that was pointing a pistol at him; a Tory driving a bayonet through the chest of Captain George Logan, who had ridden eighty miles that day to join the troop; Luke splitting a bewigged head like a pumpkin. Then there was a burst of colored stars.

When Bill came out of it Luke was splashing water on his head and Mac was rubbing his chest.

"Lawdy Lawd! He done riz frum de daid!" Tears ran down Luke's face.

"He played possum till the shooting stopped," Mac jibed.

"What hit me?" Bill asked, and wondered what had happened to his voice.

"Luke says it was a musket butt. You're always getting it on the melon."

"Ah wuz jes' one hop too slow," Luke apologized. "But dat Philisteen won't pester hones' folkses no mo'."

"Where are the Tories, Mac?"

"Oh, here and there — dead, prisoners, or in the swamp, according to their individual tastes."

"You won the battle by setting fire to that haystack and giving us light."

"You're delirious, little man." Mac stood up. "Take care of him, Luke, I must go and hunt up Selim."

Marion smashed the Tories decisively in that night battle on Black Mingo, but he lost a considerable number of men and many of the survivors were in need of repair. To such as had left their families unprotected he gave permission to return home and meet him later at Snow Island on the Pee Dee. With the others, he jogged over to visit his friends on the Waccamaw. Those friends, the Hugers and Trapiers and Alstons, managed to live in comparative luxury despite the war. Half a century later Peter Horry, in his memoirs, would still be enthusing over the food and drink, the mahogany and silver, the stables and pastures and various other favors Marion and his ragged command received from those warm-hearted patriots.

They begged the colonel to relax and he promised he

would, when he found time. That time never came. With an ease that amazed Bill, he turned from saddle to writing table. By couriers who knew every road and bypath he sent letters to planters, professional men and partisan leaders, and from all he begged cooperation in the plan he outlined. That plan was as primitive as Indian warfare, for the state's resources could support nothing more ambitious: turn out, though you have only a shotgun or an ax, harrass the enemy wherever you find him, cut his communications, give him no security day or night, make his life so miserable he will be glad to leave the country.

"It is our only chance," he said to Bill, who was helping him copy letters. "We can't cope with British regulars in open battle. War is an art and those who master it must have a long apprenticeship."

"But we can outride and outshoot the redcoats," Bill said.

"Right. And as I believe in God I believe we can break them, though we lack equipment and discipline."

"Is discipline so necessary, sir?"

"Discipline in a body of troops, in civil life, in a family, in an individual, is like a bridle on a horse. Our militiamen are too free to accept it willingly. That is why we can't expect too much from them. They must be managed rather than commanded. Understand?"

"In part, sir."

"Some day you will be a militia officer, Bill. When you turn out against the enemy and see your men in high spirits all itching to go, that is your time. Close your columns, sound your bugle, and sail in."

"I get the idea." Bill nodded.

"But" — the colonel wagged a finger across the table — "if they get the worst of it and start running, you mustn't fly into a passion. You must run faster than they do, so you can get ahead of them and stop them. That's the way to handle militia."

Marion stood up and stretched his arms. "I would much rather be instructing you in the art of raising rice or indigo than how to kill your fellow men." He took a long look through the window. "I love the woods. Tomorrow I am going to the swamp alone and rest for a day."

A light knock sounded on the door and a house servant asked, "A young gen'man says kin he see Kunnel Marion?"

"Yes, send him in." Marion swung around.

A boy, perhaps fifteen years old, stepped into the room lightly after the manner of woodsmen. He was tow-headed and poorly dressed, but as honest-looking as a stook of corn.

"Who are you, lad?" Marion asked.

"Dick Birdsell, mister. My father lives on the upper Pee Dee. He fit the Britishers with you at Fort Moultrie an' got shot in one laig so he hain't did no more fightin'."

Marion smiled. "I recall Birdsell." He remembered all his men. "He was a gunner in the south bastion that day."

The boy continued: "My father says to tell you the Tories're after your hide. They've been down to George Town an' fetched back two wagonloads of new British muskets, an' they're holdin' a big powwow up our way tomorrow night to fix up a scheme to git you. My father says kin you be thar tomorrow night you'll make a big smash because they won't be expectin' you. I'll guide you the road back kin you come."

"How far is it?"

"My father said seventy mile."

"And you will be ready to start back soon?"

"Sure, mister. We don't like the Tories, they killed our sheep."

"Bless their hearts!" Marion smiled with one corner of his mouth, then added hastily, "Yes, Dick, I will be there tomorrow night. Make yourself comfortable till we start."

When the boy was gone Marion said to Bill, "He appears sound, but it's never safe to say who is not a spy these days. You and Mac feed and flatter him and try to fox him with questions."

Before noon young Birdsell's reliability had been established by two men from the vicinity of his home. Marion gave the order to prepare to march and the troopers fell to work. Every weapon was put in fighting trim. Every piece of harness tested, every horseshoe examined for loose nails. Messengers were sent off to bring in such men as lived near the road to be traveled. At dusk, after a rousing supper under the magnolias, the hunting horn sounded and the troop of thirty fell in. They paused at the gate to give three cheers, then rode down the highway in double column, singing a marching song, and lighted on their way by a full moon. For a few minutes, even to the colonel, war seemed almost like a holiday.

Ten men joined them during the night. They rode steadily except for brief breathers, and gradually the sounds of gaiety faded out until nothing was heard but the roll of hoofs, the creak of saddles and the clink of weapons. At daybreak Birdsell said they were ten miles from their objective and deep in Tory territory, so they turned into a swamp and settled down for the day. Sentries were posted and the rest of the men slept, while the sun came up and all was peaceful as a Sabbath morn.

About eleven o'clock Marion sent Mac and Bill up to the main road to take the pulse of the community. They watched the artery all the afternoon and, in the evening, reported scores of horsemen, presumably Tories, carrying new guns and riding gaily in the direction of the rendezvous Birdsell had mentioned.

"Scores on one road, and there are several roads hereabouts." Marion looked at his forty men. "Get out the rations, boys, then we'll be on our way."

As soon as it was dark they moved out of the swamp and took the road at a sweeping gallop. Their spirits were high and for a while they sang, with their heads thrown back and the moon in their faces. Finally they were ordered to use caution, all except Luke, for they loved his bass rolling along like a river of melody, and a Negro singing on the road was nothing to excite suspicion. Even when they sighted the Tory campfires in a field he kept on alone, singing until he was well past, then left his horse and stole back.

"Dey hain't got so much ez a dawg on guard, suh," he reported. "Nice new guns ez clumped up like cohnstalks."

"It will be almost like murder," Marion said to Horry.

"Kunnel," Luke put in, "don' have no tender feelin's fer dem Philisteens. Roun' de ben' in de road ez a house burnt down an' de air stink wid daid cows an' sheep."

"Thank you for mentioning it." Marion dismounted.

They left the horses with a small guard and walked through the woods to within fifty yards of the fires. There were about a hundred and fifty Tories in sight and they were having a grand time tipping up jugs and playing cards. One shouted a toast to King George and another proposed the destruction of Marion's Men. Good men and good neighbors until war poisoned their brains.

"Take aim, boys," Marion ordered in a low whisper, and the cocking of firearms sounded like a flurry of hailstones on a windowpane.

He fired his pistol, and the woods spat death with a roar. It was not a battle because not one Tory put up a fight. Twenty-three of them fell dead, thirty were badly wounded, and thirteen were too dazed to resist or run. The others escaped, for it was impossible to follow them far in the dark woods.

Marion threw a ring of pickets around the place, set his two doctors and their helpers to aiding the wounded, then counted the booty. It was considerable: close to a hundred new English muskets with bayonets and ammunition, a hundred horses wearing new British army saddles and bridles, and miscellaneous equipment including two fiddles with bows.

Horry bent over one of the Tories, who lay dead with his cards in his hands — an ace, deuce and jack.

"Tough luck," the major mused. "With high, low and jack you were in a fair way to do well, but Francis Marion came down with a trump that non-suited you forever."

"I didn't deal the cards, Pete," Marion said sadly.

"Kunnel," Luke appeared beneath a huge grin, "us done foun' t'ree roas' pigs, ten turkeys an' a heap of journey-cakes." He came nearer and whispered, "De angels likewise show me half a bar'l ob peach brandy."

"The angels or the Tories?" Horry grinned.

"Ah cain't tell which frum tudder when dey tells me where de brandy is."

"Roll it out." Marion made a wide gesture. "Bring on the food. We will feast in the name of civilization."

"You're bitter, Francis," Horry remarked.

"Puzzled, Pete. I had planned to have the day alone in the woods and I have spent it killing my neighbors. I can't understand such things."

He was silent as they rode back to the Waccamaw the next day. By winning three victories in succession Marion had demonstrated that his plan of campaign was best under the circumstances. He knew by what his spies said that the Tories feared his name above all others and were demanding protection from the British regulars. That was good inasmuch as every soldier he could pin down was one the less to be dealt with elsewhere. In that way it was possible to build up a threat that would influence not only the fate of South Carolina but the whole Union. Yes, it was good, better than he had anticipated, but its responsibilities were timber for serious thought. The higher the stakes, the clearer the head and the steadier the hand must be.

When they reached the plantation he went straight to his room, but ten minutes later he was back with papers in his hands.

"News from President Rutledge!" He waved the papers

over his head. "He thanks us for what we have done and requests me to present this" — he held out one document — "to Colonel Peter Horry."

"Eh?" Horry jumped. "What did you say?"

"You are a colonel, Pete." Marion smiled broadly. "This is your commission."

"A great moment for me!" Horry took the paper reverently.

"Lieutenant MacDonald — Lieutenant Barlow, allow me on behalf of his excellency to thus acknowledge your services to your country." Marion handed the boys their commissions and the men whooped.

Marion looked at the other paper in his hand and then at his troopers. "Boys," he swallowed hard, "I owe this to you, for without your loyal support I could not have come by it. It makes me a brigadier general."

Then the men really cheered.

CHAPTER XVIII

THE fact that Marion was now a general made little difference to anyone. It was the man, not the rank, that counted. Had he been reduced to a private his men would have followed him as readily and the enemy would have feared him as much, for the name of Francis Marion had taken on magic.

It was, naturally, especially odious to the British in South Carolina. A few months before they had considered the state completely subjugated, but now, largely because of this homely little soldier, rebellion was cropping up everywhere again. Many of their supposed friends had gone over to the upstart's banner, being Whigs at heart who had pretended to be Tories in order to save their necks. In widely scattered sections other patriot bands, inspired by Marion's example, were raising Cain with communications and transport, gaining confidence and storing up supplies for more ambitious campaigns. Something must be done about it or British prestige would be knocked into a cocked hat.

Lord Cornwallis, who after the battle of Camden had proclaimed himself master of the South, was outraged to learn that the South Carolina yokels dared dispute his authority. By all the rules of European warfare they were licked and should have the decency to stay licked, yet here they were, popping in and out of swamps and causing jolly havoc among the good friends of the king. It was an insult to British dignity that could be wiped out only with fire and blood. Or so he thought, for to him opposition to royal will deserved annihilation. So he issued orders that, in his opinion, fitted the crime.

Bill heard about it from Marion. They were camping in the woods again and the general sat on a log reading despatches, while Bill waited for possible orders.

"Listen to this." Marion glared at a paper in his hand. "It is from a letter written by Cornwallis to Colonel Cruger, commandant at Ninety-six. Major James took it from a captured courier."

He coughed and took a drink of water from a gourd. "Here are parts of the letter. *I have given orders that all the inhabitants of this province who have taken a part in this revolt shall be punished with the greatest vigor; that they shall be imprisoned and their whole property taken from them or destroyed.*" The general's fingers trembled as he turned the page.

Bill commented, "We are fighting to defend our lives and he calls it revolt!"

"It is revolt," Marion said, "but show me an Englishman who wouldn't fight for the same thing. Listen to this: *I have ordered, in the most positive manner, that every militiaman, who had joined the enemy, should be immediately hanged.*" Marion looked up with blazing eyes. "And those orders are being carried out, Bill. Hugh Horry, who has been into Camden in disguise, says they hang a batch of prisoners every morning in front of the jail."

"Can't we attack Camden, sir?"

"Sixty militiamen against two thousand regulars?" Marion returned to the letter. "If this had been written by a bigoted Tory it might be laid to ignorance, but coming from an educated gentleman — a nobleman, with an archbishop for a brother — it is inexcusable. By the Eternal, if the British Empire tolerates the plundering and hanging of patriots it is doomed."

"But, as you have said, it will help us win the war, sir."

"So it will, Bill. The harder they lay it on, the more people will rebel. There are so many among us who still respect the mother country that if the British had fought like gentlemen they would already have won. But when they fight like savages — Harsh medicine, but this country needs it."

The most cruel of the enemy leaders were Rawdon, Tarleton and Wemyss. The last named, whose dirty work was largely between the Black and Pee Dee Rivers, aided Marion most. There was seldom a day that did not bring men and boys to his camp begging to fight. Each had his tragic variation of the same story. They had not been active in the war because of indifference or an inherent regard for England, but some member of the family had at one time or another borne American arms. That was enough to set Wemyss upon them. With the stealth and suddenness of Indians, he and his dragoons had swooped down on the defenseless plantation, driven off the Negroes, slaughtered the stock, destroyed the crops, burned the buildings, and shot or hanged everyone who resisted. Time after time these stories ended in nearly the same words: "And I alone am left to tell you."

Marion gave them what they craved, action against the enemy. He moved down nearer Black River and made one of his favorite camps in a swamp. From there he sent scouts and spies in all directions. When they spotted game, relays of horsemen rushed the word to headquarters, the hunting horn sounded, and the troop was away at a gallop. Whether their mark was a supply train, a batch of reinforcements, a military camp or a Tory rendezvous, they hit it with a whoop and a bang and were back in the swamp before the British officers knew what had happened.

Tories were their favorite meat, being considered renegade Americans, and they hit them right and left. One good haul was made the night Marion led ninety men sixty miles against a company of Tories on Black River. Thirty-three were killed and forty-six captured, including the colonel in command. They also picked up all the baggage and horses. Thus over an area of intense strategic importance to military operations in the South, that of the Charles Town-George Town-Camden triangle, Marion's Men were keeping their enemies awake nights.

As his command grew in numbers the general gave more responsibility to his younger officers. He expected to be killed in a skirmish or shot from ambush, for he knew he was a marked man, but he had no intention of allowing such a stroke to halt the work he had started. One of his staff, preferably Peter Horry, would take over the leadership and carry on, but everything would run more smoothly if the youngsters rehearsed their parts.

So two days after the Black River brush Marion gave Mac and Bill command of fifteen men each and sent them out toward George Town to see what they could find. They crossed the river about midnight and rode quietly until dawn, when they hid their men in the woods and went back on foot to the road. They were too close to the enemy line to take chances, so they made themselves comfortable in a fence corner behind a screen of bushes, hoping that a supply train would pass on its way to the interior.

"I wouldn't object to a wagon load of pork," Bill said longingly.

"With salt." Mac rolled his eyes. "After all these months of corn and sweet potatoes and wild meat without salt I could eat the stuff clear."

"Lack of it doesn't seem to harm us."

"We're tough, Bill. We eat anything or nothing, drink ditch water, sleep on the ground without tents, and none of us gets sick."

"When the war is over we will live in houses and pine away."

"Let's not live in houses."

"What do you mean, Mac?"

"Let's cross the Alleghenies and see that new country. They say it's endless. You can go thousands of miles in a straight line."

"No one ever crossed all of it."

"They will some day. I haven't a thing in the world but my horse and rifle, but that's enough to start with. I can get along in the wilderness."

"I have a house in New York, but who wants to live in a city? I'll go with you, Mac."

"And if we — " Mac broke off abruptly. "There's a redcoat down the pike."

Two officers cantered toward them, one a regular, the other wearing the uniform of a Tory regiment.

"Small fry," Mac muttered. "Can't bother with only two when more may be coming. Though I suppose we might pick 'em off."

"That's too much like murder," Bill objected.

"Right. Let 'em pass."

As the horsemen rode by, not forty feet away, Bill gripped his rifle and breathed hard. When they had passed he whispered, "The Tory is Harold Graves!"

"The one who sold you to the pirate?"

"Yes."

"Why didn't you shoot the buzzard?"

"I can't shoot even him in the back."

"Shucks!"

"And, besides, I'd like to get him alive. He may have learned something about the gold."

They lay in the fence corner until noon and nothing more passed except an occasional Negro carrying a few yams or pieces of fruit to market.

"We should seize the food in the name of the united colonies," Bill said.

"Steal from an old Negro?"

"We're too easy, Mac. We're officers now and should provide for our men."

"Our men would lick us if they knew we robbed the poor."

"Was there ever such an army! Too soft-hearted to grab a bushel of potatoes and too poor to buy one. Then we must beg. Well, it's been done before. There's a good Whig planter a mile back. Come on, we'll see what we can work him for."

They got their men and rode to the plantation. The owner was known to be on their side, though he was so near the British line he was afraid to say so. The house was beyond sight of the road and when Bill knocked on the door it was opened by an old man in white wig and knee breeches.

"Sir," Bill told him, "we come from General Marion."

"Ye do, eh?" The old gentleman's voice was a surprising bellow. "Well, I've nary kernel o' corn or drop o' water for you blasted rebels. Get out of here!"

"I was told — "

"Told nothin'!" He stepped onto the porch and gave Bill a sharp wink. "I said get out of here!" he roared, and motioned toward the horses.

Bill had seen such tricks before. He retreated in pretended confusion, and the other followed hotly until they were a considerable distance from the house, then he whispered, "There's spies amongst my servants — damn 'em! You must draw your sword and demand my keys. There's plenty of food for you and your horses."

Bill saw faces in the background and pulled his sword with a flourish.

"Now I've got you where I want you!" he thundered, grabbing the old man by the collar. "Out with your keys, you old reprobate! This instant, too, or I'll let the blood out of you as I would kill a pig."

"Yes, sir, yes, sir! Spare me, for I am feeble." The old gentleman handed over the keys with a shaking hand, and said under his breath, "Post sentries. The country's filled with vermin."

The boys threw out a circle of guards and then took possession of the place in high-handed fashion, ordering the slaves around at pistol point, and threatening the owner with enough death to wipe out a regiment. The result was a good meal all around, corn and hay for the horses, and ham and eggs, with salt, and hearth cakes, butter and milk for the men.

"Contrary to our custom, we won't burn your house," Mac said to the host, who was backed against the wall twisting his hands nervously.

"Thank you, sir, thank you!" The Whig ventured another wink. "Heaven will reward you for your mercy to an old man."

Shots outside ended the play. As the men ran from the house they saw their pickets coming in with a swarm of British dragoons hard after them. Commands weren't necessary, each man found his horse and, as they swung into solid column, the pickets sailed over the fence into the yard. The dragoons did not follow for they were only about twenty in number and their surprise had failed.

"At 'em, boys!" Bill yelled and took the fence.

The British turned down the hill toward the woods and the chase was on. The Americans were well mounted, and horses and men were at their best in such going. In close battle, where maneuvers counted, they would have been outclassed by professional troops, but where the action took the nature of a fox hunt they had the edge. And they knew how to keep it. With a whoop and a yell they swept down the hill like a thundergust, pistols blazing and swords flashing. As the redcoats neared the woods they scattered for cover and the hunters followed, each choosing his game to run down.

Mac's Selim was the best horse on the field and for all his master's weight he outdistanced the others. Three lagging Britishers were his mark. Mac rose in his stirrups, looking twice the size of a man, and waved his great sword three times around his head. The three dragoons shot at him, tried to parry his blows, ducked, dodged — and went down one after another. The homespun troopers rode over them, spreading out, and filling the woods with their charging shout, "Marion's Men!"

Bearing fresh memories of burned homes and butchered families, the Americans were not looking for prisoners. Only one dragoon left the woods alive and Mac brought him out by the collar.

"Willie," he called to Bill, who was changing his saddle to a captured horse, his having been killed by a bullet, "Hey, Willie! Here is a present from Uncle Mac."

He tossed Harold Graves to the ground as he would handle a bag of grain. The Tory had been roughly used and was, for the moment, thoroughly scared.

Bill looked at him and snapped, "Stand up."

Graves stumbled to his feet and seemed rather surprised to find himself in one piece.

"Salute."

"Yes, sir." He did.

"Can you give one good reason why you should not be immediately hanged?" Bill asked him.

"I have done no wrong, sir."

"Since when?"

"I never did."

Mac snorted, "I'd better clip the angel's wings before he flies away from us."

"Graves," Bill said slowly, "you don't recognize me."

"I seem to have seen you before, sir."

"Not only have you seen me, you have tortured me and sold me to a pirate."

"Ah!" Graves was staggered. Then in a flash he was himself, for he knew he must fight for his life with his wits. "This is a fortunate meeting," he purred. "I have long wanted to tell you that only by pretending to go along with Bottle was I able to save your life."

"You are a liar," Bill said contemptuously. "Help me tie him up, Mac."

"By the neck?"

"No. We will take him back to camp and work on him."

Graves began, "I wish to say that — "

"Silence!" Bill picked up a rope. "One more word out of you and we leave you for the buzzards."

Graves obeyed to the letter during the ride, for well he knew he was on thin ice. Even when they reached camp that evening and he was shackled to a tree amid not too comfortable surroundings, he continued to be a model prisoner.

Marion received the report of his lieutenants with open satisfaction. They had pulled off a nice piece of work under the nose of the George Town garrison, which would not induce tranquility in the enemy camp. A small engagement, it might be called, yet Cornwallis could not fail to note that his best dragoons had been tied in a double bowknot by the despised rustic militiamen. Perhaps, even in the councils of the mighty, Marion's Men were not the subject of light conversation.

"What will you do with Graves?" the general asked Bill.

"Is he my property, sir?"

"I understand Mac presented him to you."

"Free of all encumbrance," Mac added.

"I'll question him about the gold, though I can't believe what he tells me. Then I'll turn him in with the others to be held for exchange."

"Why don't you shoot him?" Mac suggested. "It's the least you can do to even the score."

"You know we don't murder prisoners."

"Then try him in military court for inhuman conduct."

"He's not worth the bother. And, too, a trial would make him feel important. Put him through the mill with the rest of the prisoners. Am I right, General?"

"Charity can't be wrong," Marion answered. "Neither can justice. The question is up to you, Bill."

"If you will excuse me, sir, I'll go over and talk to him."

"Certainly."

"Coming, Mac?"

"No, thank you. I'm too tired to take on the added burden of being civil to a Tory."

Bill was dog-tired too, but the sight of Graves had stirred up thoughts about the money that would not be quieted. He took a pitch-pine torch and walked over to the prisoner.

"Graves," he said, driving the stick in the ground so the light would show the other's face, "things have changed since we parted company."

"The fortunes of war," Graves answered pleasantly. It was the same smooth voice, the same sly narrow face, though tanned by outdoor living.

"Call it that." Bill squatted on his heels.

"I am not complaining, inasmuch as I have been privileged to contribute my humble bit to Mother England's victory," Graves said piously.

Bill didn't like the tone. "I am not here to argue about the war," he said brusquely. "What about that buried treasure? Have you a line on it yet?"

"Oh, no." Graves looked surprised at the question. "I dropped it when you refused to cooperate with me."

"If you know which side your hoecake is buttered on you'll stick to the truth."

"My dear friend — "

"Don't use that word. It stinks in your mouth."

"Pardon, my dear sir. Since we parted in Charles Town I have been too busy for treasure hunting."

"But perhaps not too busy to locate the island on paper."

"I have made no inquiries — none at all."

"Mr. Stewart didn't help you? Think hard."

"Mr. Stewart and I parted company long ago."

"Because he is an honest Tory."

Graves continued in a tone as impersonal as though discussing the weather, "I was hasty. I should have waited until you and Mr. Stewart had pooled your knowledge of the island. Then I should have forced it from you."

"What do you mean by that?"

"Neither of you knows where the island is, but together you may find it. I should have gained your confidence and worked with you until the gold was uncovered."

"Then you would have slit our throats and all would have been well."

"I am fated to be misunderstood." Graves sighed. "By the way, do you know what has become of our friend Bottle?"

Bill stood up. He knew Graves was playing with him and he was too tired to take more of it that night.

"We will settle a few things in the morning," he promised and walked away.

But in the morning Graves and his guard were gone.

CHAPTER XIX

DURING the next few weeks Marion established a permanent camp on Snow Island. It was a triangular piece of land, bounded by the Pee Dee on the northeast, Lynch's Creek on the north and Clark's Creek on the west and south. It was an ideal headquarters for such a command, being practically safe from attack, surrounded by friendly neighbors, and within striking distance of the enemy's communication lines from the coast to the interior.

It was also the center of a smoothly working intelligence service. Choosing his men carefully from among his Whig friends, Marion built up a model spy ring. Its members were posted in the main British strongholds such as Camden, George Town and Charles Town, where they worked inconspicuously at all sorts of occupations. If a Britisher or Tory let fall an indiscreet word within hearing of the man who sold him vegetables, ferried him across the river or tapped his boots, it might be reported to Marion within a few hours. Such news traveled at great speed by relays of mounted messengers, whose horses stood saddled day and night. Thanks to his growing reputation, the general by now usually had on Snow Island a considerable striking force that acted instantly on tips. Out of the night they would gallop, cut up a force ten times their size, and vanish into a swamp where no dragoon dared follow.

The British officers raved and ranted until Cornwallis sent his best cavalry to rid the country of that pest. Tarleton, the smartest and bloodiest of all, rode himself ragged and returned to report, without apology, that it was impossible to corner the Swamp Fox. From one end of the South to the other and far into the North, the silent little man and his riders became legendary heroes who gave new hope and supplied new courage to others in the fight.

Bill had a hand in many of those adventures, too many to be mentioned except in a large book. Just how much Marion's activities had to do with it is questionable, but in September of that year, 1780, Cornwallis began falling back toward Virginia. On October seventh a thousand of his men were wiped out at King's Mountain by militiamen from Virginia and North Carolina. The tide of war had turned in the South, though few people realized it. Bill certainly did not or he would not have asked Marion's permission to ride to John Stewart's plantation.

"Commerce with the enemy, Bill?" The general smiled with one corner of his mouth.

Bill explained: "I want to talk with him about the gold while he is still within reach."

"You think he may have located it?"

"No, sir, but I have been pondering what Graves said."

"A rotten stick to lean on, by accounts."

"I'm not leaning on him. But it is possible that Mr. Stewart and I each know something about the island that the other doesn't know and so if we pool our knowledge, or our guesses, we may get somewhere."

"Possibly. How many men do you want for the trip?"

"Only Luke."

"You intend to ask Stewart for information, not try to force it from him?"

"Yes, sir. My father trusted him as a friend and so do I."

"The right attitude, Bill. Take Luke and good luck to you."

"Thank you, sir."

"Give my regards to Stewart, if you please."

"I will, General."

When Bill and Luke approached the plantation they scouted it carefully for possible enemy visitors, but there was no sign of them. Nor was there scarcely a sign of life, for Stewart was waiting out the war in seclusion, asking only to be let alone by both sides.

Old Noah met Bill at the door but did not recognize him. Bill did not identify himself, for though he trusted the old man, he knew that even in the best households there might be a servant in enemy pay.

"Is your master home?"

"Yes, suh."

"Be pleased to announce Lieutenant Barlow."

"Yes, suh." He was back in a minute. "Marse John say come up to de libury." He led the way upstairs.

Stewart was as solid and florid as ever. "Drop me down!" he burst out. "Young Barlow! I'm pleasured to see you, William. Are you alone or have you brought an army?"

"I have a boy with me, sir."

"Take care of him and the horses, Noah. Good care of 'em, too, or I'll skin you."

"Yes suh." Noah grinned as he left the room, for he had been promised a skinning for the past forty years.

"Be seated, William, be seated." Stewart swept an arm toward a chair. "How are you faring? How is Francis Marion? There's a rebel I'm proud of, deuced proud of, though I risk my neck by saying so. Have you heard the story of Watson's flag officer?"

"No." Bill sat down.

"Colonel Watson, who commands the British in George Town — you know."

"Yes, sir, I know. But not about the flag officer."

"Ha! This is good. Good! Watson sent a flag officer to Marion's camp to treat for an exchange of prisoners."

"Yes, I remember, though I was not in camp that day."

"Well, y'know, the chap had heard such tales of Marion he expected to meet a mixture of Lucifer and Hercules in flaming regimentals. Said so himself, he did. My word! When they took the blindfold off and introduced him to that smoke-dried little rascal in ragged homespun he all but swooned." Stewart slapped his thigh and roared.

"The general is better dressed now," Bill said. "We found him a shirt and trousers on a clothesline."

"Did, eh? Good!" Stewart wiped his eyes. "Well, the chap stayed to dinner. Nothing but sweet potatoes served up on a piece of bark. 'We're faring well today,' says Marion. 'Often there's not enough to go around.' "

"True enough," Bill commented.

"The chap says, 'Yes, sometimes an officer has to buy food

out of his pay.' 'Pay!' Marion gives the chap a laugh. 'Not one of us ever drew a cent of pay.' 'My word!' says the chap. 'All this fighting for no pay and no provisions but potatoes! What are you doing it for?' 'For liberty,' says Marion."

Stewart paused and blew a sharp toot on his nose. "You know, William, when the chap got back to George Town, Colonel Watson says, 'Why do you look so serious, old feller?' And the chap says, 'I have cause to look serious.' 'What d'you mean?' asks Watson. 'Well, sir,' says the chap, 'I've seen General Marion and his men living on roots and drinking swamp water, without pay and almost without clothes — all for liberty. What chance have we against such men?' "

Stewart realized he had gone too far, for a Tory, and explained hastily, "Marion is on the wrong side of the fence, of course, as all you blasted rebels are. You're all misguided and stubborn and unreasonable — *all* of you. But I admire any man's spunk, in particular when he's an old neighbor."

"General Marion is a wonderful man," Bill said fervently.

"Nonsense! But what fetches you here, William? This is no social call."

Bill gave him the story. Before Stewart made any comment he opened the door and looked up and down the hall.

"In these times I can't trust my own people," he said, with a touch of sadness. "Remember my boy, Ham?"

"Yes. I took a fancy to him."

"Smart as a whip. Ideal servant. I can't pin a thing on him, but I suspect Graves has set him to spy on me. Deuced irritating. I'd sell him, but I can't buy another these days."

"Why should Graves spy on a fellow Tory?" Bill asked.

"Oh, he hates me because I bounced him — and for other reasons. And Ham has a wife and children. I shouldn't sell him. I never had a family, but I don't want to break one up. Tell me what you know about the island, William."

"I have told you all I know," Bill answered. "It is the largest of a group of three small uninhabited ones off the coast between George Town and Charles Town. The gold was buried under a great cypress, on a point at the south end of the island."

Stewart leaned back and closed his eyes. "I've been up and down the coast many times in sailing ships. Thought much about the islands since I met you. Much — at night. Don't know if they're named. Believe they're nearer George Town than Charles Town. If we had a small ship. But we haven't. The blasted Brit — that is, all ships have been confiscated. After the war we will find that money. Sorry I can't help you now. You see how it is, William."

"Yes, I understand," Bill said, with disappointment.

"What will you do when the war is over?"

"Go west, perhaps."

"As a refugee?"

"No, sir. The United States is bound to expand that way."

"United States — pooh! Two poohs! There's no United States except on paper."

"It seems real to us," Bill said stoutly.

"Huh! Stupid of you chaps. You can't lick the greatest nation on earth. Can't do it. Why don't you change sides before it's too late? Swear allegiance to the king and after the war I'll do the handsome thing by you."

"I'll never bend my knee to any man who is no better than I am," Bill answered evenly.

"What! What's that? You're as good as King George?"

"Yes, sir, I am better than he is."

"Drop me down!" The old Tory leaned forward and stared.

"Any man who fights for liberty is better than a king who denies liberty to others." Bill stared steadily back at him.

"Am I to sit in my own house and listen to treason!" Stewart threw up his hands.

"I will be going, sir." Bill stood up.

"You will not! You are my guest for tonight and as much longer as you will stay. I lead a lonely life here and crave news. Tell me more about that traitor Francis Marion. He warms the cockles of my heart — I mean he makes my blood boil." Stewart tried to look fierce and only looked comical.

Bill stayed and sat up late talking. The novelty of being in a bed again was so overpowering that he slept like anything but a woodsman. He did not hear the sound of horses' feet at dawn, or voices, or steps on the stair.

"You must pardon an intrusion at this hour," was the first thing he heard. He opened his eyes on a pistol close to his face, and behind the pistol was Harold Graves and two British dragoons. "Don't be distressed," Graves said smoothly. "There is really nothing you can do but obey orders."

As Bill sat up he saw that the soldiers had his sword and pistol.

"I am not distressed," he said honestly. "I am boiling mad to be caught flatfooted this way."

"War is so unpredictable," Graves murmured. "Yesterday one was free, today he is a prisoner."

"And tomorrow he will be free again," Bill added defiantly.

"Dress," Graves ordered.

Bill obeyed, thinking furiously. Stewart had not betrayed him, he was sure of that. Probably Ham was the one. It didn't matter. He was in a box and he must get out before Graves could tighten the screws. Given power, a bully of his kind was the worst of masters. Bill glanced out the window and saw dragoons posted at intervals. A few Negroes were about, but Luke was not with them.

"I should have hanged you when I could," he remarked casually to Graves.

"Is that an indirect plea for mercy?"

Bill forced a laugh. "Mercy from you? I'd sooner expect milk from a rattlesnake."

"We will go down now," Graves said pleasantly.

"Don't I get a chance to shave first?" A razor would be better than no weapon.

"No. In your nervous state you might cut yourself. Down the stairs."

There was nothing to do but obey, so Bill followed the soldiers down, with the muzzle of Graves' pistol suggestively between his shoulder blades. The little procession entered a parlor where Stewart, his hands tied behind his back, was pacing up and down and tongue-blistering two dragoons who had been set to watch him.

"This is a pretty kettle of fish, William!" he roared. "A handsome way, a deuced handsome way to be treated by a — I almost said gentleman. Drop me down! In my own house, too! Is there no decency left on earth?"

"Not in certain quarters," Bill growled.

"Pray be calm, gentlemen," Graves purred.

Stewart wheeled on him. "You ditch-bred puppy! What do you mean by this? What do you mean by violating the laws of God and man in this infamous and high-handed manner?"

"Leave the room," Graves ordered the soldiers, "but guard the doors and windows." When the door closed behind them he drew another pistol and stood with one in each hand. "I mean," he answered coolly, "I have you where I want you."

"A dashing figure," Bill sneered. "If you could steal a sash and earrings you might understudy Bottle — though Bottle is no windbag."

"Shut up!" Graves snapped. His face twitched with anger, for the ridicule stung.

"You scurvy whelp!" Stewart thundered. "To insult my guest in my own house! If you were a gentleman I'd demand satisfaction. As it is, I'll have you flogged."

"Shut up, you old fool!" Graves glared at him. "I'll hang you from your balcony if you don't meet my demands."

"Hang and be damned to you!" Stewart roared.

"Later." Graves was calm again. "First, I want to know where that gold is buried."

"So do we." Bill said.

"The very question we'd give a pretty penny to have answered," Stewart seconded.

"Bluffing will cost you dear. Between you, you know where the money is. Out with it." Graves waited threateningly.

"But we don't know," Bill insisted.

"And if we did know d'ye think we'd tell you?" Stewart kicked a chair. "By mighty! I'll report you to the British commandant."

Graves gave him a cold, bitter look and answered, "Before Lord Cornwallis left for the north he issued a proclamation to the effect that all those who once were with us and later turned against us are to be hanged and their property seized or destroyed. That order is still in force, Master Stewart."

"What if it is in force?" Stewart demanded. "I haven't turned my coat."

"You have been apprehended in communication with the enemy."

"The enemy — you ninny! You know William is the son of an old friend."

"He is one of Marion's Men and you have befriended him. You are a traitor to the king and shall be dealt with as such." Graves' voice rose to a triumphant pitch, for this was his moment.

But Stewart would not believe it. "You white-livered rat!" he bellowed, tugging to free his hands. "If you lay a finger on me or my property I'll have you hanged as a brigand. Yes, sir, I will! Do you hear me?"

"I do." Graves laid one pistol on the table and blew on a

small whistle. Six dragoons appeared. "Take these prisoners to the yard," he ordered. "Bind them to the magnolia tree facing the house and place a guard over them."

Bill went quietly, realizing it was the wise thing to do, but Stewart raved and kicked as they dragged him to the tree.

"You might as well save your strength, sir," Bill finally said. "Graves hast the whiphand for the present."

But for what seemed like hours the old Tory shouted and swore as he watched Graves and his men go through the rooms, looting and smashing.

"Oh, my God!" The words were a sudden cry of pain. He bowed his head and tears ran down his face, joining the streams of sweat. The house was on fire in a dozen places.

When Graves sauntered over to the tree Stewart was crushed almost to unconsciousness.

"You had better cut him loose if you don't want to answer for his life," Bill said.

"I don't care a fig for his life." Graves eyed the old man without a trace of emotion. "I shall hang him, as well as you, if you don't tell me where the gold is."

Bill knew it was no idle threat. Graves was too drunk with revenge and power to stop at anything. Only the prospect of money would interest him.

"We are licked," Bill said quietly. "I'll tell you all I know."

"Begging for mercy at last!" Graves leered at him, a fifth-rate demon against a background of flames and smoke.

"I am begging for Mr. Stewart. Neither of us knows exactly where the gold is, but we will tell you what we know. You may hold us as hostages while you search for it."

Graves' small black eyes lighted. "Now you talk like a reasonable man. So I make you a reasonable proposition. If you direct me to the treasure, I release you both. If you don't, I hang you both. Do you agree to that?"

"Yes," Bill promised. It was the only way he could play for time.

"Excellent!" Graves rubbed his smoke-blackened hands together. "I will take you to George Town for safe keeping."

Within half an hour they were on the road.

CHAPTER XX

MOST of the men were asleep, a drowsy afternoon on Snow Island, for they had been busy. Scarcely was Bill on his way to the Stewart plantation when a rider brought word that Colonel Watson was moving out from George Town with horse, foot and artillery to surprise the island. This would be, he said, the last of the Swamp Fox. Marion disputed the statement. In fact, the whole command disputed it so hotly that if Watson had not done a neat bit of covering with his field guns he would have been wiped out along with his promise. As it was, the British returned to George Town on the run.

Marion sat on a log writing a report of the engagement.

"Pete," he asked Horry, who was dressing a bayonet scratch on his leg, "What were their losses at Black River ford? You had a better view from your end of the line."

Horry answered through a bandage he held in his teeth, "I counted seven dead and I believe three others sank in the water."

"Ten. Help you with that bandage?"

"No, thanks."

"That totals thirty-four known dead. Their wounded filled several wagons. A fair return for us."

"Including the return of Mac's clothes."

"I didn't get the particulars on that."

"It happened after dark while you were flanking their guns. Mac swam the river to feel out their pickets. Carried his clothes on his head. A patrol jumped him before he could dress, so he had to leave his clothes and swim for it. Got over, but was he vexed? He made a trumpet of bark and roared across the river like a bull, promising to kill eight men if they didn't return his clothes. And, by George, they sent 'em over on a raft!"

"Another American victory." The general laughed and resumed writing.

A minute later his head came up with a jerk. Horry was on his feet, and both were watching a bend in the path that led across the island. Luke came in sight, running in long strides, and swung toward them. He bowed from the waist, which was his way of saluting, and gave them the story of Bill's capture. Marion's eyes began to snap as he listened.

"The British set out for George Town by the main road?" he asked, when Luke paused to breathe.

"Yes, suh."

"Pete," the general grew tense like a spring, "we can take the swamp road and beat them."

"If we ride like Jehu, Francis."

Neither officer asked Luke how many dragoons they might expect to find. It didn't matter. Marion took a hunting horn from where it hung on the limb of a tree and blew three long blasts. Men rose on all sides, carrying rifles, and buckling on sabers.

"Bring in fresh horses," the general called to Mac. "Bill

has been captured and is being taken to George Town."

"Yes, sir!" Mac was away, his red hair rising in the wind.

"By the way, Luke, where is your horse?" Horry asked.

"Ah lef' him two mile 'crost de fo'd," Luke said. "Ah wuz in a sweat to git along."

Sixty men left the island and disappeared down the swamp road. It was a mere trail used by hunters and horsemen who were in a hurry, so narrow they must travel single file, but firm under foot at that time of year. Marion led, setting a pace that was sharp for all except Selim and Mac. The big horse and his big rider were itching to break out of line and gallop away on one of those mad missions they both loved. Guessing as much, the general finally sent them ahead to scout and, if there was nothing to report, continue to the junction of the trail and the main road. Mac rode away, his face more grim than they had ever seen it. Heaven pity the enemy that crossed his path that day.

They traveled steadily all the afternoon in the great gray swamp. Even so many men and horses were completely swallowed up by that wilderness. Occasionally they stopped for water where one of those rare clear brooks danced over golden sand before losing itself in the languid yellow waters. There was something primeval, something indescribably ancient, in the way the closely packed gum trees and the cypresses with their bottle-shaped trunks looked down at the passing horsemen, as they had regarded other creatures coming and going for so long. And the towering old sycamores, white as marble, looked like the very bones of the past. In that tangle of land and water, sunny pine ridges and dismal black morasses, there was nothing to care if fish ate fish, animal preyed on animal or man hunted man. Marion always felt the spell of such places even in the midst of war.

It was approaching twilight when Mac returned, Selim loping lightly as a fox. Not half an hour before, Mac said, he had seen Graves and his dragoons pass the corner, thirty-two of them. Bill and Stewart had their hands bound and their horses were being led. They were traveling at a rate that would take them to George Town within two hours. Marion looked back along the line and raised his saber high above his head, the signal that the hunt was on.

When they reached the road they formed double column and swept on, knee to knee. Mac was out of sight ahead and Marion and Horry rode together, squinting into the slanting light to spot the rising dust. They saw it floating lazily above the trees and twisting east as the breeze caught it. At the same time Mac reappeared, in a little cloud of his own, to say he had completely circled the enemy without being seen because of woods on each side of the road, behind which were open pastures. Marion gave him fourteen men, and as many more to Horry, with orders to bypass the British and block the road, while he attacked from the rear.

He gave them a long start and then led his troopers down the road at a sharp trot. Around a bend and they saw the enemy. The hunting horn rang out and the trot changed to a gallop, pounding to the war cry "Marion's Men!" The dragoons wheeled in perfect order. Graves sent two of them ahead with the prisoners and then spurred to the head of the line. Shots popped, horses reared, one went down on each side and then the gap closed.

The general rode at Graves, but Luke was ahead of him. The big Negro struck with enough force to fell a tree, Graves parried, and the blow bent him sideways in his saddle, pulling his horse around so it blocked Marion's for a moment before the battle swept them apart. Luke kept on through the line and into the open. He had a slash in one shoulder and a swath had been burned through the hair on top of his head by the flash from a pistol, but his sole thought was to liberate Bill. Riding a black horse, he tore on like a thundercloud, sent Bill's guard flying into Kingdom Come, and pulled the led horse to the roadside.

"Set still, suh, so kin Ah cut dese ropes 'outen diselbowin' yo' arms," he shouted. And when he had freed Bill's hands he added, "Hit take more'n a passel ob Philisteens ter stop dis boy."

"Help Stewart," Bill yelled, waving his arms to restore the circulation in them.

As he spoke a bullet came out of the melee up the road and dropped Luke's horse dead. Luke jumped, landed off balance, and rolled over. Thinking he was hit, Bill leaped down beside him to pull him away from the thrashing hoofs.

"Praise de Lawd!" Luke whooped, and bobbed up so suddenly they collided.

"This is no camp meeting," Bill shouted. "Give me your sword. The boys need help."

He snatched the saber and turned, to see his horse galloping across an open field. Farther away, Stewart and his guard were disappearing in the woods. Couldn't follow without a horse, blast the luck! Up the road was a boiling mass of dust, plunging horses and fighting men. It flashed through Bill's mind that the trouble was due to him and he was taking no part in it. He started running toward the fight, though he knew a man on foot had no chance in that maelstrom.

"Outen de way, suh!" Luke grabbed his arm and pulled him to one side. He glanced over his shoulder as Mac galloped by on Selim.

"Mac, help Stewart!" he yelled, but Mac did not hear him.

A few lengths behind came Horry and the troop that had made the circling maneuver. When they hit the battle, it flew apart like a broken wheel, flinging British dragoons in all directions. The pursuit took off across country fox-hunt fashion and disappeared in the twilight.

Having no horses, Bill and Luke did what they could for the wounded who could not leave the field. There were about a dozen, besides six British and two American dead. The dragoons were youngsters from a regiment recently out of England and expected to be killed on the spot. When they found themselves being bound up by supposedly bloodthirsty barbarians they looked at each other in amazement.

"Bloody liars!" one boy cried, in a near-hysterical voice.

"Who's a liar?" Bill wanted to know.

"Our officers. They told us — they told us — Marion's Men butchered prisoners."

"Never believe a British officer," Bill said gravely. "We patch up our prisoners and exchange 'em for — "

"I don't want to be exchanged," the lad screamed. He

was shot through the body and was going fast. "I want to stay here."

"You may," Bill said.

"Promise me that?"

"Yes."

"Thanks, mate." The boy's round face strained taut with pain. "I hate their lies — and their wars. I want — peace." He drew a long breath and died.

It was nearly dark when the men began coming back, some with prisoners, others leading horses with empty saddles.

"We couldn't endure leaving one of our officers in bad company." Marion looked down at Bill and smiled. He had a handkerchief bandage on his right wrist.

"I was a fool to get caught. They got me flat-footed." Bill kicked a bush spitefully.

"Where was Luke? I thought he went along as nurse-maid." Mac rode up with three dragoons' helmets swinging from his saddle.

"Dat fool Luke's conscience ez jes' one pain," Luke answered from the shadows.

"You finally saved my neck," Bill told him. "Did Graves get away?"

"By the width of a Junebug's whisker," Mac grumbled.

"And Stewart?"

"No tally for him."

"They'll hang him in George Town, Mac."

"Who will?"

"The British."

"But he's a Tory."

"Graves will swear he is a traitor, if he doesn't tell where the gold is buried."

"Does he know where it is?"

"No, but Graves thinks he does."

"Well, it can't be helped."

"But he's my friend, Mac. I got him into this scrape and I must get him out."

"I don't see why you should worry much about a Tory."

"Can't you understand anything? He risked his neck for me because he knew my father before the war."

"The war has changed things."

"It hasn't changed his honesty."

"Sure he didn't turn you over to Graves?"

"And lose his property and perhaps his life? Don't be such a fool."

Mac shrugged. "For all that, I don't trust a Tory."

"You don't have to. But I can't leave him in the lurch."

"What can you do about it?"

"I don't know yet."

"Count on me, if you need help."

"I'll paddle my own canoe, if I take a Tory aboard." Bill walked away.

That night they camped in a piece of woodland owned by a Whig. Bill and Marion talked together during the evening, and before dawn Bill and Luke went farther into the woods together.

"I'm going to George Town to learn what happened to Mr. Stewart," Bill said. "Help me rig up a disguise."

"Now or when we git nigh de town, suh?"

"Now. I am going alone."

"Dis am a me-too journey, suh."

"I don't need company, Luke. I can't let you risk your hide for a Tory."

"Yo' gwine spy fer de genr'l too?"

"Well, he asked me to keep my eyes open."

"Dat make two jobs. Dey need two mens. Ah go."

"Oh, all right. Now disguise me so my own mother wouldn't know me."

"Yo' mammy in Jawdge Town, suh?"

"No, no, no! But Graves is."

"Ah reckon he hain't so hard ter fox ez wuz ole man Bottle an' ole man Lord Bob."

Soon after sunrise those who watched the George Town road saw two men plodding toward town. One was white, obviously a small farmer who, like so many others, had been caught between the millstones of war and ground almost to extinction. He was too poor to ride a mule, his clothes were in rags, his right arm was in a sling and a bandage passed under his chin and over the top of his head, covering half his face and one eye. The other man was a large Negro who carried a sack of sweet potatoes on his shoulder.

"Effen dese yams fetch two shillin' we buy ourselfs hog meat," Luke remarked dreamily.

"The Book says the devil is in swine," Bill said solemnly.

"Pow'ful sweet meat ole Satan be."

"After the war you should raise hogs, Luke. Give 'em a start and they would grow as fast as you could eat 'em."

"What yo' do aftah de wah, suh?"

"Going west. Want to come along?"

"Ah's gwine to Africa."

"Still thinking about that?"

"Yes, suh. All ma kinsfolkses is in Africa. Dat de place fer a black man ter live. De Lawd put black folkses in Africa an' white folkses some udder place, like yo' plant rice in de water an' cohn on dry lan'. Yo' mix 'em an' yo' git a crop ob trouble."

"You may be right," Bill said thoughtfully.

As morning advanced the road came to life: countrymen bound for town with chickens and vegetables, soldiers driving a herd of beef cattle, Tory planters and miscellaneous Negroes. A troop of cavalry, escorting a string of hospital wagons, looked none too cheerful.

"You there!" the captain hailed Bill. "Have you seen any enemy horsemen today?"

"Naw, suh," Bill answered in a singsong whine. "I hain't seed none terday, but yistday I seed 'em, I did."

"Who did you see?"

"That ole Swamp Fox is out agin, suh. He lef' th' road full of daid corpses an' wounded sojers. He beated me up when I wouldn't jine his varmints."

"Has he gone?"

"E-yah."

"Which way?"

"South."

"No'th," Luke contradicted.

"That way." Bill pointed west.

"Dat way." Luke jerked a thumb east.

The captain swore. "I've seen idiots in a dozen countries,"

he said to another officer, "but never one to equal these natives." They clattered on.

When the town was in sight Luke asked what they were to do when they got there.

"Find Mr. Stewart," Bill told him. "If he is in jail, try to learn his sentence. If he has been paroled in a tavern or private house take him away by force in the dark. He won't violate his parole to go with us, but we can force him at the point of a gun. That reminds me." He glanced about to make sure they were alone, then undid the bandage on his arm, showing his right hand fitted around a pistol. He examined the priming and replaced the bandage loosely.

As he finished, a woman shouldered her way through the roadside hedge and stared wide-eyed at them.

"There is no cause for alarm, madam," Bill assured her.

"No cause for alarm!" Her voice was high and tense. "You say that when they are hanging my son this morning."

"Who is?" Bill walked over to her.

"The British." She came out into the road and they saw she was mud-stained from tramping a long way. She began to tremble.

"Please talk freely, if we can help you," Bill suggested.

"You can't help me." Her eyes were dry. "They shot my husband a year ago. He was one of John Rutledge's agents. My son and I carried on the work. They took him last week. He is only eighteen."

Bill could sense her agony. "Where are you going now?" he asked.

"To George Town to plead with the commandant. I

have walked all night. They took our horses. They took everything we had."

Bill nodded miserably. "It has happened before."

"God will strike them down. But what will it matter then?"

"May I escort you to George Town?" Bill offered.

"I should not inflict my trouble on a stranger, and one who is suffering."

"My injuries are of no consequence," he said. "Let's be going."

"Effen Ah had me a mule caht Ah'd haul de lady," Luke said. He was so eager to help.

"Oh, I can walk." She put up her chin. "I could walk around the world if it would help him."

George Town, with its streets of houses and shops, its public buildings and wharves, looked like a city to the plantation people. Bill saw only one thing: midway of the street, in the market square, a body was swinging on a gallows. He knew, even at that distance, it was John Stewart's.

"Oh, God!" The woman caught at her throat with both hands.

"It is not the one you think, madam," Bill said, in a strange-sounding voice.

"You know — him?"

"Yes."

"De Lawd hab mercy on dis worl'!" Luke muttered.

They walked down the street, irresistibly drawn to the focal point of agony. Something began tightening in Bill's brain. He could imagine what the old Tory had suffered at

Graves' hands. Frustrated in his quest for gold, arrogant with temporary authority, cruel enough to delight in such work, he had denounced his former employer and friend as a traitor who had sheltered Marion's Men. That had been enough. Without reason or justice the commandant, who had known such humiliation by Marion, had struck, as Graves knew he would.

Bill was sickened by the thought that by visiting Stewart on the plantation he had brought this to pass. The Tory might have turned him over to the British and saved himself, but his code had been rigid. A man was either a friend or an enemy, and he had chosen to be a friend to the last.

"De Philisteens am comin', suh," Luke whispered.

Bill pulled himself together and looked across the square at a platoon of redcoats marching a prisoner briskly toward the gibbet. The officer who commanded them was Graves. That something in Bill's brain tightened more. A silent crowd had gathered and when it parted before the soldiers the woman saw their captive. Without a sound she walked toward them and, as though a malicious fate had arranged the rendezvous, met her son at the gallows.

"Out of the way, old woman," Graves ordered.

"Sir," she said quietly, without moving, "I am here to beg mercy for my son."

"You swine are always begging." Graves glared at her. "Had you reared your son to fear his king he would not be paying a traitor's price."

"I reared him to fear no man," she answered.

"Least of all an English tyrant!" The boy's voice rose

high and clear. "Don't cry, mother. It's a privilege to give all we have for liberty."

Some of the onlookers cheered and Graves raged at them to be silent.

"To your office!" he shouted to the guards. "Stand back, hag!"

For all her courage, she fell on her knees at his feet.

"In the name of our Saviour," she pleaded, "I beg time to present his case to the commandant. All the facts have not been given. I ask only justice."

"There it is, you rebel witch!" Graves kicked her in the face.

The something in Bill's brain snapped. His bandaged arm went up and the pistol barked. At a distance of three paces he could not miss.

CHAPTER XXI

THE shot cleared Bill's brain. He knew, without conscious thought, that an instant's delay would lose everything. He wheeled, but Luke was ahead of him clearing a lane through the crowd. No one tried to stop them, and when they had passed, the gap between them and the soldiers closed. Sentiment was so strong for the prisoner that when the guards left him, perhaps intentionally, and tried to follow Bill, the boy and his mother disappeared.

Bill was unaware of that, for he was completely busy keeping up with Luke. There were shots and shouts behind them, then a swelling hubbub of voices as though a giant hive of bees had been overturned. Given horses, the fugitives could have left town without trouble, but as far as they could see there was not a horse on earth. They crossed the street, dodged behind a hedge, sprinted down a garden path, ducked in the front door and out the back door of an empty stable, vaulted a wall and cut back along it to the open basement of a house. Bill tore off his bandages and threw them almost in the face of a fat man who sat on a stool winding a fishline.

"Quiet!" Bill covered him with the empty pistol.

"Take your own advice," The man said, unperturbed. "I am a Whig myself, so put up that gun."

"I need a change of clothing," Bill said, watching him closely.

"So do I, but the confounded Tories have gobbled everything in town."

"An old coat?" Bill suggested.

"Slip into my fishing clothes there." The fat man motioned toward a peg. "And you," to Luke, "will find a prewar red shirt in that closet. You can squeeze into it if you don't button it. Throw your castoffs into that tub of water." He went on winding his line.

Bill put on a woolen shirt and long trousers that were stiff with fish scales, blood and grease, while Luke was partly covered by a flannel shirt such as sailors liked to wear.

"We are obliged to you for your aid," Bill said warmly.

"And I to you for yours," the fat man returned.

"We have done nothing for you."

"It's plain as a pikestaff the enemy has you on the run. Therefore you must have caused them trouble. He who annoys the Tories does me a favor."

"That is our business." Bill grinned.

"You want to leave town?"

"Yes, immediately."

"Then don't hurry. They will be watching. Take this fishing pole and sprawl on the wharf. Return here tonight for food. You, black boy, keep in sight of him, but not too close. When you get away give my regards to General Marion."

"What makes you think — "

"I don't," the fat man interrupted. "It is a gambler's instinct and I am betting ten to one you are Marion's Men. Here is your pole. I will let you out the front door to dull suspicion."

"Perhaps some time I can repay you, sir," Bill said as he took the pole.

"Drop a Tory for me." The man slid off the stool and waddled to the door. As he opened it his voice rose boastfully, "Yesterday I caught eighteen off that wharf — eighteen I say!"

Two red-coated soldiers were passing almost within reach.

"You always were an awful liar." Bill laughed.

The soldiers stopped. "In the king's name," one of them said, "have you seen a villain with a bandaged head and one arm in a loop?"

"Yesterday as I was — "

"Damme! Not yesterday — ten minutes ago."

"No, sir," said the fat man. "What is he wanted for?"

"Murder. It's death to harbor him."

"Gad! Only a fool would harbor such a character. Thank Heaven good King George's men are here to protect honest folk."

Bill shouldered his pole and sauntered down the street behind the soldiers, trying to show only a casual interest in things. The military portion of the town was hopping, bugles sounded, orders snapped, aides galloped, squads of infantry and cavalry marched, and even the commandant himself dashed about on a white horse. To have one of their most efficient Tory officers shot down in the public square while on duty was a blow in the face no Briton would tolerate. So the town was being turned inside out for the man with an injured arm and a bandaged head.

The most inconspicuous occupation for one with a fish pole is fishing, so Bill drifted down to the wharf and cast his line. After a while Luke shambled past, reeling with laziness, and lay down on a pile of lumber in the sun. Many ships were tied up in the harbor and the nearest one, a small black craft, was taking on a cargo of mixed merchandise. It looked to Bill like army stores, suggesting that the British might possibly be pulling out of town. That was worth looking into, so he loafed along until he was fishing almost under the bow of the ship. He fished and fished and looked and looked and listened and listened. Obviously the master was away and loading operations were going badly. So badly as to be almost at a standstill. Then someone sang out guardedly, "Heads up, mates, here comes the old man!"

Two minutes later Bill heard such a burst of vivid profanity as he had not listened to in years. It was a masterpiece of its kind, a gem of sailors' art. And he knew that voice, sounding as though it had rusted in salt water — Bottle's!

The fisherman hunched his shoulders and studied the water, trying to think of the best way out. The tirade continued on the deck close at hand. Judging by the captain's remarks, he was short of help and was suggesting to the crew that they do a bit more work or be shot and fed to the wharf rats. Or, if they preferred, he would beat them to jelly and grease his boots with it.

The familar, hated voice came nearer. Bill dared not

retreat or turn, so he went on fishing. Then a hand clapped him on the shoulder and he had to swing around. He looked Bottle squarely in the eye and held his breath, but there was not a flicker in the pirate's face to show that he saw any resemblance between the hulking loafer and the lad he had known years before.

"Here, you!" Bottle roared. "Lend a hand with this cargo and be quick."

"I am a free man," Bill retorted.

"Free, eh?" The captain shook his earrings furiously. "Ask the redcoats if you be. I'm loadin' my ship for 'em and it's lend a hand, me lad, or I'll send you up in irons."

Bill had no wish to see the inside of a British military prison after what had happened.

"Fishing is poor so I don't mind accommodating you," he said.

"You sound a mite eddicated." Bottle looked him up and down. "Can you write?"

"Yes, and read and cipher."

"You'll be me supercargo. Come aboard for orders." He led the way over the side, across the deck and into his little dirty cabin. "Now, me lad," he said, when he had closed the door, "take my orders and you won't be sorry."

"What are your orders, Captain?"

"Simple as tossin' a cat o'er th' rail. For every three bales that comes aboard you tally two on th' papers I turns in to th' British. That's all. See?"

"Perfectly." Bill grinned knowingly. "You reserve a third of the cargo for your own use."

"A clever lad!" Bottle slapped him on the back. "I'm a

hard-workin' sailorman, I be, a honest sailorman who has to make his livin' where he finds it. King George two bales, me one bale — square's a beam end. I'll do handsome by you, me lad, when we make port."

"What port, sir?"

"Charles Town. Th' army's shiftin' some from here to there. We want to help 'em, don't we, mate?"

"Certainly."

Bill could see no wrong in relieving the enemy of supplies, even if Bottle would profit by it. And this would be a safe way for him and Luke to leave town. When they reached Charles Town they would take French leave and rejoin Marion in short order. Also they might pick up considerable worth-while information on the trip. He would like to even an old score with Bottle, but perhaps the most he could hope for was to fox the pirate into serving his ends. And, too, the disposal of Graves had quenched his thirst for vengeancc.

"We'll waste no more time." Bottle clumped across the cabin floor. "Action means money for us, mate."

"Your crew is short-handed, Captain?"

"Aye, but I'll drive 'em."

"There's a big Negro asleep on a pile of lumber on the wharf."

"Which way? I'll fetch him alive or dead."

"I had some talk with him. Perhaps I can persuade him to work."

"Persuade! Blast him, kill him if he refuses."

"I will," Bill promised and ran up the stairs.

They worked steadily throughout the afternoon loading

the ship. By keeping his eyes open, Bill learned that the British were not evacuating George Town, but merely shifting surplus supplies from there to Charles Town. How Bottle had cut in on the job was not obvious, but evidently the old reprobate knew his way around.

Late in the day two companies of infantry descended on the dock and posted guards in a businesslike manner. The others searched the ships and warehouses. The soldiers looked hot and tired and it was easy to see that their combing the town had not been pleasant.

"Line up your crew," a lieutenant snapped at Bottle. "Failure to report every man will cost you dear."

"I'm servin' o' my king, but, for all that, wasted time means money to a poor sailorman," Bottle complained.

"Line 'em up. Step lively."

The men stood with their backs to the rail and the officer walked up and down the line.

"You don't look like a seaman." He stopped in front of Bill.

"I'm not," Bill said and glanced at Luke, signaling him to stand by for a break.

"What are you?" The lieutenant glared at him.

"Dock hand."

"Do you know this man?" The officer wheeled on Bottle.

"Him? Sure. He's loaded many a ship for me, sir."

"Did he work for you this morning?"

"Sure. And yesterday."

"Hold out your right arm, what's-your-name."

"Higgins," Bill told him," putting the arm out straight.

"Is that his name, Captain?"

"Sure, Jack Higgins, sir."

"What is his name, Higgins?"

"Bottle," Bill answered, wondering if that was the one the captain still used.

"Is that right, Captain?"

"Sure. You'll find it on th' army books this four year past."

The officer had been examining Bill's arm without satisfaction.

"Off with your cap," he barked.

There were no marks under it to suggest a wound, so he passed on. He had been on the jump for ten hours, without being too keen about the search in the first place. The dead Tory had been a cad, anyway, and deserved what he got.

Bill let the others return to work first, then said under his breath to Bottle, "Why did you lie for me?"

"Gratitood, mate." The pirate winked.

"What do you mean?"

Bottle stepped nearer and whispered, "I seed what you done this mornin'. A body as rids th' earth o' Harold Graves deserves th' thanks o' mankind."

Bill felt suddenly cold. "My disguise — "

"Tripped 'em all but Bottle. Nobody trips Bottle." He chuckled and swaggered up the deck.

Bill and Luke slept on deck. They held a council of war and decided that, considering the intensity of the search, it would be wiser to stick with Bottle as far as Charles Town, as Bill had first planned. If the captain had not already recognized them, the chances were he never would.

Bill lay awake a long time thinking about John Stewart

and blaming himself for his death. There was a man who had been above party, and the memory of him would be something to tie to in the days ahead. War had wiped him out as ruthlessly as though he had been a beast. That was war, created by intelligent men, yet once started as cruel and unreasonable as a river or a wind.

The next day they finished loading the ship and, when the tide was right, dropped down the river to the sea.

"Ever been on the deep before?" Bottle asked, as they sat in his cabin going over the tallies. He was in genial humor for he stood to make a fat profit by his thievery.

"No." Bill looked away through a porthole.

"Ever hanker to?"

"Yes. I would like to go cruising for buried treasure, if I knew where to look."

"Aye, it would be sport to dig up money. They say th' wicked pirates has stowed away heaps of it."

"I suppose you have heard convincing yarns about it."

"Aye, dozens. I knowed a lad who had a true secret to buried treasure."

"Did he find it?"

"Nope. Poor lad, blowed up on a ship he was."

"And took the secret with him?"

"Aye." Bottle's voice was sad. "Seein' 's how it turned out, I wish I'd pressed him for it. But I was too honest a sailorman. 'If he wants to tell me he will,' I says, an' I nary pressed him. Blowed up he was, an' I loved him like a brother." The gentle captain sighed.

They sailed south that day, keeping near shore and occasionally sighting a British patrol vessel that recognized them at a distance and made no comment. The ship was loaded beyond the danger mark to accommodate the stolen goods, which comprised a third of the cargo. Bill wondered what Bottle's next move would be and got the answer late in the afternoon when they sighted a small island and headed for it.

"Tonight," Bottle remarked blandly, "we'll unload our surplus yonder. Tally each bale an' have th' tallies balance th' ones you didn't tally when we loaded."

"I understand," Bill said. "You want the figures shipshape when you dock at Charles Town."

"If they ain't — " Bottle paused significantly.

"You will drop a word about me to the British," Bill finished.

"Oh, now, now, now! You wouldn't say that of a honest sailorman."

"Not of an honest sailorman! No." Bill smiled pleasantly. "Let's agree to respect each other's private affairs, Captain Bottle."

"Sure, a gentlemen's private agreement always suits me." Bottle moved down the deck.

Bill stood leaning on the rail. The ship was tacking and a second island appeared near the first. Then a third. The middle one was the largest, but all were small. He bent forward for a better look, seeming to hear again his father's words: "Three little islands up the coast from Charles Town. We buried it on the biggest, which was between the other two, under a great cypress on a point extending north."

He never knew before that a ship could move so slowly.

The sun had almost set before he made out the long low point stretching north from the largest island. Not until the last minutes of daylight did he see the cypress near the end of the point. When he did, he turned his back, fearing he had been staring at the islands in a way to excite suspicion. Whistling carelessly, he found Luke and edged him out of earshot of the crew to tell him.

The big fellow rolled his eyes. "De angels done lead us ter de Promis' Lan' like us is Moses."

"Perhaps so."

"What us do now, suh?"

"I'm not sure."

"Jes' set?"

"For the moment."

The ship moved in as near the first island as possible and began discharging cargo. Under the captain's lashing tongue the men worked fast and the boats plied back and forth. Bill did not go ashore, but he understood the bales were piled on a natural platform of rock and covered with tarpaulins, making them quite snug until Bottle could return for them.

An hour or two before dawn the job was done and the crew was asleep. When the sun awakened them they found that the supercargo, the big Negro and a small boat were gone. They searched the islands and then bore away toward Charles Town, while Captain Bottle paced the deck and cursed himself for a fool for not keeping the Whig in irons until he could turn him over to the British at a profit. Such a loss was a sad blow to an honest sailorman.

When the ship disappeared Bill and Luke rowed out from the mainland to the middle island and there, as easily as digging a hill of sweet potatoes, they uncovered the gold. Just like that! After years of anticipation it was a downright prosaic climax. No chart marked with a mysterious X, no midnight adventure, no bloodshed, no dead men's bones, none of the trimmings of a first-class treasure hunt. And yet, for all its humble setup, it paid off, for there were the ten buckskin bags each holding a thousand British guineas.

"Lawdy Lawd!" Luke clasped his hands. "Ah nary expec' ter see so much gol' dis side New Jeerooserlum."

Bill stared at the money his father had earned piece by piece and buried there with his own hands so many years before.

"We will put it back," he said in a husky voice. "When the war is over we will come again."

CHAPTER XXII

ONE December afternoon, in the year 1782, Bill left his horse in front of the State House in Charles Town and went up the steps two at a time. A Negro porter met him in the hall and smiled broadly. Everyone was smiling these days.

"I have an appointment with General Marion," Bill said. "Has he arrived yet?"

"Yes, suh. Genrul Marion an' Genrul Greene an' Gov'nor Rutledge all havin' a visit in de big room."

"I will wait. I am Captain Barlow, in case anyone asks for me."

"Yes, suh."

"Have you seen Captain MacDonald around here?"

"Ah' don' know him, suh."

"A big fellow with red hair."

"He ain't been visible terday, suh."

Bill went down the hall to a small room and stood by a window in the sunshine. He might have sat but, strangely enough, amid the security of peace he felt more uneasy than he had during the war. Off in the east the harbor wimpled in the breeze and set memories running like waves. It had been a long while since he first saw that piece of water from the ramparts of Fort Moultrie. The world had moved since then! And he with it. When he had landed on Sullivan's Island that night he had stepped from boyhood into manhood. Most lads made the change gradually, but he had been given no time for the customary approach. Bang, bang! And he was there.

Better than six years it had been since then. Long, tough years for the most part, yet, looking back, they seemed to have flashed past. The most impatient months were those after he had found the gold and been obliged to leave it on the island, for it would have been folly to attempt to move it in a small boat in those days of war and lawlessness. It had been nerve-wracking to think of the fortune on that small muddy nub of land, but there was little time for brooding.

So many other things had happened. Operating from Snow Island, Marion struck the British again and again and again, forcing the evacuation of George Town in August, 1781. The other American leaders in the South were also driving hard. Before that, in January 1781, had come the victory at Cowpens, when General Morgan ended Tarleton's bloody career in South Carolina. Then, in October, they heard of Cornwallis' surrender. By the first of the next year the British were driven back and penned up in Charles Town and on James Island. The troops and refugees were so crowded and so hungry that General Leslie had killed two hundred of his horses. And now the beautiful city that had suffered so much for so long was free. And so was America.

Busy days, glorious days. Bill walked up and down the room, too titillated by memory to keep still. The door opened, and Mac strode in, a dashing figure in new uniform and jack boots.

"Hi, cub of the Swamp Fox!" he sang out. "How goes the world?"

"Fine as cat hair." Bill swung around to meet him. "How's the North?" For Mac had been on courier duty to Virginia.

"A good enough country, but I'm glad to be back." Mac sat down. "I nigh wore out Selim trying to get here for the big day. Tell me about it."

"It was a big day, Mac!" Bill looked out at the war-scarred town. "We had waited a long while for it."

"Not exactly waited," Mac said. "As I remember, we didn't sit around twiddling our thumbs. But what happened at the last?"

Bill leaned his back against the window ledge. "By an agreement between General Leslie and General Greene we moved in as their rear guard moved out, after firing the morning gun on December fourteenth."

"No actual contact?"

"No."

"Too bad we couldn't have run 'em out with bayonets."

"Greene is a gentleman. So is Leslie, for that matter."

"Still, we can't forget some things."

"I know. But it's victory that shows a man up. For weeks after they began pulling out, Marion wouldn't let us attack. He said enough blood had been shed."

"That's Marion, Bill. Even Cornwallis and Tarleton and Wemyss couldn't tarnish his humanity."

"It's been a mighty privilege to serve under him, Mac."

"Right." Mac switched the conversation for fear of sounding sentimental. "Did the redcoats act licked?"

"They marched in good order. It took them four hours to go aboard their ships. We got to the State House at eleven in the morning. The city was wild."

"It must have been. How did the Tories take their medicine?"

"Most of them weren't there. Nine thousand of them left with the British."

"I thought the air seemed sweeter just now as I rode in."

"You have letters for headquarters?"

"Two saddlebags full. Luke is guarding 'em in the hall."

Bill held up his hand and looked toward the door as General Marion entered.

"Mac!" He stepped forward lightly. "Welcome home again."

"Thank you, sir." Mac took the offered hand almost reverently.

"A pleasant journey?"

"Yes, sir. I will fetch the despatches." He went out.

Marion shook hands with Bill. "I hear you brought back the bacon."

"Yes, sir. The gold is in the vault in the cellar."

"Splendid! Well done!"

"As I said before, General, it is all at your disposal for the cause."

"A magnificent offer, Bill!" Marion's voice was soft, then it rose proudly: "It may be acceptable as a loan, but, thank God, the state of South Carolina, as one of the United States of America, is able to honor its debts."

Bill looked at the man who had grown old and weary-looking during the hard years, but whose spirit had never dimmed.

"General," he said, "the battle lanterns were kept burning, as you said they must be."

"Yes, Bill." Marion looked far away. "But there are battles of peace no less than of war. May it be the Almighty's will that we and those who follow us shall find the courage and the wisdom and the faith to keep those lanterns burning."